A MAN OF
LITTLE EVILS

A MAN OF
LITTLE EVILS

STEPHEN DOBYNS

New York 1973 ATHENEUM

Copyright © 1973 by Stephen Dobyns
All rights reserved
Library of Congress catalog card number 73-78408
ISBN 0-689-10567-3
Published simultaneously in Canada by McClelland and Stewart Ltd.
Manufactured in the United States of America by
Kingsport Press, Inc., Kingsport, Tennessee
Designed by Kathleen Carey
First Edition

FOR MY PARENTS

A MAN OF
LITTLE EVILS

PROLOGUE

HENDERSON HAD ALWAYS been afraid of falling. Consequently, even now, waiting for the Underground in Charing Cross Station, he stood back against the wall. It made him almost as uncomfortable to see others approach the edge, although at this late hour the station was nearly empty.

Down toward the main exit an old busker with a harmonica was playing for a pair of American tourists. The song was a ragtime version of "Yankee Doodle," which the busker either didn't know or had decided to play creatively. He was supplementing the song with a little dance. The busker was a small ragged man and wore a new bowler hat. Pink and blue ribbons hung from the hat over the man's ears, and as he danced the ribbons bounced up and down like the ears of a sloppy dog. The tourists, who were heavy and middle aged, were too tired to be amused.

Farther on a drunken man was lying on a bench, snoring and embracing his umbrella. Near him a young couple were staring at each other.

Henderson knew he had never seen any of them before and would never see them again. Even still he was foolishly pleased that he had decided to wear dark glasses; that he had gone so far as to bring a stout cane for protection. He felt that tense elation he remembered feeling as a young boy when he had once come secretly into London and prowled the streets of Soho searching for knowledge of the World. But now, leaning against the wall, he kept telling himself: You are forty-seven years old. You are a respected man of business. You are about to do something which is extremely dangerous.

Looking at his watch, Henderson saw it was nearly midnight. The last Queen's Park train would be arriving at any time. Henderson told himself to remain calm. The man he was to meet would be in the last car of the train. And if he wasn't? Henderson forced the thought out of his mind. The man would be in the last car. He had blond hair and was in his early twenties. He had five rings on his fingers. He would answer to the name of Frank. And if he wasn't there?

Henderson switched his attention to a large poster across the tracks, in which a benevolent copy of Mao Tse-tung urged him to join the Red Revolution. It advertised beer. He was still thinking of the word "revolution" when the guard began shouting, "Last train, last train." Despite the warm and stuffy wind which precedes the trains, Henderson felt decidedly chilly as he moved away from the curved and sloping wall. Then he paused and slipped his cane behind a candy machine. After all, he told himself, I'm not the person who needs protection.

The red Bakerloo cars jumbled to a halt smelling of oil and dust. Henderson walked quickly toward the last car, glancing briefly at the others, which were almost empty. The guard shouted at him to hurry, adding the inevitable Please.

He stepped past a West Indian, who was waiting to shut the doors, and into the car. There were two other people in it. The first was a very large woman sleeping with her head thrown back and her mouth wide open. The second was a young man sitting back toward the middle door.

Henderson felt a moment of complete surprise. Although he had known Frank was young, his mental image had been of a much older man. Even now, while seeing the garish rings and the blond hair, he doubted this was the right person. It occurred to him that if it had not been for the war, he might have had a son this age. The thought struck him as ridiculous.

Still, as he sat down beside him, nearly losing his balance as the train bounced forward, he found it difficult to speak, wished he had remained on the platform and watched the train pull away without him.

"You're . . ." was all Henderson could bring himself to say.

"Yes."

Henderson remained silent, careful not to look directly at Frank, while watching him out of the corner of his eye. The rings were certainly garish. Two had large red stones while a third had a wax seal of the peace symbol. The other two were entwined snakes with ruby eyes. The train pulled into Trafalger Square, took on a few passengers and pulled out again.

Frank turned his head angrily, but not far enough to face Henderson. "Are we going to do business?"

"Yes, certainly. I only wanted to be sure."

"Sure of what?"

"Of the person with whom I am dealing . . ."

"Shit."

But it wasn't a matter of being sure of Frank; it was a matter of other alternatives. Even though he had the money in his pocket and the arrangements had been made, he kept searching for other alternatives. Just as he had searched for them all week, ever since he had first missed the ledger and heard Jacobs calling the American reporter. What alternatives had there been? If there had been the slightest

5

chance that Jacobs would have accepted money . . . But where would that have led?

Fortunately Ahmed had been in London. Should he have even gone to Ahmed? Ahmed had been too quick in his decision. He had known about Frank. He had known what Frank would cost. But after all, the situation was equally threatening to Ahmed. He, too, could go to jail, although Henderson doubted Ahmed would be bothered by the scandal.

"Well," said Frank, "are you just going to sit there?"

The train had now reached Piccadilly Circus. Quite a few people were getting in and out of the other cars, although the last car remained relatively empty.

Henderson found a small, hard place in his mind: some place of resolve, some place without hope. He began to wrap himself around it. At last he took two envelopes out of the inside pocket of his suit coat. He handed the smaller of the two to Frank.

"This is the man's name and address. I have also included his working hours and what I know of his habits. That isn't much of course."

Frank took the envelope, putting it in the pocket of his blue windbreaker without looking at it.

Henderson gave him the second envelope. "This is the money."

Frank opened it, glanced at it briefly and put it in the pocket containing the first envelope.

"Aren't you going to count it?" asked Henderson.

"Why? It's a thousand pounds, isn't it?"

"Yes, but . . ."

"You're not going to cheat me." There was no element of question to the statement.

The train was now approaching Oxford Circus. The large open-mouthed woman stopped snoring and woke up. Slowly she got to her feet, staring all the while at Frank and Henderson. "My bleeding feet are killing me." Her voice was a kind of groan. "We all have to live, ducks." Then she turned and staggered a little toward the door.

"Tomorrow," Henderson said, "I am taking an early morning plane for Tangier. Part of my business is there. You should be able to find an opportunity any time after that."

Frank nodded but didn't speak. He still hadn't looked directly at Henderson. After a short, inexplicable wait, the train pulled out of Oxford Circus.

"I . . . I really have no choice," Henderson continued. "You see . . ."

Frank turned away. "Don't tell me your problems."

Henderson nodded. "Just make certain you get the ledger. That's all that's important. But you must do it quickly." Henderson felt a wave of words flow through him. "Even now it may be too late, but you must try, there's no other alternative. You see . . ."

"Your reasons disgust me. Don't involve me in them." Frank leaned back and closed his eyes. They were very blue. "Your stop is Baker Street," he said.

Henderson nodded again. Now that he had done it, he wanted to stop it. He wanted to say, "No." But he was afraid of the young man beside him. Not that he felt the other man would hurt him physically.

The train stopped at the Regent's Park Station. No one got on or off. Henderson was filled with a desire to explain himself, and the knowledge that he couldn't only increased the desire. He wished he were in Tangier right at that moment. He could almost smell the mint tea and the overripe fruit in the central market. It would be cooler now, in September. He would drive out to Cape Spartel. Perhaps he would go swimming. The train began slowing down for Baker Street.

Henderson got up quickly. "Goodbye," he said. Frank

7

appeared to be asleep. "If you have any trouble . . ."

Frank opened one eye and focused it on Henderson. It was like a weapon. "There won't be any trouble," he said. He closed his eye again.

The train stopped and Henderson got out, walked quickly toward the exit. The train pulled slowly out of the station, leaving behind its musty smell of something confined too long.

1

ALTHOUGH HE WAS LATE, Trevor refused to hurry. He had no desire to see Jacobs, no desire to hear Jacobs' small tale of suspicion and intrigue. The feeling of self-satisfaction he received from doing something unpleasant didn't justify one step in Jacobs' direction. It seemed to Trevor there were too many people like Jacobs around the edges of his life. But that was probably true of most reporters.

Trevor was also irritated that he had had to come all the way out to Jacobs' flat in West Hampstead. He was irritated that Jacobs refused to tell his story over the telephone. This wasn't entirely fair. Trevor could have easily met him in the city during the week. They had in fact set up two appointments, which Trevor had broken. But that didn't make it any better.

Even today, Sunday, Trevor had said he would come out in the afternoon. But then Clare had arrived, and stayed, and they had gone to bed, and would have stayed in bed even longer if the phone hadn't interrupted them around seven.

It was Jacobs' girlfriend, Eva Lipton. She sounded upset, which surprised Trevor because normally she seemed indifferent to everything around her. She was a tiny woman who worked in a pub on Chalk Farm Road. Owing to the noise in the background, Trevor guessed she was calling from there.

"You aren't going to see him," was the first thing she said. It was a flat statement.

Trevor was confused. "See who?"

"Ralph, Ralph Jacobs. You were supposed to see him. You promised." Although she spoke in a monotone, she was practically shouting, presumably because of the bar-noise.

Trevor held the phone away from his ear. "So, well, I'll see him tomorrow. What's bothering him?"

"I don't know. He won't tell me. I was with him this afternoon, then I left because he thought you were coming. You don't know how frightened he is. He just rang me up here. Can't you do something? He's terribly upset."

"All right, I'll call him."

"Right away?"

"Yes."

Trevor had hung up and then guiltily called Jacobs to say he wouldn't be coming out after all. But Eva had been right; Jacobs, who usually seemed calm, had pleaded and behaved in such an uncharacteristic manner that Trevor said he would be there at nine o'clock. But first he had dug out a little more information about Jacobs' smuggling charges.

It was now ten o'clock, and Trevor was kicking himself for his moment of weakness. To make matters worse his car had been in the shop all week and current finances made taking a taxi an impossible luxury. Therefore he had spent thirty minutes on the Underground being bounced and subject to those feelings of claustrophobia which this symbol of English efficiency always awoke in him.

As he walked along, turning off West End Lane onto Compayne Gardens, he looked like someone on his way to a fight. Trevor was a stocky, red-haired man about two inches under six feet and gave the impression of having a body that was too small for him. His features combined to heighten this effect. He had large, watery blue eyes which always looked bored. He had long teeth, high cheekbones and a nose flattened by a policeman in Chicago. His features were jumbled onto his small, bulldog head in a way that had once led an editor of his to remark: "Trevor has a face like a ghetto."

With his face, red hair, his abrupt movements, he looked constantly angry, as if he cut through the air not to places, but to targets. Actually he was a very tired man whose anger was directed mostly at himself.

But at the moment it was directed equally at Jacobs. Trevor passed a building which appeared to be a Pakistani social center, then a house with two crumbling sandstone lions in front. He charitably assumed they were lions; the weather had ground them to the point where they could easily be a pair of plump Pekingese. In any case, they weren't beasts that would consider growling.

The neighborhood gave off the aura of gray and sagging respectability. The houses had been built some seventy years before by a contractor who had been practicing making villas for a richer, better place. Now the rent was controlled and the landlords had given up. It was just the sort of place where Jacobs would live.

Trevor had met him about a year ago, although he had seen him with Eva before that in various Fleet Street taverns. Then Jacobs had joined a group of about ten reporters who met regularly to play poker. He was a mediocre player who often won. Small, dark-haired, looking like a ferret with his quick movements, he had the appearance of a man who cheated. Trevor believed that he did.

Jacobs was a man of little evils. What had first made

Trevor notice him was the way he abused Eva in public. Not that she appeared to mind. Trevor realized that even now, as he approached Jacobs' building, he was looking for an excuse to turn around. But Trevor disliked to think too badly of himself, and the penance suffered from seeing Jacobs would be good for some moral mileage. Trevor took a deep breath and climbed the steps of a particularly tired three-story structure of faded brick.

Jacobs lived on the third floor. Trevor remembered something about his intention to move because of his neighbors' complaints about his stereo. If Jacobs had one good point, it was his passion for music. He would even share it, for often he would buy records, tape them, then give them away. Trevor had always refused, although he had been particularly tempted by an early recording of *Tosca*.

But Jacobs' neighbors didn't share his taste and there had been long battles and threatened evictions over Jacobs' contention that he could play his stereo as loudly as he wished. Jacobs had gotten carried away and had been forced to capitulate by the police after threatening to poison some woman's dog. Trevor wondered what he did for music now. It was that sort of useless curiosity he found too often in his mind. He should have been a printer like his father and stayed in Chicago. He continued climbing to the third floor.

Trevor knocked on the door and leaned back against the opposite, faded yellow wall to wait. I will give him thirty minutes to talk, he told himself. I will refuse all drinks.

No one came to the door. Trevor knocked again. The landing smelled of urine and curry. There was a small, yellow light hanging from the ceiling by a frayed wire. From a flat nearby, he could hear the excited muttering of a television. Still no one came to the door.

Trevor lit a cigarette and called himself various obscene names. He turned away, meaning to leave. Already it seemed as if he had been standing on the landing for hours. Then he angrily turned back to the door and hammered on it with his fist. The door slowly swung open. For a moment he had a flash of being a small child who has done something wrong and has just been caught. Then he shoved his hair back with his hand and walked into the dark hallway, shouting, "Jacobs, where the hell are you?"

There was no answer. Trevor paused, listening. There was no sound at all. No, that was wrong. From the next room he could hear music, but very faintly, as if coming from a far place.

He walked angrily into the living room, then stopped abruptly. It was like hitting a wall. Everything went out of his lungs, and it seemed that all the air in London couldn't fill them again.

It was a shabby room with faded yellow wallpaper spotted with violets. The one window was covered by a pair of purple drapes which someone must have been proud of fifty years before. The room was furnished with a large library table, a yellowish sofa and two heavy armchairs. The room felt yellow. It smelled yellow. It was like the cage of a tired animal. There was a small oaken desk next to Trevor. The drawers had been pulled open and papers covered the floor. There were also sofa cushions on the floor.

Jacobs' stereo and record collections took up one whole wall of the room. One shelf of records had been pulled out. Records covered the floor like scattered leaves. The stereo was on, although the speakers had been turned off.

Jacobs was sprawled casually in the less tattered of the two armchairs. The only light in the room came from the standing lamp just above him. It had a round, green shade with a yellow fringe. The light seemed to devour him. Jacobs' mouth was open. His eyes seemed to be open.

He was wearing a pair of stereo headphones. They were

all that was keeping his head together. There was a gaping hole in his forehead, like the center punched out of a jar. What had passed for brains in Jacobs' lifetime were now spread across the room, hanging to the wall, mixed in with the papers, sticking to the purple drapes.

The music seemed to be coming from the hole in Jacobs' forehead. It was deafening in the otherwise perfectly silent room. Trevor found himself trying to think what it was. Then he recognized it as the opening of the third movement of Brahms' Fourth Symphony. The room was awash with trumpets. Trevor turned quickly, looking for someplace to be sick.

2

"I WAS WITH CLARE until about nine thirty. Then I left her at Marble Arch and took the tube out here." Trevor paused. He was leaning against the wall farthest from the body. Although there were eight other people bustling about the room, he was certain he could still hear music. He knew that was impossible.

Questioning him was Percy Mitchell, a detective inspector from Scotland Yard. Mitchell was bald with a thin fringe of gray surrounding the top of his head like a fur collar. He wore glasses with black frames and smoked a pipe. Tall, thin with a face creased into false smiles, he had the look of a friendly confidant and advisor. This was deceptive for at the moment he felt impatient and cross.

He made a snorting noise at Trevor. "But you had intended to see Jacobs earlier?"

Trevor nodded. "I was supposed to come out here this afternoon, but then I saw Clare instead. To tell you the truth, I didn't want to see Jacobs. He'd been bothering me all week. Then his girlfriend calls me and says he's hysterical. So I call him around seven o'clock, maybe a little after. He was really upset, and I thought, shit, well, I'll see him and get it over with. Partly it was his being upset and it seemed he might have a story for me after all."

Mitchell made some scratch marks on a dog-eared pad. "Who's his girlfriend?"

Trevor told him.

"What's she like?"

"A skinny blonde, quiet. Jacobs pushed her around a lot. I don't really know her. She seems all right."

"What did you do between seven and nine thirty?"

"I've got to eat, don't I? Jesus."

Mitchell shrugged and glanced at the body. Five police technicians were fussing around it, measuring, photographing, looking for fingerprints, taking microscopic samples of small discoveries and generally behaving like children on a beach. Mitchell's assistant, Sergeant Fawcett, an eager and open-mouthed man, was poking behind records looking for clues. A young constable with huge eyes guarded the door. He looked ill.

Mitchell turned back to Trevor. The two men had met professionally about a year before. Both had originally intended to be historians, and in talking they discovered a shared passion for certain aspects of Scottish history. Since then they had had dinner together a few times.

After finding the body, it seemed perfectly natural to Trevor to telephone Mitchell. It didn't, however, seem natural to Mitchell, who had just closed a case concerning a double murder in Kilburn. He was due for a rest. Now here was Trevor giving him the responsibility for a whole new murder. Mitchell wasn't pleased.

"Did Jacobs mention anything in particular about smuggling?" he asked Trevor, who was staring at the body.

Trevor forced his eyes back across the room. "It's as I say. First he wouldn't talk at all, just vague hints about somebody smuggling. Then we set a luncheon date, which I broke. He was so upset that we made another date. There were more hints but nothing concrete. I had to break the second date, too. There was a Common Market meeting that needed covering and Wolfe, who usually does that sort of thing, was sick. Maybe he was drunk. I don't know. Jacobs kept calling, insisting that I see him. I guess what put me off originally, along with the personality of the man, was that he said he had a great story for me. You hear that all the time. It's amazing the number of people who believe they have front-page stories concealed within them. . . ."

"But Jacobs?"

"Well, I guess he really had a story. As I say, I called him at seven. He was the sort of person who always pretended to be very cool. But when I talked to him, he was right over the edge, practically hysterical. I told him I was busy and that I wasn't going to come all the way out here without some idea of what he had to say. He started babbling about somebody called Henderson. There are thousands of Hendersons in London so I got angry and threatened to hang up. He goes on to tell me that Henderson was the man he worked for as an accountant. He says that Henderson has been smuggling, hashish apparently, and has been making a fortune at it for years. This Henderson, he says, is a big, respected businessman. I was still skeptical and asked if he had proof. Jacobs said he had all the proof I needed. So I decided to come out."

Mitchell made some more scratch marks on his pad. "And you found him like this?"

"Yes. . . ."

There was a bustling at the door. Sergeant Fawcett hurried over to be of service. He returned moments later with a beaming man whom Trevor recognized as the medical examiner. He was in his late fifties and wore a dark pin stripe suit which seemed a few sizes too small for him. It covered his portly figure like a rubber glove. He bustled

17

over to the body and the stereo, looking at them intently. Suddenly there was a swell of music which Trevor recognized as a Beethoven quartet.

"Turn that off!" Mitchell was furious. "If, Dr. Fenton, you can contain your irrepressible sense of humor long enough to examine your patient . . ."

Dr. Fenton flicked off the stereo. He wore a grin which seemed painted onto his face. "Isn't there an expression—I am not well versed in these matters—but isn't there an expression 'Keeping your head together'? I should think that without these objects on his ears my poor patient . . ."

"Just examine him, don't discuss him," interrupted Mitchell. "I don't wish to hear about it." He turned back to Trevor. "Bloody doctors."

Dr. Fenton began poking and prodding Jacobs in an unscientific manner. "Are your men through with him?"

"Yes," said Mitchell without turning around. "Get on with it."

Trevor noticed how the police had tracked through the blood. He felt ill again.

"So if you had seen him before, even this afternoon . . . ," said Mitchell.

"You don't have to tell me that. I never liked the man and now I dislike him even more. Goddammit, he's involved me."

"Involved you?" Mitchell looked up again from his pad. Trevor was surprised to see he was drawing a sailboat.

"I mean by my not being here, by my not coming earlier. Don't you see that?"

"No."

Trevor would have liked a fuller response. He was beginning to feel tied to the body of Jacobs, could almost feel the touch of Dr. Fenton's hands. "If I had come earlier, he wouldn't have been killed."

18

Mitchell looked bored. "Don't be sentimental, Trevor. It may have been something else entirely. What sort of person was this Jacobs?"

Trevor glanced toward the body. The doctor was still prodding it. Occasionally he would mutter, "Aha," in a happy tone.

"He was a small, unpleasant person; always in the midst of quarrels, petty fights; always trying to enlist your sympathies. I had seen him a number of times in some Fleet Street bars and at the New Chelsea Club. He's an accountant but he had decided to hang around with newspapermen. God knows why. I played poker with him a few times. I . . . People said he cheated, but he was never actually caught. There was also talk that he was involved in blackmail. I don't know." Trevor felt terribly tired. He also wanted a drink, maybe three or four.

"But that's the sort of person he was," Trevor continued. "Even if he wasn't actually blackmailing somebody, he'd probably do it if given the chance. But that's not a capital crime and neither was cheating at cards. He was little. He was an ass-pincher, always talking about his way with women."

Mitchell raised his eyebrows. "Did he have a way?"

"Only with the dumb ones. It was something he did almost ritualistically, if you know what I mean. Jesus, what more do you want? I want to get out of here."

Mitchell turned to the medical examiner. "Can you give me an estimate of when he was killed?"

Dr. Fenton made a complaining noise. "I'd have to see the contents of his stomach. There's his dinner time to consider. The temperature of the room . . ."

"Perhaps just a guess," interrupted Mitchell. "For instance, I would say he was killed about eight o'clock."

"Oh, no," replied the doctor, "earlier than that, but not

by much. Perhaps between six thirty and seven thirty. You see, it's . . ."

"Thank you," said Mitchell, turning away.

"Who's Henderson?" asked Trevor.

"An importer."

"Is there anything on him?"

"Not that I know." Mitchell paused, looking at Trevor. "Well, off the record, our tax fellows had a look at him about three years ago. Seems he was spending more money than he was declaring. But before they learned anything, Henderson apparently got the wind up and became very tight with his money."

"The money could have come from smuggling."

"Not necessarily."

"But possibly? I mean, he seems to be your best bet."

"Possibly, although it's rather clear he didn't do the actual killing."

Trevor was surprised, even disappointed. "Why not?"

"Too professional. Nobody heard any shots and amateurs rarely have silencers. Also the flat was searched by a professional. The killer arrived, found Jacobs wearing his headphones and unable to hear a sound, shot him at point-blank range, searched the flat, found what he was looking for—as you see, the flat is only half-searched—and left after perhaps fifteen minutes. . . . Excuse me a moment, won't you?" Mitchell walked over to Sergeant Fawcett and the two began talking.

Trevor remained leaning against the wall. Apart from feeling depressed, he felt a growing anger with Jacobs for dragging him into his death. It seemed that wherever he looked in the small dismal room, there was Jacobs' blood or brains. It astonished him how the police never seemed to notice. Even if they throw up, as he had seen once at a massive traffic accident in Chicago and another time during an autopsy, it never seemed connected with what was being investigated. Trevor always felt ill, and the memories lingered for months, lodged in some neon part of his brain.

But here it was worse. He wasn't an observer but a kind of accomplice. There was a feeling of being terribly separated from everyone else in the room. Mitchell came back, with Fawcett close behind him.

"You may leave if you wish," said Mitchell, sounding bored. "I'll ring you up if we learn anything."

Sergeant Fawcett looked surprised and made a slight grunting noise. "Shouldn't you take a proper statement, Sir? Down at the Yard?"

Now Mitchell grunted. "Whatever for? You don't suspect Mr. Trevor of planning to leave the city, do you?"

Sergeant Fawcett twisted his face into a deprecating smile. Trevor suddenly realized that Sergeant Fawcett had tagged him as the murderer. It surprised him, but he was even more surprised to realize that he didn't care.

"Anything else?" asked Trevor.

Mitchell shook his head. "Not unless Sergeant Fawcett wishes to make a formal arrest."

Sergeant Fawcett looked embarrassed but stubborn. He was a none-too-bright man of fifty who had gained his promotion by not only looking under every stone, but also digging great pits around them. "We can never be too careful, Sir," he said.

Trevor began buttoning his raincoat. "I'll be in touch." He turned to leave.

"Just a moment," said Mitchell. "How do you plan to write this up?"

Trevor looked back over his shoulder. "I don't. It's not wire copy. It looks like a killing during a robbery. That and Jacobs' personality make it a two-bit murder. I can't touch the Henderson angle and I don't want to get involved myself. Eventually I may do a story, depending on what you find out, or . . ." He paused and looked again at Jacobs, apparently comfortable in his overstuffed chair.

"Or what?"

"Or what I find out."

"Don't do anything without contacting me," said Mitchell. "This sort of thing usually solves itself within forty-eight hours. The only thing that troubles me is the silencer. Well, perhaps everyone in the building is deaf, or perhaps wearing headphones."

Trevor managed a smile and left. He had to hurry in order to catch the last train. There were more police on the stairs and other landings. Occasionally they would shoo away tenants who felt they had the right to know what was going on.

It was drizzling outside, but a small crowd of the curious had gathered anyway. They huddled under their shiny umbrellas that reflected the streetlight and the lights from a police car. Trevor recognized some hovering reporters. One of them, Dermot from *The Post,* called to him.

"How did you get in, you slippery goon? Buy off the police?"

Trevor smiled, waved and kept on walking.

Dermot ran up to him with a few other reporters on his tail. "Not so fast, my friend. Let's have a few words for the press from the press. What happened in there? Who was shot?"

Trevor stopped walking. The only thing he could do now was to protect himself. "Do you remember Ralph Jacobs?"

"Who's he?" asked Dermot.

"Jacobs. A little ferrety guy who hung around The Two Lions and the New Chelsea Club, always pinching the help."

"Oh, yes," said Dermot, "an unpleasant chap."

"A bleeding nuisance," said someone whom Trevor didn't recognize.

Trevor nodded. "He was shot between six thirty and seven thirty by a person or persons unknown. The killer searched the flat but the police don't know if anything was taken. Mitchell's in charge of the case."

"How did he happen to get it?" said someone else. "He just finished with those Kilburn murders."

"Beats me. Anything else?" Trevor looked at his watch. It was eleven forty-five. He had fifteen minutes to catch the tube.

"How many times was he shot?" asked Dermot.

"Once. In the back of the head, at close range."

"Was he tied up?"

"No. He'd been wearing stereo headphones and the killer walked right up to him. Jacobs never knew he was there, probably."

"Did you see him?" asked the reporter whom Trevor didn't know.

"Come on, fellows," he complained. "The police will issue a statement soon. There's nothing in it. Jacobs probably deserved shooting and somebody finally got him. I got a date. See you later and all that." He started to walk away.

"Just a moment," said Dermot. "What were you doing there?"

Trevor had always admired Dermot's ability to ask important questions. Now he could kick him. "I just happened to be in the area and got in before the police set up their line." He moved closer to Dermot. "Look, you know how it is. Woman trouble and all that. Don't tell Clare, okay?"

Dermot just looked at him. "Who found the body?"

"I don't know. Some neighbor. Come on, I've got to split."

"Want a ride?" asked Dermot.

"No, my car's around the corner. Work hard and don't quote me." He began to walk off again.

Dermot shouted after him. "Hey, what sort of story do you have?"

Trevor turned around quickly. He suddenly felt angry, as

all the feelings he had been sitting on for two hours bubbled up. "Story! Shit, man, I'm not interested. Can't you get that through your head. Some two-bit fucker gets killed. Why should I break my ass chasing that? Keep it. It's yours. I don't have the slightest interest. Not the slightest interest."

Without waiting for a reply, he walked off, angry with himself for losing his temper. Soon they would know he had found the body, but hopefully by the time they bothered him about it, it would be just another old story.

Trevor jogged back down West End Lane to the West Hampstead tube station. There were dozens of feelings spinning around inside of him. He was careful not to define them. But constantly, as if the picture were flashed on the dark buildings around him, he saw Jacobs in his chair with the earphones clamped to his head, blood and brains on his face, in his eyes, on his clothes, on the floor, on the furniture, on the wall, on those awful purple drapes, over and over until Trevor shut his eyes and tried to think of something else. He wasn't very successful.

He got to the station only moments before the train. Reaching a seat and collapsing, he tried to occupy the next fifteen minutes staring at faces, reading the same old ads promising better beer and fulfilling jobs, wondering why anyone would want to live on Finchley Road, wondering if the Swiss Cottage was still a good place to pick up girls, swallowing frantically as the train went deeper just before St. John's Wood, making his ears pop, generally wondering what he could do to clear his mind. He got off at Oxford Circus.

The station was practically empty and the last Central Line train which would have taken him back to Notting Hill Gate and to bed had left fifteen minutes before. A guard told him to hurry so he could lock the doors. Trevor climbed up to Oxford Street and began looking for a cab. There seemed to be dozens but none would stop. At last, just as he was beginning to feel neglected and invisible, one drew up to the curb beside him. It was late and he would have to be up early the next morning, but instead of going home, Trevor directed the cab to the New Chelsea Club. The drink which he had been wanting for hours would turn into four or five.

But along with the pictures in his head, and the music, and the confusion, there was the feeling of being tricked. He was a professional observer who had become the object of his own observation. He was the nonparticipant who was suddenly involved; as if a football had been thrown into the stands, forcing him to run. Often in his work there could be a very fine edge between observing and taking part, but mostly he was able to remain aloof. The major exception had been a murder he had once covered in Chicago. He still couldn't think of it without wincing.

Someone had broken into a slum apartment, had raped, beaten and finally strangled to death a twenty-five-year-old hillbilly woman, had beaten her fourteen-month-old son to the edge of death and disappeared. The husband and the caretaker had found the body when the husband returned from work at six o'clock. Trevor had been sent out with a photographer at seven thirty. The body was gone, the police were gone and the father was with his child at the hospital. There was only the caretaker left, plus the woman's older children, who were sleeping in the caretaker's apartment.

The area had been so bad and the apartment house so dark that the photographer had refused to go in. Trevor had walked through pitch-black hallways knocking nervously on doors and expecting to be shot. At last he found the caretaker, and the photographer had come up to waken the older children for pictures. The caretaker had arrived from Tennessee three months before and kept calling Trevor

"Sir." Both men were twenty-seven. Trevor desperately wanted to tell the man not to call him Sir. The caretaker's accent was so thick that Trevor could barely understand him. As they talked, the photographer kept fidgeting, refusing to sit down because of the cockroaches. Trevor had been filled with a desire to take the caretaker's hand and say, "No, I'm like you." The thought of it embarrassed him terribly.

Instead, he had quickly concluded the interview and had hurried off to the hospital to talk to the father. As he did, he was aware of other reporters and photographers from other papers crossing and recrossing his path, searching for better information while trying to slow down Trevor. This was part of the game.

Trevor dreaded that particular hospital, which was the dumping ground for practically all accident cases. Emergency was a battlefield; people standing around in partial shock, amazed at the sudden turning of their lives.

Trevor had been followed in by a black man in his sixties whom he had barely noticed. Ignoring Trevor, a doctor had asked the man what he wanted.

The man was drunk and pointed vaguely at his leg. "Shot," he said.

Aware of him at last, Trevor saw that his left pant leg was completely soaked with blood. A pool of blood was widening on the floor. It was as if the doctor had given him eyes. Trevor was so startled that he jumped back, nearly falling. But the doctor only turned and said in a voice of absolute calm, "Nurse, GSW." Gunshot wound.

Trevor had wanted to say, "But how can you be so quiet? How can you act like that? How can you be such a person?"

As it turned out, that was almost what the doctor had said to him. He had refused to let Trevor go up and see the father. He had refused to let Trevor call upstairs. He had refused to call himself. He had refused to let anybody take a message.

Trevor made the mistake of asking, "Why not?"

The doctor looked at him with obvious disgust. "Here's a man who has just discovered his wife naked, raped and brutally murdered, and whose baby was assaulted, beaten so badly that he will either die or suffer irreparable brain damage. And you want me to drag him down here so some fucking reporter can ask him questions. What kind of person are you anyway?"

Trevor had been shocked, not at the doctor, but that he had been so caught up in the game he hadn't thought of anything else. His photographer said, "Sometimes it does a person good to talk." Trevor had taken him by the arm and they left.

The whole scene was very vivid for Trevor, although it had happened ten years ago. He had seen himself as one of the tormenters, on the same side as the killer. He could still hear the doctor's voice whenever his work led him into positions that disgusted him. Although after all these years, it now took a lot to bring out that response. Jacobs' murder brought it out. Here more than ever, he was a participant and there was no way to keep his hands clean. He had become the person he didn't want to bother. If only Mitchell could clear it up in those promised forty-eight hours. There must be a real killer somewhere, someone to accept the legal responsibility.

The cab arrived at the club. Trevor moved as if in a bad dream and without thinking gave the driver an extra pound. Once inside, he ignored the few people he knew. He sat at the bar and ordered a double Scotch, then another. He was humming quietly to himself. Then he realized what he was humming and went to the lavatory to be sick for the second time that night.

3

"HENDERSON WAS IN TANGIER for the whole time. There was no way he could possibly have killed Jacobs." Mitchell was tilted back precariously on the hind legs of his chair. Trevor was sitting across the desk from him. His watery eyes were bloodshot and he needed a shave. On the other side of the room, Sergeant Fawcett was sitting with an air of grim disapproval. This was difficult to maintain because he kept sneezing. He had caught a cold in the drizzle four days before, searching for somebody who might have seen Jacobs' killer. The office was small and Fawcett's sneezes were large. He neglected to cover his mouth.

Sergeant Fawcett disapproved of the fact that Mitchell was taking Trevor into his confidence. He felt it undignified of Mitchell to lean back in his chair. Mitchell was aware of this. It was why he was leaning back. It was also partly the reason he was talking to Trevor.

"Henderson announced Friday afternoon that he was going to Tangier the next day. As you know, Jacobs was killed on Sunday. Henderson returned on Wednesday. He was highly visible during his entire Moroccan stay. Actually, his business requires him to take month-long trips to Tangier and Fez in the spring and fall, but never has he left on such short notice."

The information disappointed Trevor. He would have preferred to put Henderson at the scene of the crime, even though the professional nature of the murder indicated that Henderson hadn't done the actual shooting. But Henderson's sudden trip was obviously suspicious. Trevor needed that, because in the four days since Jacobs' murder, he had decided, almost as an act of faith, that Henderson bore all responsibility for the crime.

"More than that," continued Mitchell, leaning back in his chair still farther, "Henderson's man in Tangier, a chap by the name of John Carlton, says he knew nothing of the visit until Henderson arrived."

"You've talked to Henderson?" asked Trevor.

"Oh, yes, twice as a matter of fact. He said he wanted to make a spot inspection of Carlton's work. The only problem is that Carlton appears to be a model employee of ten years' standing."

Sergeant Fawcett sneezed abruptly. Mitchell looked at him with distaste. "Sure you won't take the rest of the day off, Sergeant? Clear up that cold?"

Sergeant Fawcett wiped his face and the front of his brown suitcoat with a red handkerchief the size of a small flag. Then he stuffed it back into his hip pocket. "No, thank you, Sir. Something might come up." He scowled at Trevor.

Mitchell looked as if there were little chance of that. Trevor ignored the interruption. "Then you think he's lying?"

"I'm not certain, but I rather feel he is. On the other hand, our investigation into Jacobs' life shows quite a few people who would prefer him dead. But I assume Henderson is your choice?"

"That's right."

It had been a difficult four days for Trevor. Dead drunk

on Sunday at the New Chelsea Club, short tempered at the bureau—even to Clare, which was a mistake because she was both a friend and the woman he slept with—then more drinking and anger directed at those around him. Whenever he paused in this round of excitement, he could hear Jacobs' whining voice on the telephone, first asking and then begging Trevor to meet him. Whenever he didn't hear Jacobs' voice, he heard that damned music.

He had expected Mitchell to telephone all day Monday. Trevor would have called him but he didn't care to admit the extent of his preoccupation. That was foolish. He would have given a lot to stop thinking about Jacobs.

Finding it impossible to wait, Trevor had decided to do some investigation of his own. He thought it might be profitable to talk to Eva Lipton and he wanted to have a look at Henderson, just to see what he was like. Early Tuesday afternoon, Trevor called Eva at the Coach and Horses, where she worked, and said he wished to talk to her. Although she sounded depressed, she told him he could come to her room after three o'clock. She had a bed-sitter on Ferdinand Street, off Chalk Farm Road.

Trevor had then telephoned Henderson's office, identified himself and said he wished to talk to Henderson about trade agreements with non-Common Market countries. He had been told that Henderson was out of town but would return Wednesday.

The moment Trevor entered Eva's room that afternoon, he realized he had made a mistake. Eva was sitting in a rocking chair by the only window. The shade was drawn and the small room was dark and stuffy. Eva rocked back and forth staring at the shade. She was wearing a blue bathrobe.

"They wouldn't let me see him," she said without turning around.

Trevor stood between an uncomfortable-looking single bed and a small table. "Who wouldn't?" He didn't know what she was talking about.

"The undertaker. He said he couldn't allow it. I asked over and over. He said I wouldn't want to see him." She continued to stare at the shade. "You'd think I'd know best, wouldn't you?"

"It wasn't very attractive," said Trevor helplessly. He wished he could go away.

"He liked me. Ralph played around with other women but he liked me."

"Did he ever talk about Henderson?" asked Trevor.

"Sometimes I'd see him out with other women. He'd bring them into the Coach and Horses as a joke. But I didn't care."

"Eva, did he ever talk about Henderson?" Trevor took a step toward her.

She turned her head, seeming to notice him for the first time. "Henderson?" Her face was so thin that her high cheekbones looked like marks made by a black crayon. Trevor guessed she was in her late twenties, although now she looked much older than that.

"The man he worked for. Did he ever talk about him?"

"Sometimes. Aren't you going to sit down?"

Trevor sat down gingerly on the edge of the bed. "What did he say about him?"

"Nothing in particular. He said he was conceited."

"What else did he say?"

Eva raised her hand slightly as if pushing the question away. Then she glanced sharply at Trevor. "Why didn't you see him when he asked you to?"

Trevor winced. "I was busy."

"If you had gone there, they wouldn't have shot him." She said this very flatly. "He told me he had something awfully important to tell you but that you couldn't be bothered. Why couldn't you be bothered?" She had stood up and was facing him. Trevor doubted that she weighed a hundred pounds.

"I was busy. I couldn't see him." Trevor was sweating. He disliked sitting and having her standing over him.

"He liked me. He even said I was pretty. Do you know what that means? Do you?"

"Sure you're pretty. Look, Eva, this is important. Did Ralph give you any idea of what he wanted to talk to me about?"

"You bastard." Eva opened her bathrobe. She had nothing on underneath. There were stretch marks on her small breasts. "Do you want to fuck me?"

Trevor had to restrain himself from jumping back off the bed. "What do you mean? Of course not." He tried to keep his voice calm.

Eva shrugged and walked back to the window. "I just wondered. I'm lonely. Now there's no one at all." She turned, facing Trevor again. "He could be horrid at times, but he liked me. Why wouldn't they let me see him? I don't understand it. . . ."

Trevor didn't want to hear any more. He got up quickly and left the room.

The interview had shocked him. Not so much because of her accusations, but because she was letting herself fall apart. He also had been shocked by her blatant attempt at seduction, even though in the back of his mind, he had suspected that she was mocking him. He was much more willing to accept her charge that he had killed Jacobs. It was more or less what he had been telling himself ever since he had discovered the body.

Wednesday morning Trevor called in sick. He wanted to see what Henderson looked like. Although he might blame himself for Jacobs' death, he wanted a real person to whom he could attach the actual killing. Seeing Eva had made that very necessary. And Henderson was the plausible choice.

Therefore when Henderson left his office at 5:00 P.M., Trevor was standing across the street watching. Henderson's business was in four modest rooms on the second floor of a three-story brick building on Chesterfield Street near Berkeley Square. A small brass placard in front announced "Thomas Henderson, Ltd."

Henderson walked down to a parking garage on Curzon Street to get his car, a dark-green Bentley. He was a tall man who stooped a little as he walked. His face was thin, with thin lips and a long straight nose. He had gray hair. Trevor was reminded of some sort of tree, perhaps a birch. There was an angular scar on his left cheek.

To Trevor he looked like a person who had gone to Eton and Oxford, been active in sports and had stayed fit ever since. His clothes were very conservative: dark-blue three-piece suit, bowler hat, a perfectly rolled umbrella. He looked a little like a World War II bomber pilot whom Trevor knew: a man who carefully attended all the reunions and told endless stories that no one cared about anymore.

It didn't occur to Trevor that Henderson's appearance had been designed to placate the English prejudice against anyone who dealt exclusively with Arabs, or "Wogs," as they were generally called. Actually Henderson's father had been a greengrocer in Wembley. But Trevor had a strong streak of the true believer. Leaving the man and taking the image, he went away satisfied. He even stayed sober for the rest of the evening.

The next morning, deciding not to wait any longer for Mitchell's promised call, Trevor went over to police headquarters: a bland, modern building on Victoria Street across from Parliament Square and in constant view of tourists swarming into the Abbey. Other than being unnaturally communicative, Mitchell had not reacted to the visit at all. This made Trevor faintly suspicious. Of course Sergeant Fawcett had objected.

Fawcett sneezed again. Trevor saw Mitchell wince and close his eyes before he continued speaking. "But Jacobs' personality has certainly increased our problems. Much of it is the usual routine, bringing us nothing but more work. Correct, Sergeant Fawcett?"

Fawcett was startled at being spoken to. "Very much, Sir."

"For instance," Mitchell paused to take off his glasses, search them for smudges and put them on again. "For instance, Jacobs was playing around with another man's wife. Therefore, time must be spent investigating the husband. The same is true of Jacobs' gambling debts. There is also evidence that he was involved in blackmail, but we haven't found any list of names. I'm afraid we probably shall. You certainly know disreputable people, Trevor."

"Did you talk to the girlfriend?"

"Eva Lipton? Yes, a dreary girl. Jacobs doesn't seem to have confided in her."

"I talked to her Tuesday. She didn't seem to know anything."

Mitchell glanced at Trevor curiously. "Why should you talk to her?"

"I thought she might know something."

"And did she?"

Trevor remembered Eva standing naked before him in the dark stuffy room. "No, she got hysterical."

Mitchell continued to look at Trevor as if he were trying to decide about something. Then he shrugged. "As for the scene of the crime, as it's called, we have found no one who saw or heard anything. People were out. They were watching the telly. They were sick in bed. They were in the bath. We have no evidence that the murder wasn't committed by a trained chimpanzee wearing spats. Isn't that so, Sergeant Fawcett?"

Again Fawcett was surprised and nodded quickly behind his red handkerchief. Mitchell took off his glasses a second time, held them up to the light, found the annoying smudge and removed it with his own immaculately clean handkerchief

Trevor felt restless. He wasn't interested in Mitchell's games with his sergeant. "What's Henderson like?"

"He's a pleasant enough chap, trying to be helpful, or at least appearing to be."

"What's his history?"

"Nothing unusual. Actually he had a rather good war record. Decorated and all that."

"RAF?"

"No. The infantry. I believe he was a corporal. Got in early, lying about his age in 1942. Saw action in Africa and then with McCreery in Italy. Took part in the show at Cassino, was badly mauled and received a Distinguished Service Cross."

There was a slight mocking quality to Mitchell's tone which Trevor decided to ignore. "So there's nothing suspicious. He's an honest businessman. Come on, Mitchell, there's got to be something."

Sergeant Fawcett sneezed again.

"I didn't say there wasn't. For instance, there's that tax business. We're checking into it but I doubt we'll find anything new. However, as you pointed out, it could suggest smuggling. There is also Henderson's Moroccan partner. It might interest you to know that this chap, Ahmed, was in London last week."

Trevor looked up. "And?"

"And he left for Morocco two days before Henderson. There are some stories about him, however. Nothing definite. I'm still waiting for information from Interpol and the Moroccan police. The point is that someone had to know how to hire a professional murderer. I doubt that Henderson has that knowledge. Ahmed might."

"But what are you doing about Henderson?" asked Trevor. "If you believe he did it?"

"He's the most suspicious, naturally. Let's assume that he was smuggling. Let's assume that Jacobs found proof of this. He could then either blackmail Henderson or go to the police. Instead he tries to contact you, which suggests he would rather hurt Henderson than get money from him. This brings us to a final bit of information.

"Henderson has a rather attractive secretary, Sandra Coates, whom he hired in July. Jacobs made various overtures to her. She ignored them. He dramatically increased these overtures, apparently believing she was being coy. She responds by slapping him. This all takes place in Henderson's offices exactly four weeks ago. Jacobs grabs her, threatens her and accuses her of sleeping with Henderson. At this point Henderson walks in, sees the girl nearly hysterical, grabs Jacobs and offers to put him through the window. Being a typical sort of bully, Jacobs wilts. Henderson tells him to apologize. Also in the room is another secretary and Henderson's sales agent: a Mrs. Clavering. Jacobs gets stubborn and Henderson increases his hold. Therefore, in order to save himself from a brief journey through the window to the street below, Jacobs apologizes.

"This was relayed to me by Mrs. Clavering, a rather mannish woman in her early forties, who took delight in describing the discomforts of all. In any case, Jacobs then left in a fury and Henderson returned to his office, while Mrs. Clavering took the hysterical girl in hand."

Trevor felt there must be more to the story. "Why didn't he just fire Jacobs?"

"Presumably he didn't realize the extent of the problem. Henderson is not the imaginative sort and I doubt he ever had a thought about this Sandra himself. But you see the situation. Now where does that leave us?

"Let's assume that Jacobs has proof of the smuggling and plans to use it to get even with Henderson; that Henderson learns about it and contacts Ahmed, who is in London; that Ahmed then supplies a killer who disposes of Jacobs and removes the proof after both Ahmed and Henderson are safely in Morocco. What can we prove? And in the meantime we have to sort through the rest of Jacobs' sordid life for other possibilities."

Trevor shifted in his chair. He had no wish to accept Henderson's personality as portrayed by Mitchell. "What about the hired killer?"

"I very much doubt that he is still in England. We'll keep looking, of course, but right now the strongest point is that we can't prove Henderson's innocence."

"I want to see him. I mean, talk to him."

Mitchell took off his glasses again. "Why?"

"I want to see what he's like. I'll tell him I'm doing a Common Market story. Or maybe . . ."

"Maybe what?"

Trevor had the feeling that Mitchell was waiting; that he had carefully led the conversation around to this point. "Maybe I'll tell him I'm doing a story on business irregularities and that Jacobs told me to look him up. Perhaps I could make him jump."

"An interesting idea, but I think you underestimate the man. It might take quite a bit to make him jump, as you say."

Trevor doubted that. "But it might be worth a try."

Mitchell sat looking out the window. The drone of London traffic was quite loud in the room. Fawcett seemed uncomfortable and kept shifting in his chair.

"I'll tell you what," Mitchell said at last. "Give us a week. If we don't find anything, then you can make him jump or at least have your chance. . . ."

"Sir," interrupted Fawcett.

Mitchell ignored him. "But it will have to be delicately done. You can't just bully the man. If he reported you to the police then that would be the end of it. Evidence is such a nuisance. Oh, well, give us a week or ten days. It's surprising how these things can suddenly clear themselves up."

But Trevor didn't want it to clear itself up. He wanted to make Henderson jump.

4

FOR A NORMALLY quiet man, Henderson was feeling almost bouncy. He felt as if weights had been taken off him. It was nearly five o'clock and he was just finishing up the papers on a large carpet sale which he hoped to complete in a few weeks. Two hours before, he had completed another interview with Detective Inspector Mitchell. Hopefully, the very last, thought Henderson.

He was looking forward to the drive back to Hampstead and a quiet evening at home. Perhaps he would take his wife up to the Cruel Sea for a drink. They hadn't done that for some time. On the other hand, perhaps he would give up drinking entirely. Not that he did much, of course. He could get back in shape, play some tennis. It was time that his daughter, Elizabeth, who was thirteen, learned the game. It amazed him that she had never learned it in school. John, who was a year older, had been playing for years. But he wouldn't be back until the holidays.

Across the office, Henderson's secretary, Sandra Coates, was returning some files to the cabinet. She had apparently caught Henderson's infectious good humor and was humming quietly to herself. Henderson recognized it as some popular song by a group whom his daughter liked. The Ginks? He couldn't remember. Sandra was twenty-seven. There was no reason she shouldn't like that sort of music. As a matter of fact, thought Henderson a trifle condescendingly, those early fellows, the Beatles, had written some rather good tunes.

Henderson continued to stare at the girl as she knelt in front of the file cabinet. He realized she was very attractive. The thought surprised him because he rarely looked that individually at women. Certainly he saw them as good looking or bad looking, but he didn't usually single them out for particular attention. This was true of his reaction to most people. Unless they suddenly impinged on him, they were only shapes moving through his environment. He wished them well, but had no curiosity about them. Henderson was self-perceptive enough to know he did this and it seemed perfectly natural. In fact, it made his dealings with people much easier.

Therefore, he was surprised by his interest in Sandra. Sitting at his desk, he was very aware of watching himself watching her. He wondered if he would have noticed her in that way if Jacobs hadn't made those accusations.

Sandra had a soft, nearly oval face, which hid the cheekbones, and large blue eyes. Like small wells, Henderson thought. She was short with a model's figure. Her blond hair was also short. Henderson assumed it was naturally blond. But what particularly struck him was the naturalness of her movements. It was almost as if she glided, as if she lived in perfect comfort with her body. There was a pleasure to it which Henderson himself had never experienced.

Henderson was also attracted by her American accent. Actually, she was Canadian, but it didn't matter. They know a lot about sex over there, he thought. The idea surprised and even embarrassed him. He stopped looking at the girl and put his papers away in his desk.

Not that there was anything wrong with sex, he told himself. It just wasn't his particular sport. On the other hand, he certainly wasn't a model of fidelity to hold up as an example to the unhappily married. There had been that woman in Tangier, two, as a matter of fact. But that had been different. It had been Tangier, and for years Marie had been part of his vacation, until she had decided to return to Toulon. She had asked him to visit her there, but he couldn't imagine doing it.

The other woman, Henderson couldn't think of her name, had been a rather sudden acquisition. They had started talking one afternoon in the Café Paris. Then followed a few pleasant days together before she disappeared. Henderson assumed she had been visiting the city and that her stay had come to an end.

Fortunately, Henderson's wife, Harriet, didn't care for Tangier, or Morocco in general. She thought it was rather unclean. Henderson knew, but was indifferent to the fact, that she faintly disapproved of his dealing with Wogs. He didn't think she had minded so much before he had bought the house in Hampstead a few years before. But it wasn't a subject which they discussed, and Harriet lacked the strength of character to actually say anything about it. It was enough for her to live on Church Row in Hampstead.

But Sandra was a creature of London. She and her sisters flooded Oxford Street and Piccadilly Circus clothed in purple and lavender, wearing those excellent short skirts and long hair. Not that Sandra's hair was long, of course. Perhaps . . . Henderson stopped himself. He must be getting home. Had he ever known a woman in London besides his wife? There was that girl during the war—when was it?—in 1943, just before he had left for the invasion of Sicily. What was her name? He couldn't remember. That bothered him a little.

When he had come out of the hospital over a year later, he had gone back to the pub where they had met, hoping

41

to find her. All he found was a massive crater. He had thought of asking around the neighborhood for her but felt people might laugh at him. She had been worried about getting pregnant and he had wondered . . . But that was the war and he had been eighteen. Now he was forty-seven and respectable. Looking briefly again at Sandra, he got to his feet and picked up his briefcase and umbrella.

"I'm off," he said, walking to the door. "Don't stay out too late dancing." She smiled at him, while he wondered why he had said such a stupid thing. What business was it of his?

Mrs. Clavering was in the outer office. "You'll lock up?" he asked. She was a short, heavy woman wearing a solid two-piece gray suit and, to Henderson's surprise, long false eyelashes.

She nodded. "Certainly, if you wish."

He smiled and gave her a short wave as he left. He didn't particularly like the woman, but he felt he had no reason not to. Therefore, he was always friendly. Also, she was extremely efficient and Henderson was often amazed at the number of sales she could make to, for example, resort hotels in Bournemouth. He suspected she was a lesbian. Well, what of it, as long as she didn't make advances to Sandra as Jacobs had done. That had been rather unpleasant.

Henderson trotted down the stairs and out onto Chesterfield Street. It was an unusually warm September day with pure white clouds scudding across a dark-blue sky. Henderson always liked the weather to reflect his own mood and so was satisfied with what he saw. Up and down the street, people were hurrying out of their offices in an attempt to reach home before everyone else. Henderson consciously slowed down as he walked toward the parking garage where he kept his car.

Now that he thought of it, he supposed that Sandra bore

some of the responsibility for the whole Jacobs problem. He realized that ever since he hired her two months before, Jacobs had been circling her like a band of Indians around a wagon train. It was not something to which he had given much thought. Certainly this showed something about Sandra, since the other secretary, who worked mostly with Mrs. Clavering, had been spared Jacobs' attentions or at least that seemed to be true. But Cecilia was a little mousey and too prone to giggle. Also she was only twenty. But although these were subjects which Henderson knew little about, he felt that those apparent drawbacks wouldn't have dissuaded Jacobs. However, he couldn't be sure, since he had hardly ever thought about Jacobs, and what he now knew came mostly from Mitchell.

He ought to have fired Jacobs months ago. Henderson had even suspected that Jacobs was taking too keen an interest in his affairs. But not being a curious man, he was very slow at suspecting curiosity in others. Besides, Jacobs had been a good accountant and it would have been difficult to get someone else on that permanent half-time basis. It occurred to Henderson for the twentieth time that day that he had been extremely fortunate.

Henderson got his car from the garage. He and the attendant, Mr. Cameron, briefly discussed other Septembers they had experienced. They both agreed that, while this one was better than most, it still wasn't to be trusted. They parted amicably. Each Christmas Henderson sent Mr. Cameron a bottle of Scotch.

Henderson drove along Curzon Street to Park Lane, bordering Hyde Park, then past Marble Arch up Edgeware Road two blocks to Seymour Street, then east until he turned north on Baker Street at Portman Square. The heavy traffic seemed to make such maneuvers necessary. Usually Henderson enjoyed driving in the city, a pleasure he seemed to share with no one else, but today he wanted to get home and relax. Perhaps he would take Harriet up to the Cruel Sea after all. But then if he was going to take up tennis again, perhaps . . . He was suddenly surprised as a red double-decker bus sporting a massive advertisement for Harrods pulled away from the curb at Marylebone, practically running him down. A West Indian conductor waved cheerfully from the back. Henderson felt a moment of anger, then smiled and returned the wave. Public transport in London would stop entirely without these foreigners.

The best thing about driving a Bentley was that other cars allowed you a lot of room, not wanting to pay for bumping into you. Buses, however, were an exception, buses and taxis. He continued up Park Road, past Lord's Cricket Ground and St. John's Church, an elegant white and gold affair, to Wellington and then Finchley Road, which shot north like the barrel of a gun. It had been quite attractive before it had been widened and the trees had been cut down.

If he had only known what Jacobs was like earlier. But Henderson was the sort of person who, once in a situation, takes it for granted and leaves it alone. He liked to let his environment make the choices of his life, after he had first carefully arranged his environment. Now that he knew about Jacobs, he felt quite indignant, to the extent that he had an absurd wish the man were alive just so he could fire him. As for Jacobs' murder, he had almost put it out of his mind; just as he had done with the death of his friends during the war. When such things impinged too much, he would switch his mind to something else.

What had happened after all? He had flown to Tangier. He had spent five pleasant days wandering through the Medina and having excellent meals at Le Detroit, absorbing the city stretched out before him through the restaurant's huge glass walls. He had driven out to Cape Spartel along one of the most beautiful roads he knew, past the Governor's mansion, with its guards armed with machine guns: a road lined with pine trees, while through them to the south he could see the mountains rolling up and up to the very top of the horizon. This time he had even climbed the lighthouse, or rather had been escorted by a small boy who lived in that amazing house of blue tiles beneath it. The view of the sea and the rock-torn coast, the view of Spain and Portugal growing up out of the water miles and miles away like the back of some awakening beast—he could have stood there for hours.

Occasionally Henderson wondered why he didn't retire and move to Tangier right away. It was his wife, of course, and perhaps his children. Well, Elizabeth could be packed off to college in five years. Then he'd move to Tangier, wife or no wife.

He turned at Swiss Cottage, which was already jammed with early evening drinkers, onto College Crescent and then onto Fitzjohn's Avenue. Traffic was abominable and unfortunately the road was filled with Rolls Royces, other Bentleys, Mercedes, Jaguars, Daimlers—all driven by people who felt smug and protected by their wealth. Henderson considered buying a Land Rover. Certainly he would buy one when he moved to Tangier. Traffic there was even worse, besides being filled with people who would try to be hit on purpose, hoping to collect huge sums of money.

Henderson had felt better after learning from Mitchell what Jacobs was like. Then he felt guilty for feeling better. The petty evil of the man certainly didn't justify his death. If he thought about Jacobs' death at all he could only justify it in terms of pure survival.

Henderson had also been pleased by his handling of the interview. He had been in perfect control from beginning to end, and although it was their fourth interview Henderson never deviated from his original story. Yes, he had had words with Jacobs about Sandra, but good Lord, the man was practically assaulting her. Mitchell had learned about that from Mrs. Clavering, of course. She had been only too glad to tell him. She called it her duty.

Had he been aware of anyone who had particularly disliked Jacobs? Well, no. You see, they had only met at the office. Did he dislike Jacobs? Why, he doubted that he had ever given the matter any thought. They moved in completely different circles. Jacobs seemed to be a sort of sporting man. Actually, he doubted that he spoke to Jacobs in a conversational way more than once a month. No, their only run-in had been the incident with Sandra. If there had been anything like that before, he certainly would have fired him.

There had been nothing for Mitchell to hold on to, no point of contact. All Henderson said had been true. And Mitchell, fortunately, didn't know about the ledger, although he must have known about Jacobs' attempts to contact the press. But perhaps he didn't. Certainly he didn't mention it.

Just the thought of the ledger turned Henderson cold. He had been a fool to let Ahmed talk him into the smuggling venture. But the money had been so good. Besides, Ahmed had been using Henderson's business for smuggling almost since they had begun. If he was going to do it, then it was only fair that Henderson should reap some of the rewards. When Henderson had accused Ahmed of smuggling, eight years before, it had seemed much easier to join him as a kind of silent partner than to dissolve their association completely. Also, Ahmed could have made trouble. It wasn't as if hashish were actually a narcotic. He had smoked it himself in some of the cafés, not here in London of course.

Fortunately, they had stopped smuggling in April after the growing interference of the French and American authorities had made it too dangerous. The bribes, too, were becoming more and more costly. Also, he felt that Ahmed was being a little greedy, taking more than his fair share. Well, it was over now.

He turned the Bentley onto Church Row and began looking for a parking place. The street was rather short and began with an expensive French restaurant, Cellier du Midi, and ended with the oak-surrounded church and graveyard. Between was a distinguished row of early Georgian houses. Henderson found a space just past his own house and maneuvered the Bentley into it. His daughter was just going out.

"I'm going over to Kathleen's, Daddy," she said, blowing him a kiss. She was a chubby, friendly girl who would probably end up like her mother: a worrier.

Henderson went into the house and looked over the mail on the hall table. Although he wasn't expecting anything, he would have liked to have word from Ahmed. Perhaps he ought to send him some small present.

"Is that you, dear?" his wife called from the living room, a trifle nervously. There had been a few robberies in the area during the past month and Harriet was a little upset. She blamed it on the American influence, as she called it.

Henderson wondered how many burglars would begin by rifling the mail. For a moment, he considered saying, "No!" in a gruff voice, but thought better of it. Harriet wouldn't think it a bit funny and might scream.

"Yes," he said at last.

"Shall I make you a drink?" Harriet came into the hall to look at him. She was forty-one, and although she had been quite cute when they married in 1954, her face received no support from the bones beneath it. Consequently, it had been moving downward for the last twenty years.

Henderson kissed her casually on the nose and picked up the paper. "None for me, thank you. It's time that I get back in shape."

5

LATER THAT EVENING, Trevor was returning to his flat with Clare. She was still a little touchy about his recent indifference, as she interpreted it, and he planned to show her her mistake. They had had dinner together at the Gay Hussar on Greek Street. Hungarian food always gave Trevor gas. He had suffered from it during the entire evening.

After dinner they had walked over to the Academy Theatre, on Oxford Street, to see an old Japanese movie: *The Seven Samurai.* As Trevor climbed the stairs to his flat, he kept seeing the faces of the actors who played the terrified villagers, trying to fight off the bandits with sharpened poles. For some reason he was reminded of Jacobs. Trevor decided that he needed a drink.

"What are you thinking about?" asked Clare, as he unlocked the door and let her precede him into the flat.

"Just those faces in the movie." He couldn't express what he wanted to say.

"Character actors," said Clare, taking off her coat. "They're the foundation of Japanese films. We've never been quite able to equal it here."

"Let's go to bed," said Trevor, taking their coats to the

closet. He didn't want to get into a discussion of films with Clare who knew a hundred times more than he did, knew the names of all the actors back for years and years. She would often talk about it while thinking of something else, having the ability to turn it on and then send her mind off in another direction: someone to tend the shop, as it were.

She was a tall woman of twenty-nine with the sort of face that would remain exactly the same for thirty years: thin, high cheekbones, small mouth and jaw. It was attractive, although the jaw jutted out a little too much. Trevor thought she had a perfect body, designed for and by his own hand.

"Sometimes," she said, "I wonder if you really like films."

"Sure I do. Let's go to bed."

She was office manager at Trevor's bureau, and the best thing for her, he thought, would be to be given the title of Editor, even Assistant Editor. Why not, since she did the work? Without it she felt too much like hired help and compensated by adopting a knowing manner which could be irritating.

She was using this knowing manner now. "I thought you'd lost interest."

The remark bothered Trevor because it brought Jacobs back to mind, and with Jacobs came Henderson and Mitchell. It had been a week since they had talked about making Henderson jump.

He took Clare by the arm and kissed her roughly. His hand settled on her left breast like a great crow. She pulled away, smiling. "Hey," she said, and began unbuttoning her blouse. Trevor took off his shirt, paused and then went in to prepare large glasses of Scotch. He could hear Clare making comfortable noises from the bedroom.

Getting ice from the kitchen, he filled two glasses and then poured in triple shots. So far, they hadn't argued and she hadn't come down too strong about the way he had been neglecting her, although she didn't mind that as much as she minded his work interrupting when they were together. Whenever he was called to the phone in a bar, she became angry and wanted no part of him. Being called Editor would change that, he thought.

He walked over to the radio and flicked it on, then moved the dial back and forth looking for something suitable. The radio was an old Telefunken, which theoretically could pick up any station and band in the world. He got a classical station and turned up the volume. Suddenly he went cold. He quickly turned off the radio and stood staring at it for a moment.

"I liked that," called Clare from the bedroom. "Could you turn it back on. . . . Please?"

"I don't like the Fourth," said Trevor, walking over to the record player.

"That was the First, silly."

He stopped, a little surprised. "They're all the same," he said quietly.

"I beg your pardon?"

"I said they're all the same." He spoke angrily. Then, looking through his records, he selected an album of Thelonius Monk solos and put it on. He badly needed a new needle. In a moment of self-pity, he decided he badly needed all sorts of things. On the long table by the record player was a pile of unread books which he had bought at Foyles three weeks before. There were five books on chess, including one of the Fischer-Spassky games of the previous summer. Although the game didn't excite him and he was at best a mediocre player, he had decided he needed a new hobby to fill up the time. But Trevor always liked the idea of doing something much more than the actual doing. His bookcase included many unread books on antique cars, old coins, hiking and other hobbies of a nonfrivolous sort. Sometimes he wondered if it weren't the same way with women: the idea being better than the act, that after verbal capitulation body contact became unnecessary.

Picking up the glasses, he shrugged and walked into the bedroom. Clare looked at him curiously. "Is something the matter?"

He wanted to tell her about Jacobs and Henderson but realized it would be very much the wrong thing to do, especially since she was lying there naked. He stood looking at her lying on his large Victorian bed. Monk's solo piano sounded like pebbles dropped at random in a tin drum. Trevor felt he could look at Clare for hours. Her skin was perfect and her bones, ribs, pelvis were outlined as if covered by a thin blanket. He wanted to touch her, move his hands roughly across her large breasts. Then he thought of Eva, remembered her thin naked body. He could almost hear her asking in her flat monotone about Jacobs.

"Is something the matter?" Clare asked again.

He handed her a glass of Scotch. "No. It just seems like a long time." He couldn't clear his mind. Clare lifted her arm and gently touched his leg, then her fingers fastened on it firmly.

Trevor stopped thinking and practically fell on top of her. A bit of his drink splashed over the pillow.

"At least you could take off the rest of your clothes," she said. "Your belt buckle scrapes."

He twisted around and began taking off his shoes and socks. That could never be done casually. The shoelace of his left shoe caught in a knot. He pulled at it impatiently, finally breaking it. She put her glass to his mouth and he took a long drink; then quickly he finished getting undressed.

"You have the hairiest body," she said, smiling.

"That's because I'm an animal." He made a growling noise.

They sat looking at each other for a moment as they finished their drinks. To Trevor it seemed he could actually feel his eyes touching her skin, touching her like a soft glove moving back and forth across her body. They put down their glasses. Trevor slowly reached out his arm, touched her breasts lightly and then tucked his hand behind her neck. Her eyes were fastened on his. He began pulling her toward him, still very slowly, keeping his eyes locked on hers. Then she touched his leg again and her fingers moved up it like a small animal. All the air went out of his lungs. He pulled her to him roughly and they toppled over on their sides as Trevor sought out her crotch with his hand, still roughly and impatiently.

"Take it easy," she whispered.

He stopped and then moved his hand lightly across her belly. She arched her back and he began kissing her neck and mouth, softly at first, then harder, forcing open her mouth. She began twisting her body against his, pressing her pelvis against him, pulling him tightly against her, as he slowly moved on top of her.

The telephone rang. At first they ignored it and tried to continue. It kept ringing. They stopped. Trevor was still breathing heavily. The phone kept ringing.

"Goddammit to hell." Trevor walked across the room and picked up the phone on the bureau. "Yes?" he said curtly. He looked at his hairy white body in the mirror, disliking what he saw.

It was Mitchell. "Good evening."

"What do you want?"

"Am I disturbing you?" Mitchell sounded bored.

"Us."

"I beg your pardon?"

"I said, Us."

"Ahh . . ." There was a pause. Trevor could hear Clare rustling around in the bed, probably searching for a cigarette. He carefully kept his back to her.

Mitchell spoke again: "Are you still interested in Henderson?"

"You called me at eleven o'clock to ask me that? Who in the hell . . ."

"Don't be sharp with me, Trevor. This is a delicate situation which has required some thought. Are you interested?"

"What do you have on him?" Despite his anger, Trevor was interested. He also felt cold. Clare was still moving about behind him.

"Less than ever, actually, although there is still nothing against him. Well?"

"Sure I'm interested. What do you want done?"

"Make him jump." Mitchell's voice was hard.

"Now? Jesus Christ . . ."

"Tomorrow will do, but be careful. Remember what we talked about. We want him to think we're no longer interested, but at the same time we can't afford to have him call and complain about you. Understand?"

"Sure, I'll get right on it." Trevor felt better already. He felt almost vindicated.

"And, Trevor, come and see me afterward, all right?"

"Sure thing. Sometime in the afternoon."

"And, Trevor, sorry about the Us." Mitchell hung up.

During the latter part of the conversation, Trevor had forgotten about Clare. Now he felt guilty about it. He turned around.

Clare was dressed and facing him, smoking a cigarette. She didn't look pleased. "Can't you get a switch for your phone?" It wasn't really a question.

"I wasn't expecting any calls," he said lamely.

"You never are, that's the point. Do you realize how often this happens?"

"Come on, Clare, cut it out. . . ."

"Dozens. Either here or in some bar, even at the theater. I sometimes wonder if you don't do it on purpose. Is there any time when you're not working?" Her voice was quite bitter.

Trevor felt uncomfortable standing naked before her anger. "Sure, right now. Let's go back to bed." He took a step toward her.

"I don't feel like it anymore." She evaded his hand and began walking out of the room.

"For Christ's sake, Clare, I . . ."

"Don't swear at me, if you please." She walked into the living room and got her coat from the closet.

Trevor wanted to say something but instead he stood in the doorway and watched. He felt like a fool and wished that he had some clothes on. He wasn't, however, going to show her his discomfort. For a moment he considered grabbing her and dragging her back to the bedroom.

She opened the door to his flat. "Cheerio." She left, leaving the door wide open behind her.

Trevor walked to it quickly and slammed it shut. "Goddammit to hell." He wished he had something to throw or to punish.

6

THE NEXT MORNING at eleven o'clock, Trevor was sitting in Henderson's outer office, ostensibly waiting to talk to him about how being a member of the European Economic Community would affect trade with non-Common Market countries such as Morocco. The warm September weather had broken and it had begun to rain heavily as Trevor left the tube. Now he was damp and uncomfortable, while his dark-brown Harris tweed sport coat gave off the unmistakable smell of wet wool.

For most of the summer, Trevor and Clare had had a mild running argument on whether or not he needed a new raincoat. She contended that the one he had—a khaki affair with belts, buckles and flaps that he had purchased in Washington six years before—was too tattered and seedy for his work. He was aware of this, knowing that people respond more readily to innocuous dressers, but he liked the tattered and seedy effect. Moreover the coat was almost an exact copy of a coat that Mountbatten had worn during the war. Trevor had an unvoiced preference for costumes, which existed uncomfortably with his own self-image as a dour, cynical reporter. Therefore, with Clare he argued that while the coat was old, it did an excellent job of keeping out the rain. This morning, however, the coat not only refused to keep out the rain but seemed to attract and absorb the drops at an astonishing rate.

It was now hanging from Henderson's coatrack, while a whole family of ducks could have found contentment in the pool which had gathered beneath. Trevor looked at it and felt cross. He also felt cross about Clare who had refused to speak to him that morning, apparently because of the interrupting phone call of the night before. Trevor took this anger and let it flow in the direction of Henderson, but he kept thinking about Clare.

He wondered if England would deport him if he kidnapped Clare, took her to his small cottage in Surrey and raped her steadily for four days. Only if he did it during the workweek and didn't give her a fair wage, he thought. Then he wondered a little bitterly about what would constitute a fair wage. He tried again to stop thinking about her.

Instead, he looked appreciatively at Henderson's secretary. Trevor saw her as an extremely sensuous woman. Her slow sure movements reminded him of a cat stretching, while the slightest working of her muscles seemed to give her pleasure. Good bones, thought Trevor.

He wondered if Henderson slept with her. Why would he hire a woman who looked like that unless he intended to sleep with her? He wondered if she minded sleeping with a man twenty years older than herself. Trevor remembered, however, that Henderson was in pretty good shape. Trevor at thirty-seven was conscious of having a growing potbelly from too much lager: a malady common to journalists. Occasionally, he considered getting rid of it, but the idea so exhausted him that he never had energy to begin. His only concession was to drink more Scotch.

Trevor continued to look at Sandra who was typing away rapidly. Then he realized he was humming. He stopped suddenly, nearly biting his tongue as he clamped his teeth together. Slowly he realized he had been humming something else, something completely innocuous, but he was now so suspicious of himself that humming even "Yankee Doodle" would make him nervous.

He breathed sharply through his nose, making a kind of snorting noise. Sandra looked at him. While appearing fairly relaxed before, Trevor had taken on the look of someone whose whole body was pointed, aimed and ready to go off. He felt very alert as if listening to something faint and far away: miners tunneling beneath the city, pigeons pecking at each other's eyes. He didn't notice that Sandra was looking at him strangely.

The intercom buzzed and unintelligible words crackled from it. "Mr. Henderson will see you now, Mr. Trevor," said Sandra.

Trevor nodded and got to his feet. He felt a surge of anger at Henderson for making him wait, for interfering in his life. He disliked this tastefully decorated outer office with its pictures of Venetian canal scenes and real plants and flowers. He disliked Sandra's assurance. Trevor was filled with a wish to turn the entire room upside down. Henderson opened the door to his office and the two men stood facing each other.

Henderson's face was calm and emotionless. If he felt anything about Trevor, he gave no sign of it. Possibly there was no reason that he should, although he must have known of Jacobs' attempts to contact the press. Perhaps he didn't. But Trevor wanted him to; he wanted the man to feel fear, to show something. Trevor was so tense and angry that he was sure it must show. He disliked not being in complete control of his appearance, and noticed with growing irritation that Henderson apparently had that knack.

Henderson smiled. "Won't you come in?"

Trevor walked into the office without speaking. It was quite elegantly and tastefully decorated: managing to be very English and show off Moroccan imports at the same time. A blue Moroccan carpet with triangular designs in dark grays and reds covered the floor. There was a pair of lamps made out of tall bronze incense burners. There was a small coffee table made from a bronze tray covered with geometric patterns. Trevor guessed the room was about twenty by fifteen feet. There was a very Victorian couch covered with what Trevor suspected to be Moroccan leather. There was nothing foreign about the large oaken desk and four straight chairs. There was a photograph on the wall behind the desk, of some city with white buildings perched on a hillside over a bay. Actually some of the buildings were pink. Trevor could see small minarets.

Henderson followed his glance. "That's Tangier. Quite attractive for a port city."

Trevor sat down in one of the straight chairs without speaking. He hadn't looked at Henderson since first entering the office.

Henderson perched himself on the edge of his desk and smiled affably. He picked up an amber paperweight with a carved silver base and began rubbing it. "People don't realize how easily the foreign can be adapted to everyday life. They somehow expect everything Arabian to smell of camel."

Henderson smiled slightly. Trevor felt that the phrase came from an old stock of mild but polished witticisms which Henderson used to show himself off as a casual man of the world. He put it down as another mark against Henderson, wondering if the man would go into a whole routine.

"Of course, as you know," continued Henderson, apparently unphased by Trevor's silence, "they aren't Arabs but Berbers. They call themselves Imaziren. Actually related to southern Europeans, although there is also a strong Hamitic element, even, surprisingly enough, a kind of Nordic element. There are thousands with blond or red hair. Perfectly natural and not the by-blows of occupying armies, although they have certainly had enough of those in their time."

Trevor had the feeling that Henderson could go on like this endlessly. It was like paying your money for a movie, then sitting down and letting the scene take over. First came the Moroccan travelogue, then the main feature. He wondered what form that would take. Trevor leaned forward, took a cigarette from a green leather box on the desk and lit it. Even the cigarette was Moroccan and very harsh. Slowly exhaling the smoke, he looked up at Henderson. He wondered how long the man would talk if he himself remained silent. He wondered if Henderson were playing some sort of game. Trevor could feel his dislike for Henderson growing. He was so self-contained, perfectly comfortable, thoroughly respectable in his dark-blue three-piece suit.

"I suppose one could see Morocco as a country of invaders," continued Henderson, "in which case the survival of Berber independence is rather remarkable in its way. There were Carthaginian colonies along the coast, while in the first century B.C. Moroccan Berbers fought in the armies of Pompey and Sertorius. The city of Tangier, or Tanja, as the Moroccans call it, stands nearly where the Roman city of Tingis stood when Morocco was the Roman province of Mauretania. Augustus made it a free city." Henderson paused and smiled at Trevor. "I hope you don't mind my going on like this. My wife tells me that I too often let the subject carry me away. But actually the country has quite a fascinating history."

Trevor refused to say anything. It occurred to him that Henderson now appeared slightly nervous, but he couldn't be certain.

He smiled at Trevor again and then took a cigarette for

himself. "The Vandals held Tangier after the Romans, then the Byzantines took it from the Vandals, then the Arabs came in 682 under Oqba.

"Tangier, of course, has been demolished quite often. The Spanish held it, as did the Portuguese and the French. Then the city was part of the dowry of Catherine of Braganza. Therefore when she married Charles II in 1662, Tangier became an English possession. Naturally we had to fight for it. Charles, however, had been too extravagant here at home, and so in 1684 he abandoned the city to the Berbers due to a lack of funds. Actually the massive gate to the Medina in the marketplace is still known as the Catherine Gate, although the Berbers call it Báb el Suk."

Trevor lit another cigarette. Henderson had stopped talking and was now looking at Trevor, who was calmly staring back. That is, he hoped it was calmly. "Actually," said Trevor after a few moments, "I'm not in the least interested in Tangier."

"I'm terribly sorry," said Henderson, apparently confused, "my secretary told me . . ."

"I misrepresented myself to her," interrupted Trevor.

"Aren't you a reporter?"

"Yeah, I'm a reporter."

Henderson got up and walked around to the other side of his desk. He stood there looking at Trevor with a small puzzled smile. It was an expression which could change instantly. "Then I'm afraid I don't understand."

Trevor was filled with a desire to hit Henderson, bring down his fist on that immaculately straight nose. "I mean I'm not doing a story on foreign trade agreements, that's what I mean." Trevor had a normally gravelly voice. Now he forced more pebbles into it.

Henderson sat down at his desk. "Then I don't see how I can help you," he said coldly.

Trevor forced his mouth into a grin. "I'm doing a story

on smuggling. Your buddy, Jacobs, told me you were the guy to see."

They both sat silently for a few moments. Trevor kept his eyes on Henderson's. Henderson was staring down at his desk. Slowly he raised his eyes to meet Trevor's. He was still holding tightly onto the amber paperweight. It would never have occurred to Trevor that Henderson might want to hit him with it. He knows, thought Trevor, he really knows.

Then, very quietly, Henderson said: "I have no idea what you are talking about, Mr. Trevor."

Trevor laughed abruptly. "Sure you do. Jacobs tells me you know all about smuggling dope out of Morocco, that you've been doing it for years. He's your buddy, right? Your business associate? He should know, right?"

"You're making a very serious error, Mr. . . ."

"Cut the shit, Henderson. I talked to Jacobs. I know what he had to say. Then he gets killed. Who stands to lose by Jacobs' talk? You do. Who stands to gain by his being dead? You do. I'm no fool, Henderson."

Henderson still hadn't moved. He sat staring into Trevor's face, speaking softly. "I have already spoken with the police about Jacobs' death. As for your preposterous allegation . . ."

"Jesus Christ, Henderson, I'm giving you a break. I only want to know about the smuggling. You want to kill Jacobs, that's no affair of mine. I didn't even like the man. But I do want to know about the smuggling. What do you say? Either you talk to me or I go to the police."

Henderson didn't speak. Trevor was certain, however, that he was coming to some sort of decision, but, except for the way he gripped the paperweight, there was no sign of what he was feeling. But just his silence is enough, thought Trevor.

Henderson slowly got to his feet, putting down the paperweight. "Get out of my office."

He spoke so quietly that Trevor wasn't sure that he heard him correctly. He was about to say, "What?" when Henderson said again, much louder, "Get out of my office!"

"Come on, Henderson, are you stupid? Jacobs told me . . ."

"Get out of my office before I call the police!"

Trevor leaned back in his chair. "You won't do that."

Henderson punched a button on the intercom. "Sandra, call the police immediately, and then come in here . . ."

When Trevor left Henderson's office a few minutes later, he was furious and didn't even notice it was raining harder than ever.

7

"IT WAS THE TIME, of course," said Mitchell, tilting back in his chair. "Jacobs was killed on the tenth. Today's the twenty-first. If you had all that information, why wait so long to use it? Also, an exclusive story on the murder would be much more of a coup than another nebulous bit of imaginative writing on the smuggling of narcotics."

Trevor was looking out the window at a busload of tourists slogging across Parliament Square toward the Abbey through the rain. They looked miserable. "Maybe I was just waiting for the police to stop bothering him," he said. He had come directly to Mitchell's office after leaving Henderson, even though he had wanted to go home and change out of his wet clothes. The office was hot and stuffy. Trevor's wet sport coat was quietly steaming above the electric fire in the corner.

"Possibly, but Henderson couldn't take that chance. Besides, he also had the evidence which was taken from Jacobs' flat. On top of that, he never called the police."

"But the girl was telephoning . . ."

"She never called. I just finished checking."

Trevor was amazed. "You mean he was bluffing?"

"Either that or he stopped his secretary from calling."

Mitchell seemed to enjoy Trevor's discomfort.

"That son of a bitch. I should have stayed there."

"No, you did much the best thing. If he had called the police then we couldn't go ahead with your plan. By not calling, he set a precedent for his own future actions. Hopefully, he'll still refrain from calling when you begin your work. Do you still want to go on with this?"

"Yeah." There were times when Trevor felt irritated by Mitchell's self-complacency, as if he foresaw everything before it happened and was never surprised. "Besides," he continued, "he killed Jacobs."

Mitchell glanced at him sharply, then shrugged. "Well, I still think you are underestimating the man."

"Oh, cut it out. He's a businessman. If he weren't you would have loosened his tongue by now." Trevor would have liked to see Henderson under the light for forty-eight hours, being forced to talk. He disliked the subtlety of Mitchell's plan, feeling that Henderson could be attacked more directly. Trevor had come out of Henderson's office feeling defeated. Now he wanted to get even.

"Come, come, we don't use such methods."

"Shit. Did you get me that bed-sitter in Hampstead?"

"Yes, quite pleasant and only three long blocks from Henderson. Although, I must say that seven pounds a week is a bit steep. Probably we should have put you on the other side of Finchley Road.

"I also took care of your office. Belton knows that you will be doing some serious work for us. I told him you were indispensable. Fortunately, he doesn't seem to feel the same way about you."

Trevor nodded. He knew his editor wouldn't be pleased, but the man was enough of an anglophile to do whatever Mitchell asked. If Trevor had asked, Belton would certainly have refused. He didn't like Trevor and felt Trevor often mocked the English. He also knew that Trevor was a better writer than he was.

Trevor hoped this official blessing on his outside work would also impress Clare, apparently giving him a legitimacy that she had previously doubted. Mitchell's intervention might even make him more interesting to her. People are absurd, he thought.

Looking out the window, Trevor noticed another group of tourists sloshing toward the Abbey. It struck him that he never saw them leave. For a moment he imagined giant machines grinding the visitors into more and more marble statues. He turned back to Mitchell. "Have you learned anything more about Jacobs?"

Mitchell was in the midst of cleaning his glasses on his yellow woolen tie. "Jacobs was the sort of person about whom there is always more to learn and most of it is nasty. What do you care to know?"

Trevor was afraid of any information which might make Henderson appear less guilty. "Anything concerning Henderson?"

"I'm afraid not. Just a great deal of information which is basically a nuisance. For instance, we found an address book. It contains about two hundred names. Many of the people only met Jacobs once and some don't remember him. All have to be checked. There are names of several people he may have been blackmailing—homosexuals. There are also the names of people with whom Jacobs wished to get even. He was an extremely vindictive man and the history of his small quarrels . . ."

"Come on, Mitchell, the man's dead. Is there anything else?"

"We still have no evidence to show that Henderson is innocent," said Mitchell irritably. "If we did have such evidence, we wouldn't need your assistance."

Trevor ignored the remark. "Anything new on that Moroccan?"

"Ahmed? Yes, I was right about him. He's been active for quite a while. During the war he did a fancy job of working for the Germans, the Vichy French and us. He was also active in the blackmarket and up to his neck in smuggling. In 1954, he joined Henderson as a kind of junior partner. There's evidence that he was still smuggling at that time. He could easily be smuggling now."

"What about the Moroccan police?"

Mitchell smiled. "The flesh is weak. The police in Morocco are transferred yearly in an attempt to stop corruption. Civil servants are transferred every two years. The police in Tangier have assured me of their undying cooperation. Presumably they'll bother Ahmed a little. At Christmas I'll send them a box of cigars. Perhaps we'll exchange humorous greeting cards."

"You don't seem to be taking this very seriously," said Trevor in a petulant tone. Mitchell's chatty manner reminded him of interviews he had had with officials in the past: men who wished to convince him that the rumors of their excesses had been greatly exaggerated and that deep down they were basically decent. There was something unconvincing about Mitchell. Trevor had noticed it before, but he could never satisfactorily explain it to himself.

"Trevor," said Mitchell quietly, "this is my case. Do you understand that? I am forty-five years old. I have been a policeman since the age of twenty-three. Although this case bores me, it is still my case and I am perfectly qualified to direct it. You are helping me for your own personal reasons, presumably because you have no internal choice. As a matter of fact, I find you much more interesting than the case itself. Murder doesn't interest me. It stopped interesting me when I was still a constable. Guilt, however, and culpability are subjects which continue to intrigue me. I once knew a man who confessed to every murder in London, saying that the victims died of his germs. An extreme but interesting example. So far, you, too, are interesting. This could change."

Trevor had no desire to discuss his own feelings of guilt. "Does Fawcett still think I'm guilty?" asked Trevor, trying to change the subject. "Where is he anyway?"

Mitchell looked at Trevor for a few moments without speaking. Then he smiled. "I have put him in charge of the address book. That is what he's best at. He is certain that the answer to the murder lies there, which is one of the reasons I favor Henderson. Fawcett's intuitions are unfailingly wrong. The reason that he is certain is because he wants us to be wrong about Henderson. The reason he wants us to be wrong about Henderson is because he desperately dislikes you. At the moment he's also feeling none too fond of me. However, all that is necessary to put myself in his good graces would be to say: 'Arrest Trevor.'"

Trevor smiled in spite of himself. "Transfer him."

"More easily said than done. Sergeant Fawcett feels he is the guiding spirit of this department. He feels I would be lost without him. These are cherished beliefs for Sergeant Fawcett. If I transferred him, to Manchester for instance, he would be crushed. Worse than that, before he left he would make my life a misery. He would explain to me how much he is giving up, but, as he would make sure to tell me, he knows his duty. The man lives for his duty as other men live for the race track. Once in Manchester, he would write me constantly, long philosophical letters on duty. No, while he is here I can always get rid of him. If I got rid of him, he would always be here." Mitchell paused, pleased with his phrase. Then he sighed and began searching for his pipe among the papers on his desk.

"Well," he continued, "I suppose that is only partially true. I know I should transfer him, but I also know that I won't."

But thinking about his own problems again, Trevor was barely listening. He got to his feet. He wanted to check out the area around Henderson's office and the route that he took home. He wanted to see what Henderson's home in Hampstead was like. He wanted to start moving out to his bed-sitter. He also wanted a drink. The pubs wouldn't be open for another hour and a half. "No," he said half to himself and half to Mitchell, "you should fire him." He paused and went on. "So we begin Monday?"

Mitchell nodded. He found his pipe and was now cleaning it. "Yes. We need to give Henderson time to think that we're no longer interested in him and let him feel that you never contacted us."

"And then we hit him?"

"In our fashion, yes."

8

IT WAS MONDAY MORNING and Henderson was driving to work. He felt uncomfortable, as if the London weather were pressing down upon him, forcing him into a tiny box. Actually there was a stiff breeze and the weather had changed again. The sky was one of those bright blue skies which occasionally appear over London and are only seen elsewhere in the middle of the ocean. Henderson didn't notice it.

He was considering the possibility of no longer driving into the city. On this morning more buses than usual were honking at him. More taxis dodged into his path, forcing him to slam on the brakes. He could easily take the tube from Hampstead and then with one change get off at Green Park, or even Bond Street if he wanted to walk. On the other hand, he had more freedom with a car; he could get away from places.

In the back of his mind was the image of Trevor. It was lodged there like something cut into a wall. Red face, red hair, stocky. Henderson could just feel the pressure. He had tried not to think of Trevor since he had left the office on Thursday. He realized it was unwise to try to put Trevor out of his mind, but for the time being that was all he could do. He had felt so safe!

Henderson turned off Park Street onto Upper Brook Street, driving toward Grosvenor Square. Although he wasn't sure why, he wanted to look at the American Embassy again. He felt the reason was mixed up with Trevor. Henderson was working from a very high place in his mind, beyond conscious thought and motivation. It seemed that he was keeping his mind a blank. Instead, he was running with his eyes closed.

The first he saw of the Square were the massive trees, then the white monument with its tall bronze statue of Roosevelt. He turned on South Audley Street and slowed down by the Embassy. A taxi honked behind him but he ignored it. It was a tremendously ugly gray building with narrow windows and topped by a massive eagle. Someone had described it as expressing "almost Roman power." Henderson had once visited the bar in the basement: what seemed to be called a "cocktail lounge" where hamburgers were served on imported buns and bowls of popcorn decorated the tables. He had sat there listening to Musak and drinking Budweiser while his host, some undersecretary, waxed nostalgic about how this was the truest bit of Americana in London. Henderson wondered whether this explained American alcoholism or prohibitionism. The rest of the building seemed full of statues and full-sized portraits of presidents and folk heroes.

Henderson accelerated down South Audley Street, glancing at the pseudo–early Georgian buildings which housed offices and several other embassies. At one time Grosvenor Square had been the most fashionable square in London. Now it was known as Little America. Eisenhower had taken over a great hunk of it as his headquarters during the war.

Henderson suddenly found himself thinking of the Italian campaign, his own participation in it, his wounds, the death of his parents in the Blitz. He had a flash of seeing himself crawling toward the German hiding places, holding his bayonet so tightly that its impression remained on his hand for hours.

Henderson drove out of the Square and continued down to Curzon Street with its restaurants, hairdressers and offices. He stopped thinking about Trevor and his embassy. After all, whatever the man suspected, he had no proof. The ledger had been destroyed. There was nothing Trevor could do.

Henderson parked his car, exchanged a few remarks about the weather with Mr. Cameron and then walked off toward Chesterfield Street and his office.

He was about a hundred feet from his door when he noticed Trevor, leaning against a wall across the street from his office. That trenchcoat was unmistakable. Henderson stopped abruptly. He was sure Trevor hadn't seen him yet. For a moment he considered going back, getting his car and driving away. He didn't care where. He would just drive. Henderson told himself that was foolish, but he still didn't move. What did the man want? Slowly he felt a steady anger growing up within him. He refused to be bullied. This time he would call the police.

No, that, too, would be foolish. Trevor was nothing, only a nuisance. He could ignore him. To his surprise, Henderson found himself thinking of the Café Paris in the center of Tangier, of sitting there eating croissants and sipping café au lait, watching hundreds of people from dozens of countries surge back and forth in front of the large windows, bumping into the outside tables, brushing aside small children selling everything from the Paris *Tribune* to their sisters. German tourists with movie cameras and Bavarian caps; old beggar-women in black carrying huge piles of sticks on their backs; dapper English homosexuals flapping at each other; Moslem holy men moving through the crowd

71

as if through an invisible sea; small yellow dogs looking for bits of food; French civil servants with their minds full of Paris and a desire to be there.

Henderson began walking toward his office. He saw Trevor look up at him, but he refused to return his stare. Trevor remained leaning against the building as if he had been built into it. Henderson crossed to the other side of the street, keeping his face an expressionless mask. He could almost feel Trevor's eyes touching him. Walking briskly to his door, he opened it and went up the stairs. He began to breathe deeply as the door closed behind him.

It surprised Henderson that the secretaries and Mrs. Clavering were working as usual, that nothing was different. He somehow expected to see the whole office in chaos: desks overturned, chairs broken, papers covering the floor. But it was like the beginning of any other day. They all wished him the same "Good morning" that they always wished him. There were the same notes and reports from Carlton in Tangier and Moers in Fez, detailing the prices of carpets, metal work, leather. There was no word from Ahmed, but that could be explained. He might be too busy. Other than that everything was the same as ever. This astounded Henderson.

He went to the window and looked out. Trevor hadn't moved, although he was now looking up at the window. Henderson stepped back quickly.

"Is there anything wrong, Sir?" asked Sandra.

The question startled Henderson and he turned around. "No, nothing, just some tourists in the street."

"Tourists here?" said Mrs. Clavering, who was sorting through some swatches of Moroccan silks on Sandra's desk. She always assumed that any conversation within her hearing automatically included her.

"Yes, here," said Henderson sharply. Then he turned and walked into his office. Once inside he had to restrain himself to keep from locking the door. Instead he sat down at his desk and began going over the reports from Carlton and Moers. He could barely read them.

He wondered why he was so upset by Trevor's appearance. After all, he had been aware from the first that something like this might happen. It had been a calculated risk, and a small one, according to Ahmed. Nothing could be proved. Again Henderson found himself thinking about the police. But what would he tell them?

But there was Trevor casually leaning against a building across the street. It was the surprise of it, thought Henderson. After two weeks of feeling safe, up pops Trevor. He had even managed, he thought, to put the whole affair out of his head. What had happened? He had been bothered by Jacobs. He had gone to Tangier. He had returned from Tangier. Jacobs was no longer there. Nothing had happened. Jacobs was just gone, existing now only as some mythical creation of the police.

What did Trevor want? Money? Henderson knew it would be fatal to admit anything. It would be fatal even to show that he was nervous. He had been surprised, that's all. But even as he thought that, he was filled with an almost overpowering sense of oppression.

There was a light knock on the door and Sandra came in. Henderson looked at her inquiringly. "There was something strange in the mail and I thought you might want to see it."

Henderson took the piece of paper from her hand. Written across it in large letters was "Jacobs?" He looked at it for a moment then crumpled it up. "Some prankster, I suspect." He tossed it into the wastebasket, feeling pleased at how natural his voice sounded.

For the rest of the morning, Henderson managed to keep his mind off Trevor, or partly so, and do some work. About eleven o'clock he happened to glance out the window and see that Trevor still hadn't moved. Henderson's work slowed down after that. Again he thought of the police and again he put the thought out of his mind. There was no point in stirring things up.

At twelve thirty Sandra came in to ask if he were going to lunch. Henderson always wanted someone in the office all day and so their lunch hours were staggered. Today he felt hungrier than usual, but glancing out the window, he saw that Trevor was still there.

"Why don't you go ahead. I'm really not hungry." He felt angry with himself.

"Oh, I can stay," said Sandra.

Henderson looked at her for a moment. He felt that he really hated himself. "Come along," he said at last. "We'll go together. There's no need for us both to stay here. We'll go to the Shepherd's Tavern on Hertford Street. It's only a short walk."

"But . . ."

"No excuses now." He got up, grabbed his coat and took her arm, playfully pushing her before him while internally kicking himself for being a fool. But it was obvious that she wanted to go and so they set off. As they went down the stairs to the street, Henderson felt almost jubilant. He took Sandra's arm as they went out the door, talking steadily while taking care not to look at Trevor. He kept talking in a manic way, joking about Mrs. Clavering and her complete lack of a sense of humor, as they crossed Curzon Street and entered the small maze of Shepherd Market. As they were turning, Henderson saw Trevor about twenty-five feet behind them. He was walking slowly and looked terribly bored.

They were able to find a table at the pub, which was fancy and eighteenth century, and Henderson ordered two steak and kidney pies and two Guinesses. He then asked

Sandra if that was what she wanted. She said, "Yes."

Then Henderson shut up. He could almost feel himself falling, blackness all around him.

"Are you all right?" asked Sandra.

He smiled lamely and nodded. This was dreadful. He couldn't just take this girl out and then act like a potential suicide. He had asked her to come because he was afraid of going out by himself, but she didn't know that. Her employer had asked her out for lunch. If he sat there the entire time without speaking, she would naturally take it personally.

He searched his mind for a topic and then asked weakly: "Why did you come over from Canada?"

But the question seemed as good as any other. Sandra's father had been an RAF instructor in Ontario during the war. Her mother had been a Canadian Red Cross worker. They had met and were married two weeks later. "Which was a mistake," said Sandra, "because they were bored and lonely and being married didn't stop that."

Henderson found the story soothing as Sandra went on to tell how her father had remained in Canada after the war and then returned to England in the late fifties to start an air delivery service, which went bankrupt three years later. It all seemed very removed from Trevor and Henderson's present problems.

Sandra's mother had taken Sandra and her brother back to Toronto. But Sandra had badly missed her father and after several years she returned to London and entered secretarial school. "Daddy has his air delivery service running again, but there's only one plane and he has to spend a lot of time working for other people. I see him on weekends, and now and then we go flying. We'll fly around in circles and he'll look at me cunningly and say, 'See anything you want shot down?'"

The hour passed smoothly and when the time came for Henderson to pay for their lunch, he felt relaxed. "Shall we go?" Sandra nodded. Out on the street, Henderson saw Trevor leaning against another wall. He was pleased to find that he wasn't in the least startled. He even turned so they would walk right past him. This was foolish but Henderson wanted to take the offensive, even if in a small way. Keeping his face expressionless, Trevor followed them with his eyes. Henderson rattled on cheerfully about his intention to go to Toronto someday in order to start a Canadian branch of his business. He had never thought about it before, but the subject seemed as good as any other.

But Sandra recognized Trevor. "Isn't that the American who came to see you last Thursday?"

It irritated Henderson that this possibility had not occurred to him. "No," he said at last, "I don't believe so. He wasn't a very pleasant American." He paused and then added, "Remember that."

He had intended to take Sandra on a walk through Green Park, thinking it amusing to lead Trevor on a small chase. But it would be stupid to anger Trevor, and perhaps dangerous. They walked directly back to the office. Henderson was silent for the whole way. For a while Sandra talked about her eccentric father—how he had been forced to stop giving flying lessons after his habit of terrifying beginners with intricate back-flips had become too well known—then she, too, fell silent. Trevor walked quietly behind them. If Sandra noticed, she didn't say anything.

During the entire afternoon, Henderson was aware of Trevor leaning against the wall of the building across the street. After a while, he didn't even have to look. He grew nervous and snapped a few times at Mrs. Clavering, who would come in to ask his advice on which watt bulbs to use for her desk lamp.

At one point, he tried calling Ahmed in Tangier but there was no answer. Perhaps that was just as well. He fiddled with various reports, but barely read them. He went over and over the figures for a large, upcoming carpet sale to a hotel chain but couldn't make sense of them. At four o'clock, he decided to go home. In order to avoid traffic, he told himself. Mrs. Clavering expressed surprise, saying that he never left early. Was he sick? Shouldn't he spend tomorrow in bed? He should take better care of himself. This led Henderson to snap at her for a third time. Then he apologized, saying he had a headache.

Henderson walked briskly to the garage, ignoring Trevor and refusing to discuss the state of the weather with Mr. Cameron. Trevor didn't follow him. This relieved Henderson tremendously.

Getting into his car, he accelerated quickly down Curzon Street, forcing several pedestrians to jump out of his way. "Bleeding capitalist!" someone shouted. He forced himself into the traffic on Park Lane, driving hard, pushing his way into small places, forcing other cars to stop abruptly. He swept onto Oxford Street, making one car nearly run up onto the curb. A bobby blew his whistle at him. Turning onto Baker Street, he had to slam on his brakes to avoid shoppers hurrying back and forth between Selfridge's and Marks & Spencer's. More people shouted at him. He ignored it, pushing his car forward through the crowd, and then accelerated so quickly that his tires squealed. Stop it! he told himself. He braked, bringing the Bentley to a halt in the center of the street. Cars honked behind him. An approaching bus slammed to a stop. Its Pakistani driver waved his arms and shouted something unintelligible. Slowly, Henderson started up again, driving back into his own lane.

For about a mile, he kept his mind blank, driving like a kind of machine. Way down in his head he could hear himself talking to himself, as if overhearing a conversation across a wide expanse of water. It seemed to have nothing to do with him, although he found it vaguely soothing. He suddenly felt very tired. His body felt old, as if the words were cut into every bone. All his years seemed bunched together. He saw himself going into the import business with his uncle twenty-five years ago. He could hear their quarrels —his uncle contending they would become rich importing souvenirs while Henderson argued they must specialize in quality merchandise. Then his uncle had died and Henderson reformed the business. He could see his marriage and the doubts he had at the time, that he still had. He could see the birth of his children. What bothered him was that it all seemed so small. It was just something he had done. He had let it move him along like an old train through an uninteresting landscape, and suddenly it had let him off here. And there was Trevor to meet him, patiently waiting, as if waiting for twenty-five years.

The last real thing seemed to be the war, and as he drove north he could almost feel the bullets which had torn into his chest and arm: and the terrible surprise that it had happened and the terrible calm with which he had received them, almost as if he had been waiting for them.

Slowly, Henderson cleared his mind again. He told himself to remain calm, and felt foolish for thinking it. After all, he had been telling himself that all day long without effect. Now, however, he began to think it might work. Trevor was gone. He had left him . . .

The red Austin Mini had been behind him all the way from Mayfair. He was sure of it. He was equally sure that the driver was Trevor. He could see his red hair in the mirror. Obviously it was Trevor.

Henderson was just approaching St. John's Wood Station at the end of Wellington Road. Suddenly he panicked. He wanted to lose Trevor. He wanted to get rid of him, be free of him. He stuck out his arm and swerved to the right, across traffic onto Acacia Road. There was a squeal of brakes, but then in his mirror he could see the little Austin making the turn behind him.

He began to accelerate faster. Then he checked himself. This was just what Trevor wanted. Henderson slowed down, turned at the corner and drove sedately around the block back to Finchley Road. For the rest of the way home, he drove very quietly and calmly. Trevor stayed right behind him.

Henderson spent the evening in his study, sitting and staring at the wall. His wife had been surprised to see him home so early. He had been barely polite to her, while careful to say he felt perfectly well. Harriet lived for those small illnesses which attack a family. Vaguely aware of her husband's indifference and frightened by the fact that her children were becoming people, she retreated more than ever to those small areas where she could cope. She could bring aspirin and hover. Henderson told her he had left some important papers at home and would have to spend the evening working.

Instead, he sat and looked at the wall, although at one point, around eight thirty, he glanced out the window for Trevor. He saw him leaning against a lamppost looking bored. Henderson went back to his armchair, a large and comfortable thing covered with soft dark leather. Ahmed had given it to him in 1965.

He knew he ought to be thinking about Trevor and making plans, but he didn't. His mind went back to Tangier, and he wandered through it in a rambling pictorial way, envisioning the white trumpet flowers which produce a poisonous but enjoyable narcotic, seeing the great clumps of bougainvillaea; imagining the steep and nearly endless climb up the steps from the harbor to the center of town; walking through the tiny alleys of the Kasbah late at night, wrapped in its smells, passing whole families in tiny niches, all sewing or washing other peoples' clothing, making intricate bronze boxes for tourists or slowly closing the heavy wooden shutters which separated their holes from the street; walking down alleys no wider than his arm with total silence around him while Berbers with the hoods of their djellabahs pulled down over their noses slipped past to places of quiet violence.

In his first contacts with Morocco, Henderson had been surprised by the number of guards carrying machineguns whom he found in government offices, surrounding houses, speeding crazily down the roads in small jeeps. Then came the difficulties of 1957 and 1964.

He felt suddenly sorry for King Hassan II, that aging playboy and slippery politician who had come to the throne in 1961. In the past ten years there had been a succession of riots, strikes, plots, attacks and assassination attempts, which Hassan met with new but innocuous constitutions, and firing squads.

Henderson had met the King several times at receptions in Rabat. He saw him as a man trying to create a progressive country while hampered by a corrupt civil service, a mutinous army and air force, and his own taste for sports cars, gold and sleek women. The attempts on his life would also be obviously disquieting.

There had been the army uprising summer before last when a thousand cadets attacked Hassan's summer palace during a state banquet. Nearly a hundred persons died, including several important foreign visitors. The attack had failed after the rebelling general had been accidentally shot by his own men.

Then last month the air force had rebelled. Returning

from Paris, Hassan's royal jet had been attacked by Moroccan fighters. Grabbing the microphone and identifying himself as a mechanic, Hassan told the attackers that the pilot was dead and that the King was mortally wounded. The rebels believed him, stopped firing and Hassan escaped. In the days that followed, hundreds of airmen were arrested. The leader of the rebellion, the Minister of Defense, committed suicide by shooting himself three times.

Ahmed had been very philosophic about it when Henderson talked to him. "Why should the King fear men who can't shoot? Fortunately, they are also very brave, and when the time comes to shoot themselves, they persevere. This saves the money of poor people like myself."

But there was Hassan waiting for the marksman who someday must arrive. The thought led Henderson back to Trevor. At least he knew who his marksman was. He suddenly felt disgusted with himself for putting up with it. Again he thought of the police. He almost knew he ought to call them. But then what? Would he have to take Trevor to court to make him stop? That not only would be pointless, but dangerous. Henderson knew that while his guilt couldn't be proved, neither could his innocence. If he tried to stop Trevor legally and the matter were publicized, there easily could be a scandal. It would be disastrous to business, and customers like that particular chain of hotels might sever all connections with him.

Around midnight, Henderson poured himself a large glass of Scotch. Fifteen minutes later, he had another. Then he stopped. He refused to behave in a way which morally embarrassed him. He refused to give Trevor that power. For a moment he thought of Hassan again, using the King as a bridge to get to some braver part of himself. From now on, if Trevor continued this farce, Henderson would give no sign. He would appear perfectly calm. He began thinking about the war, especially those winter months around Cassino where soldiers were careful to appear casual and indifferent, afraid that if they showed one crack their whole selves would collapse.

He continued to think about the war and Trevor until he went to bed around two o'clock. His decision to freeze his appearance was only slightly disturbed when he looked from his window and saw Trevor under the lamppost—a red-faced bearlike man leaning into the darkness. Henderson turned out the light.

9

POINT TREVOR at a bed and he would collapse. It was now seven thirty in the morning. He had been up since six, after having gotten to sleep at three. It was bad enough to spend his waking life within sight of Henderson, without suffering insomnia as well.

Trevor was standing beside his Austin Mini which was parked across from Henderson's house, on the north side of the street. It was Friday. He was about to begin his fifth day of minor harassment. It didn't feel minor to Trevor, nor did it seem like only four days. He had been following Henderson for months.

By now he had taken a great dislike to this wealthy neighborhood of four-story terrace houses. Although the street would have impressed him at any other time, four days of hounding Henderson had made him quite socialistic. Standing there, Trevor had a short fantasy of touring the street with a crane and wrecking ball, slowly swinging it on its long cable, smashing the bow windows, watching the red-brown brick houses crumble into dust and fragments, ripping up the row of trees which ran up the middle of the street, hearing people scream.

A door slammed behind him. Trevor knew what it was

without having to turn around. A moment later a small Yorkshire terrier ran up to Trevor's car and in a businesslike way urinated on the left front tire. The dog, whose name was Butcher, then wriggled toward Trevor on its stomach while whining in an unpleasant squeaky way. Trevor looked at the dog with distaste. Every day, twice a day, Butcher went through the same routine. The dog was now on its back about a yard from Trevor, still whining and rolling its eyes.

The door opened again. "Butcher, Butcher come here this instant," cried a high female voice that Butcher ignored. "No snacks. No snacks." Butcher scrambled to its feet and hurried off. If he had had a stone in his hand, Trevor might have thrown it.

He turned back to Henderson's house. Henderson should be leaving for work at any time now. Trevor felt frustrated and was beginning to doubt the success of the plan he had formulated with Mitchell. He wanted to move on to the next steps. Mitchell wanted him to wait. The trouble was Henderson himself. After the first day, when Henderson had made what Trevor called "little tugs at the leash," he had settled down to an apparent rocklike calm. He had done nothing of interest all week, while Trevor grew more frustrated, tired and depressed.

If he could sleep it would be better. But the moment he closed his eyes, he began following Henderson again, block after dismal block. Then, subtly, the dreams would change until Henderson was following Trevor. Trevor would run, he would hide, he would crouch in dark places, he would finally feel safe and then, suddenly, there was Henderson again, just waiting and smiling. Trevor found this terrifying. Probably he would have quit if it weren't for his other dreams, the ones about Jacobs.

The door of Henderson's house opened and the daughter,

Elizabeth, came out, leaving for school. She was a chubby, cheerful girl who for some reason reminded Trevor of Butcher. As always she wore a white blouse and a blue skirt. Trevor watched her walk off down the street, swinging her books.

Up and down the street, other people were leaving their houses and walking to their cars. No one looked at Trevor, but then, in London, people rarely looked at each other. That didn't mean they didn't see him or weren't curious.

Then Henderson came out and walked to his car, which was parked directly across from Trevor's Austin Mini. Trevor watched carefully but was sure that Henderson didn't look in his direction. Then he swore to himself and got into his car.

Henderson turned his Bentley around, drove down the street and turned onto Fitzjohn's Avenue. Trevor was right behind him, following like a child's toy on a string. By now he could drive the whole distance blindfolded. The two cars merged with the traffic bobbing along toward the city.

If only something would happen to justify this waiting. Trevor was still in the state of mind where he expected something to happen at any moment. And since it hadn't, he almost wanted to drop the matter. He didn't really, but he wanted to rest. He wanted to drop everything and go down to Surrey to the cottage he had bought with Tom Bethune two years before. That had been the smartest thing he had done since coming to England. Now it was practically his, since Bethune, a reporter for the *Post-Tribune* syndicate, had returned to New York the previous year and didn't know when he could come back.

There was nothing special about the cottage other than the two large fireplaces. Actually it was an ugly five-room affair built by some wealthy industrialist for a faithful servant in the 1880's. The small gothic touches around the eaves were obvious afterthoughts which clashed with the building's naked red brick. The cottage was south of Haslemere on the Sussex and Hampshire border.

Trevor returned his attention to Henderson, who was driving calmly along Park Road. The leaves were beginning to turn in Regent's Park. Trevor wished he could stop and walk through it, walk around the lake or go up Primrose Hill, see all of London from the City to Westminster stretching out before him, off as far as Crystal Palace on a clear day. Or he would go to the Zoo. There was an old wolf with a torn left ear that he particularly liked.

There were all sorts of things that Trevor wanted to do: go to plays, movies, bars, to see Clare, to go to his cottage. Following Henderson made Trevor feel cut off from the world. It was as if his own life had been completely erased and he was now just a creature in Henderson's mind.

But to go to the cottage; to go there with Clare and spend a week in bed, maybe two weeks. They had been there before, a few times, quite successfully with no quarrels or interruptions. He and Bethune had been adamant about not installing a phone. The nearest was at the Green Dragon on the outskirts of Haslemere.

As the two cars turned right onto Oxford Street, Trevor tried to look at some raincoats in the window of Selfridge's. A cab honked at him and he swung back into line behind Henderson.

Twenty minutes later, Trevor was leaning against the wall of the office building across from Henderson's. He was wondering if there were any way to see Clare that evening. There wasn't unless he could convince her to meet him at his bedsitter at 3:00 A.M. Ridiculous.

Besides, she was cross at him again. Not because of Mitchell's interruption, which she had probably forgotten by now, but because of Eva. During the past week, Eva had called the bureau six times looking for Trevor. Clare had taken each call. When she asked Trevor who Eva was, he made the mistake of saying she was nobody important. Clare had grown suspicious.

Trevor had at last called Eva, thinking that she might have remembered something. She hadn't, although their conversation was a fitting sequel to the interview of two weeks earlier.

Eva was at work. "I can't talk very long," she said.

Trevor wondered if she expected to hear the story of his life. "What did you want?"

"I wanted to talk to you." Her voice was very flat.

"About what?"

"Just talk."

"Have you remembered anything?"

"I don't understand."

Trevor felt like shaking the telephone. "Have you remembered anything that Jacobs said about Henderson?"

"No. Why didn't you see him?"

Trevor ignored the question. "Did you want something in particular?"

"No, I just wanted to apologize."

"For what?" He felt confused.

"For shocking you. I . . . I'm not usually like that."

Trevor hadn't said anything for a moment. He could hear shouting and glass breaking in the background. "You didn't shock me," he said at last. "That was why you called?"

"Yes."

Trevor could now barely hear her. He repressed a desire to hang up the phone. "Well, don't let it bother you." Eva didn't say anything. "Ah, look," continued Trevor, "I'm pretty busy right now." Eva still didn't say anything. There was the sound of more glass breaking. "Are you there?" asked Trevor.

"Yes." Her voice seemed small and childlike.

Trevor had no idea how to end the conversation. It embarrassed him that he should feel so uncomfortable. "Look, Eva, I've got to go now. Let me call you back some other time. Okay?"

"All right." That was all she said.

Trevor gingerly hung up the phone.

Remembering it, Trevor still felt embarrassed. He couldn't think what the woman wanted, and talking to her brought Jacobs too clearly to mind. Trevor was filled with a sense of failure. If only Henderson would make the slightest break from his routine. But he wasn't even taking his secretary to lunch anymore. Probably he was balling her in his office under the photograph of Tangier. Trevor imagined splotches of dried sperm on the blue Moroccan carpet. No, the man's probably impotent. Trevor halted that line of thought. He was becoming tired of the trash he was allowing into his mind.

The day continued. Henderson went to lunch as usual at twelve thirty, meeting some other businessmen, and returned to his office at two. The only thing of interest that happened during the afternoon was that the street was cleaned. Henderson left for the day at 5:00 P.M. Trevor trudged after him.

On one day—Trevor thought it might have been Wednesday but all the days had blended together confusingly—Henderson had gone off down Piccadilly and then crossed over to St. James's Street. Trevor had been almost excited, expecting new developments, until he found that Henderson was only going to his club on Jermyn Street. It made him dislike Henderson all the more.

Mitchell, Trevor knew, was quite pleased with Henderson's inaction. Trevor had talked to him on the phone the previous evening. Mitchell had joked at Trevor's impatience.

"You Americans, you're all alike. You don't know how to wait."

"Perhaps you'd like to take my place for a while."

Mitchell had laughed in an unpleasant way. "I would but for other responsibilities and the fact that I fortunately don't look like you. After all, we don't want Henderson to think that the police are still interested. As a matter of fact, the papers will carry articles tomorrow saying that an arrest is imminent."

Trevor had thought he was joking and said so.

"No, no, it's quite true. The papers will say that the murder was mixed up with blackmail. Nothing to do with Henderson. He'll feel safer, more likely to react to your pressure. Poor fellow, I almost feel sorry for him."

"Well, he's certainly not doing anything now," said Trevor, "and I'm getting flat feet."

There was a snorting noise from the other end of the line. Trevor imagined Mitchell being strangled by a deadly assailant who wore Trevor's face. He hated Mitchell's jolly moods.

"Of course he's doing something," said Mitchell, "or rather it's what he hasn't done. Mainly, he hasn't called us. Doesn't that strike you as significant? Anyone else harassed in this way would call the police immediately. But Henderson hasn't called and now he won't."

"Why not?" Trevor knew why not but he didn't feel like giving Mitchell any help.

"Come, come, Trevor, don't be obtuse. He's set a precedent. What would he say when we ask why he didn't call before? And, too, he's afraid to call. He's afraid to let us that far into his life."

"I'd prefer a confession."

"You've got your bloody confession. What you're waiting for is the punishment."

As he followed Henderson down the street to the parking garage, Trevor had to admit that Mitchell was right. But he still wanted the confession. He wanted to see Henderson shout it out to these well-groomed secretaries and self-sure businessmen who were now leaving work. He wanted him to shout it into the windows of cabs, to bellow it at the waiters in their restaurants, the clerks in their proper shops. He wanted to see these people hate Henderson.

That evening Henderson stayed at home. Trevor was able to get away around eight o'clock to grab a sandwich at a Greek restaurant around the corner. He also mailed Henderson picture postcards of Trafalgar Square and Piccadilly Circus: one to his office and one to his home. The message on both was "Jacobs?" Then he walked back to Henderson's house. The sandwich—barbecued lamb and green peppers—had been too spicy and Trevor was now suffering from gas. Butcher scampered out about eight thirty to urinate on the left front tire of the Austin Mini and crawl toward Trevor's foot again. At the last moment, the dog dashed back after being threatened again with "No snacks." Trevor suspected Butcher of a sneaking desire to bite him.

Shortly after ten, Trevor got away for another ten minutes, to call Clare from the Green Flag on High Street. She was neither at home, the New Chelsea Club nor four possible Fleet Street taverns. In his mind, Trevor unexpectedly saw her wrapped in Mitchell's embraces; the two of them sprawled across Mitchell's desk, while down in Parliament Square crowds of revelers with horns and paper hats surged back and forth, filling the city from Chelsea and Walham Green, through the West End and Holborn, through St. Clement Danes and the Law Courts until they burst like the sea upon the old wall itself.

As Trevor was leaving the pub, a stout red-faced man

stepped away from the bar and tapped him on the shoulder. "Excuse me, Sir, you're an American, aren't you?"

Trevor nodded, while wondering what new thing had been sent to plague him.

"Well, Sir, me and my mate were talking"—at this juncture he was joined by his friend, a thin truculent-looking man. The red-faced man smiled and continued, "Me and my mate here were talking about your country and having a kind of disagreement about this past summer when I says to my mate, 'Here, that chap looks like an American, we'll put the question to him.'"

"What's the question?" asked Trevor. He hated being recognized as an American.

"We were wondering, don't take offense now, we were wondering why there were no riots in your country this past summer." Both men nodded vigorously.

Trevor stared at them, trying to decide if this were some sort of joke. And if they were serious, why had they decided that he was the one to ask? It was preposterous. After nearly a minute, Trevor decided that the man was asking what he believed to be a legitimate question. "It's the money," answered Trevor at last.

"The money? I don't believe I . . ."

"Riots are very expensive," interrupted Trevor, "so last spring the Blacks and the Hippies got together and voted to riot only every other year. You just wait, next year there'll be a jim-dandy." Trevor turned and walked quickly out of the pub. People are absurd, he thought.

He still had gas and, as he walked back to Henderson's, he leveled curses at the cook who had made the sandwich. Apart from some sirens over toward Kilburn, the night was quiet. Very few lights were on in the houses. There was a red tint to the sky and Trevor thought something must be burning. It seemed that far away the city was breaking apart.

Catastrophes occurred on every block. And here was Trevor, stranded on an island of silence, suffering from gas and being forced to be his country's representative to idiots. He walked slowly down Church Row to wait for Henderson to go to bed.

10

WHATEVER HAD HARDENED in Henderson also hardened at last in Trevor. Primarily it was a sense of defiance, and their realization that their survival as creatures who could live with themselves depended on that defiance. Both men were on the edge. But although Henderson apparently had more to lose, socially and economically, Trevor, too, was on the defensive. He had turned Jacobs' death into a symbol of what he had chosen to do with his life and how his life placed him in a certain inhuman position to other people. For this Henderson bore no responsibility.

But Trevor needed him to be responsible. He needed him to take the weight of the question off himself. At thirty-seven, Trevor couldn't afford to think that he had spent his life as a machine, or at best as a child who dispassionately investigates the lives of insects under rocks. It frightened Trevor to think he might be indifferent to them; that their disappearance wouldn't change his essential loneliness, or, more exactly, his sense of aloneness; that he would be indifferent to the death of the entire human race, even if he were left alive.

These were questions which Trevor didn't wish to consider. Jacobs' death had forced them upon him. It was probably one of the more productive acts of Jacobs' life. Certainly Jacobs' death alone hadn't caused this, but it was strong enough to be a catalyst. For instance, there was Trevor's relationship with Clare which had continued without question for nearly two years. Jacobs' death had changed that. More often than not their conversations reminded Trevor of the knife-edged conversations he had had with Louise, his ex-wife, ten years before. It was the lack of difference that bothered Trevor. He and Louise had married out of boredom, had lived through seventeen months of even greater boredom and then parted on the worst of terms. She had gone back to her public relations job in Chicago. Mostly they had been too bored and indifferent to have fights, but occasionally they erupted into vicious arguments where each slashed bitterly at the essential self of the other. It frightened Trevor that he might be going in the same direction with Clare.

His work had also reached a potential turning point in that he had gone practically as far as he could go as a reporter. The alternatives now before him were to become an editor, a columnist or a specialist in something-or-other affairs. He had had experience with all three. Or he could leave journalism for public relations or political writing. Trevor liked none of the alternatives. But to stay where he was meant doing the same thing over and over again. Even the most apparently exciting stories had become repetitious. Trevor had done them all before. He was at that exhausted stage of journalism where it is unnecessary to talk to the subject of an interview. Trevor knew exactly what the person would say beforehand. Occasionally he would amuse his pub acquaintances by carrying on fantastical interviews with celebrities of the day. Not only were the words exact, but also the tone, the nuances, the clichés, the smiles.

Jacobs' death had underlined the worst aspects of a

journalist's life. There was the cynical mask which after a while became the face itself; there was the fear of being found out, exposing the soft underbelly; there was the desire to make a small safe place of his own, a place untouched by headlines, and the realization that all places had been equally poisoned. Trevor had known ever so many reporters and photographers in the States who had purchased cabins and cottages four or five hours from where they worked. They would drive there frantically on the weekends, like creatures pursued, and then drag back unchanged on Monday. There was the feeling of terrible boredom toward the small and large tragedies of other people; there was the realization that the inner self they had carefully been protecting for years had somehow slipped away and they couldn't even remember what it had once been like.

Therefore Henderson was necessary. But not the person, who was in some ways similar to Trevor, but the myth. Henderson's acceptance of responsibility would purify Trevor, if only for a short while. Henderson became responsible for everything; and his mask of complete indifference made it easy for Trevor to give him this responsibility. He could either do that or ask irrelevant questions about himself: irrelevant because the creature they concerned had disappeared years before.

Therefore Trevor had been forced to harden himself in order to continue the hunt. He refused to ask those questions. He couldn't afford to; and so he became a kind of machine that hopefully wouldn't break before Henderson was destroyed.

Trevor followed Henderson for seven more days. He followed him when he went shopping in Hampstead with his wife. He followed him when he played tennis with his daughter. He followed him to business meetings, through drives in the country, to dinners, to pubs. He followed him on a long rambling Sunday afternoon walk through Hampstead Heath. He followed him to work and stayed there. He waited outside his house each evening until all the lights were out. He became so exhausted that he had no conscious memory of most of what he did. Occasionally he even fell asleep while leaning against some wall or lamppost or car.

On Friday afternoon, October 6th, Mitchell called him off. It was raining. Trevor was standing under an umbrella across from Henderson's office. The rain had soaked his shoes and pants. In a sleepy way, Trevor was thinking about the act of chopping wood for the fireplaces of his cottage in Haslemere. He opened his eyes to find a policeman tugging at his arm. It occurred to him that he was being arrested. This didn't surprise him.

"Inspector Mitchell says that you may go now," said the bobby, "but he asked to have you ring him up later."

Trevor nodded and walked off without speaking. He intended to go home and get some sleep. Then he changed his mind and called Clare, asking her out for dinner. She agreed to meet him at the restaurant of the National Film Theatre at six o'clock. Trevor then went home to take a nap, but he couldn't sleep.

After twenty minutes with Clare, Trevor knew he had made a mistake. He could barely keep his eyes open. She was telling him about an office quarrel between John Belton, the bureau chief, and one of the reporters, over a story which Belton wanted to kill. The story concerned a Nebraskan couple who had been cheated at their London hotel, poisoned in a Soho restaurant and finally robbed. "I thought New York was bad," said the Nebraskan, "but these people really hate us. They make fun of us. We're not even human beings to them."

Belton said it was an isolated example. The reporter, a friend of Trevor's, accused Belton of being a flak for the

English. It had been that sort of quarrel.

Trevor was barely listening. Instead, he picked at his shepherd's pie and stared out at the river and the massive concrete supports of the Waterloo Bridge, directly above them. He was thinking about Henderson.

Clare stopped talking and stared at him crossly for a moment before saying, "Am I boring you?" Her voice was tight.

"What? No, of course not. I was just . . ."

"So I saw. Did you have anything special planned for this evening or did you just intend to ignore me?"

The idea of an argument was exhausting. "Cut it out, Clare. I wanted to see you. I've been working hard and would like some company, your company. Jesus Christ, you know how I hate talking like this." Trevor felt very fragile.

Clare seemed slightly mollified but didn't say anything. They were sitting at a long table with some other couples who were also waiting for the movie to begin. Clare was fiddling with the green water pitcher. She was wearing a dress of some Indian material: yellow with brown and green elephants, tigers, soldiers. Trevor liked the dress but was too tired to say so. He pushed away his plate.

"Look," he said at last, tediously drawing the words up out of himself, "this thing I'm doing isn't going to last forever. In fact, I thought it would be over by now. But when it is, we can go down to Surrey for a weekend, okay? The trees should be turning. . . . You know how you like it there. We've always had a good time. If you'll just be patient."

Clare shook her head. "I'm tired of being a hanger-on to your life. If something happens, I'm what you drop first. I don't mean to be maudlin." She paused and sipped some water before continuing. "It just makes me feel terribly unnecessary."

Trevor wanted to take her hand but felt he couldn't. It didn't seem he could make any movement at all in her direction. His own hands seemed tied behind him. The room was hot. "Will you come down there with me?"

Clare looked up at him. Her long brown hair framed her face, reminding Trevor of a creature in a cage. "What are you working on?" she asked.

Trevor shook his head. "I can't talk about it. It's . . . I just can't talk about it. Not because it's secret." For some reason he was afraid that she would ask about Eva. He didn't know why. She had told him earlier that Eva had called again. Trevor shook his head again as if trying to dislodge something from his brain. "Will you come down there with me?"

At first she seemed angry. Then she said: "All right, but not until you're positive that nothing will interfere. Promise?"

"I promise." Trevor was frightened they would have an intimate scene, when, fortunately, the bell rang announcing the movie. They got up and went into the theater. An attractive usherette led them to their seats.

Trevor began to tell Clare a story about a New York theater up in the Nineties where he had once stepped on a rat. Then he forgot the point of the story and stopped. The lights went out and an RKO *News of the World* piece on Mussolini flickered onto the screen. It was filmed in the year of Trevor's birth. It was an entirely different world.

The main feature was Cary Grant and Rosalind Russell in *His Girl Friday.* Grant was the fast-talking editor. Russell was his top reporter and ex-wife, who was now leaving him for Ralph Bellamy, who was solid, dependable and boring. Trevor found it both tedious and callous. He closed his eyes and soon he was sleeping.

He found himself in an alley. It was late at night. The

brick buildings rose darkly on either side and then seemed to lean inward, almost meeting at the top. There were no lights in the windows. The street lights were dim and getting dimmer. Trevor was sweating terribly. He was wearing his tattered raincoat but it seemed a few sizes too small. It held him like a strait jacket.

There was someone in front of him, or there ought to be. It was necessary for Trevor to find him. He took a small flashlight from his pocket and began walking. He felt that he had been doing this for a long time.

Flicking on the flashlight, Trevor explored the gray edges of the buildings and the gutters, which were full to overflowing with tin cans, papers, old photographs of families at summer beaches, torn clothes, hats. The streetlights went out.

Trevor kept walking, swinging his light in a wide arc from one side of the alley to the other. The flashlight flickered off. He banged it on his hand. It seemed to Trevor that he had never known darkness so complete. He kept hitting the light against his palm. At last it came on.

Above him, there seemed to be hundreds of people watching from the windows. They seemed old and critical. He could almost hear them talking about him, sometimes laughing. Apart from this, the alley was silent, except for his own footsteps and a scraping noise which he couldn't identify. The noise came from all directions like a whispered warning.

The light kept going out and Trevor kept banging it against his palm. Each time it came back on it was dimmer. He kept telling himself that he had to hurry, that it was almost too late, but he didn't know why. He wished there were someone he could ask. He didn't understand what he was doing or what he was looking for. The air was very damp as if the river were near. It was like a moist hand over his mouth. He had no idea of what he should do, ought to do.

The trash in the gutters had spread across the floor of the alley. There was a torn yellow dress, a yellow armchair with the stuffing coming out, the body of a dog. There was more paper, old letters asking for money, letters saying someone had died, newspapers featuring important events of forty years before. There were toys and books, broken lamps, records, tattered umbrellas. Trevor forced his way through it.

And always there was the scraping noise. Trevor could never identify it or tell where it was coming from. It kept getting louder. Trevor kept telling himself that he had to find out what it was. But it took so much concentration just to walk that he barely was able to think of anything else. As it got louder, however, his feeling of desperation increased. By now his flashlight had become quite dim, forcing him to hold it close to the ground in order to see anything. Suddenly he realized the noise was right behind him.

He turned quickly, stumbling in the trash. He could see nothing. Trevor took a few steps forward. The noise grew louder. The trash was now up to Trevor's knees.

His foot caught in part of a broken wheel and he fell, while managing to keep hold of the flashlight. The trash was full of decaying fruit—oranges, bananas. He was enveloped in the smell of it.

He tried to move forward and, as he did, Trevor saw a pair of brightly polished black shoes a few inches from his face. Then he realized someone was standing there.

Slowly he got to his knees, keeping the light on the figure before him. The grinding noise was louder. He raised the light along a pair of dark-blue pants, then a blue vest and suitcoat, then a maroon tie with a small bronze stickpin of a Comedy mask. Trevor moved the light past the collar and terribly white neck, up to the chin, where he stopped.

The noise was caused by teeth grinding together, grinding over and over. The teeth were less than a foot away. They were large and discolored. They kept grinding together. They were broken and rough like stones. They kept grinding together. Trevor drew back the light in order to see the face. It was Henderson's face. Trevor screamed.

He must have made some actual noise because when he opened his eyes people were looking at him. But they weren't startled. Trevor was sweating. It was difficult to breathe and he didn't know where he was. Then he remembered.

The movie was over. People were leaving. He looked for Clare but the seat beside him was empty. Standing up, he saw her walking quickly through the exit. There was a large crowd between them. He hurried after her but there were too many people. He tried to push his way through. "Bloody foreigners," somebody said. Trevor kept pushing.

When he got outside, there was no sign of Clare. There were too many directions she could have taken in the Arts Council complex. It was drizzling and very dark. Trevor stopped, filling his lungs with the moist air. Parts of the dream came back to him. He started walking, trying to shake it off. He passed a door under Queen Elizabeth Hall marked "Artists' Entrance." The gray naked concrete of the buildings rose around him. He hurried up some stairs to the plaza. The concrete was textured to look like wood. It jutted out in sharp angles and dark spaces. There were few people about, although it was still early, barely eight thirty. There was music coming from Royal Festival Hall, where some Russian orchestra was playing Brahms. Trevor looked up as he passed the giant windows of the hall. There was a middle-aged usher in a maroon uniform staring at him. Trevor felt a wave of undefinable fear. He pulled his raincoat tightly around him and hurried on toward the Hungerford Footbridge across the Thames.

An amplified voice could be heard from an open tourist boat: "Given to England in 1819 by Mohammed Ali, Viceroy of Egypt, Cleopatra's Needle reached here in 1878 after many adventures too long to describe. Suffice it to say, it was built in Heliopolis in 1500 B.C. and records the deeds of Thothmes III and Rameses II. . . ." The voice trailed off as the boat continued down the river.

Trevor remembered seeing the needle's pink granite twin in Central Park years before, looking like a poor model for the Washington Monument. Trevor found himself wondering about the life of Thothmes III. His sudden intrusion into Trevor's life seemed frighteningly surreal. He hurried up the wet and slippery steps of the bridge, still trying to shake off his dream.

The bridge was empty except for a couple leaning against the railing with their arms around each other. They didn't notice him. A train from Charing Cross Station rumbled by, making the bridge shake. To his right, Trevor saw the lighted dome of St. Paul's.

He felt surrounded by incidents of the past, not only of London's but his own. He saw himself as a child in Chicago with his father standing over him, smelling of printer's ink and wearing an odd newspaper cap on his head. He was talking about "The Bosses" and child-Trevor imagined great stone men. He saw himself as a reporter on his high school paper, interviewing a sadistic history teacher who kept urging him to learn a trade. He saw himself as a young man in the army, standing guard over an empty munitions dump near Frankfurt, hating himself for not being in Korea.

Trevor hurried down the steps leading from the bridge and cut through Charing Cross tube station. Then he turned left back under the bridge toward Northumberland Avenue. There were about twenty-five people gathered there, sheltering from the rain. Some were drinking hot tea from a stand made from scrap lumber and cardboard.

They were mostly derelicts—men and several women with long filthy hair, talking to the wall in loud voices. Trevor found himself staring at them. A number of men were sleeping on the pavement, wrapped in newspapers. An old man with a face like an open sore crouched in a doorway, muttering to himself in a high, whining voice. A mongrel dog shivered by a parked car. The air seemed smoky and even the smallest sounds echoed back and forth against the bricks. The sleeping derelicts looked like packages waiting for stamps, expecting to be sent to wherever the sun had gone. No one looked at Trevor. There was trash in the street, decaying fruit, cardboard boxes.

A man of Trevor's age was leaning against a wall playing a harmonica. He had hair half way down his back and wore a gray suit shiny with dirt and grease. Trevor recognized the song as a sad, melancholy thing about Scotland. The high notes of the harmonica reverberated against the stones, seemed to hang in the damp gray air.

For an instant, Trevor had a great desire to stop and sit down on the pavement, to let the music cover him, to find newspapers to wrap around himself, to stay there in the dark area beneath the bridge. The thought frightened him so much that he nearly broke into a run, hurrying up Northumberland Avenue until he reached a pub called the Sherlock Holmes. He went in, hoping for something to distract him from his mind.

The pub was a touristy place filled with "relics" from Holmes' best cases. These included a plaster head of the hound of the Baskervilles in a glass case. Trevor ordered a double Scotch, swallowed it and ordered another. Then he paused and lit a Players. The pub was run by very young men wearing white T-shirts with "Sherlock Holmes" written

103

across the fronts. They amused themselves by throwing beer at each other. Trevor finished his drink and ordered a third. By now the alcohol had begun to circulate around his system, putting a comfortable mist between him and his environment.

He looked around for a telephone. Clare should be home soon, that is if she were going home. He would call and make some kind of apology. Perhaps she would let him come over. With the state of his feelings, he didn't wish to be alone. He felt that he had little control over his actions. At best this gave him a slight feeling of innocence. Whatever happened wasn't his fault. He couldn't help it.

While waiting, Trevor decided to call Mitchell. He had forgotten to call earlier and was faintly curious about what Mitchell wanted. It would be someone to talk to.

Mitchell answered after the fifth ring. His voice sounded sleepy.

"In bed already?" asked Trevor.

"No. What do you want?"

"I thought you wanted me to call you. Are you sure I didn't wake you up?" Trevor laughed.

"Quite sure. I want you to leave Henderson alone for a few days."

"Okay. Then what?"

"Step up operations. You can pick up the camera at my office."

Trevor was silent for a moment. "You don't think he'll call the police?"

Mitchell made a kind of guffaw. "No, it's too late for that, much too late."

Unexpectedly, Trevor felt a surge of dislike for Mitchell. It was as if he were interfering in something private and personal; as if he were giving Trevor instructions about how to behave in bed. "Anything else?" he said at last.

"Not at the moment. Except that you might be careful."

"Of what?"

"Of Henderson. It would give Sergeant Fawcett too much pleasure if something happened to you."

Trevor began to laugh. "Don't worry." He hung up.

For a moment he considered whether he should call Clare or leave. In the few days he had off, he could go down to Surrey and get some rest. But he didn't want to be alone. He picked up the phone again.

She was home but not friendly. This was to be expected. Even hostile company, however, would be better than no company at all. But she didn't want him to come over.

"Why not?"

"You'd only fall asleep." She clipped her words, speaking very coldly.

"Cut it out."

"I'm quite serious. It's embarrassing to sit through a film with someone who's not only asleep but snores as well, especially when that person is supposed to be my date. It doesn't meet my needs."

"Jesus Christ, what about my needs? I've got needs. . . ."

"Don't speak to me like that. . . ."

Trevor hung up. What depressed him was not the tone of their conversation, which was a common occurrence, but that it didn't mean anything. He could call her back in a day or so and everything would be fine. It created an isolated world.

Trevor went back to the bar and ordered another drink. His alternatives seemed to be going home, meeting half-drunken friends at the New Chelsea Club or hunting out some woman. Although he knew he ought to go home in order to get an early start for Surrey in the morning, whenever he relaxed, parts of his dream would come back to him.

Occasionally he would hear the mournful notes of the derelict's harmonica. He was jumpy and the loud noises of the pub bothered him. On the next stool an old drunk kept trying to talk to him about Norway's refusal to join the Common Market. Trevor told him to shut up.

For another half hour, Trevor sat at the bar, attempting to come to a decision. At last he got up and left. His car was still parked over by Henderson's office. He would get it. He didn't want to be alone.

It was raining harder than ever and a cold wind was blowing up the avenue from the river. There were no cabs in sight. Trevor ran up toward Trafalgar Square where he hoped to find one. A cab finally stopped after Trevor had run into the street to hail it. He directed the driver to Henderson's office.

An hour later, Trevor was sitting in his car, which was parked in front of a row of flats on Ferdinand Street. The car radio was playing a Bill Haley song that Trevor had danced to in college. He was staring through the rain toward Chalk Farm Road. There was no one in sight. Trevor tried to keep his mind away from what he was doing by cursing himself in a slow methodical way. He made no move to leave. Over the years he had become accustomed to behaving in ways he disapproved of.

Someone was running down the street toward him. It was a woman: small, thin, clutching her dark-blue raincoat around her. She ran up the steps of a three-story brick building next to where Trevor was parked. He quickly got out of the car.

"Eva," he called.

The woman turned as if frightened. "Who is it?"

"Trevor."

"What do you want?"

"You called me. Can I come up?"

"It's late. I just got off work."

"I know. Can I come up?"

She stood at the top of the steps. The only light came from a small street lamp about ten yards away. It cast a yellow circle which cut across the hood of Trevor's car. Both Trevor and Eva stood outside of it. The rain fell into the light like silver pellets. Trevor glanced up at the building and imagined people staring at them from the windows. Eva shrugged and turned toward the door. "I suppose it's all right."

Trevor followed her up the stairs, which were dirty and poorly lit. A pipe had been attached to the wall as a kind of banister. It was coming loose. Eva unlocked the door of her room and went in. Trevor followed, shutting the door. The room was small and very narrow. It had a tired, musty smell. The bed was unmade. Eva turned to face him. Her blond hair hung in wet clumps around her shoulders. Trevor almost wished he hadn't come.

"Why did you call me?" he asked.

She shrugged again and took off her coat. "Do you want a cup of tea?"

"No. Why did you call me?"

Eva seemed nervous and looked away from Trevor at some spot over his left shoulder. "I wanted to talk. You were a friend of Ralph's weren't you? I wanted to talk about him. It doesn't matter now. And I was embarrassed. . . ."

"About what?"

"When you were here before, I mean. . . ."

"Forget it." Trevor didn't really care why she had called. He had had no thought past just seeing her. Now he wasn't sure what to do. There were other women he could have seen but they were of a different world. Since finding Jacobs' body, Trevor had felt he was playing a part in a story which he knew nothing about. He barely understood his own motivations, but he knew that Eva was also involved.

She stood facing him with her arms folded across her small breasts as if comforting herself. "Why are you here?"

Trevor assumed she knew the answer to that. He stepped forward and put a hand on her shoulder, drawing her toward him. Then he kissed her. She pulled away. "What are you doing?"

He drew her toward him again. She tried to pull away but he was too strong. He kissed her again, forcing his mouth against hers. For a brief moment she returned the kiss, then she pushed him back and looked at him angrily. "No. You don't mean it. You're using me."

"I want to go to bed with you."

"Get out!"

Ignoring her, Trevor grabbed her arm, yanking her around and forcing her to fall back on the unmade bed. He fell on top of her, clumsily kissing her neck and face, undoing the buttons on her white blouse. At first she struggled, trying to scratch his face, but then she gave up and lay there like a child's toy as Trevor finished unbuttoning the blouse.

"Get undressed," he said at last. He was aware of a great well of anger inside of him.

She got up and without looking at him began taking off her clothes. He was again struck by how small she was. He could count her ribs. Then he took off his own clothes. They were damp. He was reminded of a doctor's office. A naked bulb hung from a wire in the ceiling.

When he had finished undressing, Trevor sat back down on the bed. Eva turned and Trevor was slightly surprised to see that her pubic hair was a reddish blond color. He had assumed her hair was bleached. Reaching out her hand, she touched his cheek. She no longer seemed angry and was looking at him without any visible emotion. "You poor animal," she said quietly.

* * *

Waking a few hours later, Trevor found that Eva was gone. The room was dark, although light from the street lamp came dimly in through the window. After a moment, Trevor could make out Eva sitting in a straight chair by the table. She was hunched over and crying. Trevor lay there listening to her. Each sob seemed to be a name repeated over and over. It filled the room like water. Very slowly Trevor got up and put on his cold clothing. Then, without speaking, he quietly left her room.

11

WHEN HENDERSON discovered, as he left work Friday afternoon, that Trevor was not outside his office, he experienced a feeling of tremendous relief. The feeling didn't last long.

Soon he became suspicious and as nervous as he had been on the first day of Trevor's appearance. He didn't believe that Trevor had lost interest. He knew in an odd way, they were too close for that. The game they were playing couldn't possibly end with one player casually walking off.

The sensation of sudden release made him feel unprotected. It was as if he had been putting all his strength into pushing against a door that someone else was pushing from the other side. Suddenly the other person had stopped pushing and Henderson fell forward, desperately trying to regain his balance, certain that his enemy was running up from behind.

He had been keeping himself under such tight control that now, when it no longer seemed necessary, he felt more uncomfortable than ever. Any sudden noise would make him jump. He kept looking out the window. Harriet, who had been fretting about his behavior during the past two weeks, grew more worried. But she had stopped asking about it, because when she did, Henderson became angry.

Although Henderson had calmed down by Tuesday, he was conscious of a strong waiting feeling. There was very little fear involved in this. Unlike Trevor, he had almost forgotten about Jacobs, except for the detail that the dead man kept him from going to the police. That detail made his relationship with Trevor very intimate. All that happened was between them and nobody else.

Henderson found it interesting how their relationship had altered his life, even altering things which had nothing to do with Trevor. Trevor had changed him from a creature who took his environment for granted, forcing him to focus on it, judge it. Generally, he now saw the foundations upon which he had built his life as terribly temporary and vulnerable. He still valued them, but Trevor's intrusion had lessened the degree to which he would protect them. His defense against Trevor was a negative one: He refused to act. But now even his original motivation of fear was beginning to change.

Being forced to focus on his life made him realize how little he had to protect. His family could get on perfectly well without him. His business, while still interesting, was no longer necessary to him. Henderson also began to see what he didn't have and what he wanted. Primarily these were things he had repressed before. But he now saw no reason why he shouldn't move to Tangier, if Tangier were what he really wanted. There was also Sandra.

As the importance of his business diminished, the less he saw Sandra as an employee. He had been attracted to her from the start, but now his altered values enabled him to see her as a person. Henderson began to realize also that she liked him. He was hardly conscious of this, unaware that he had begun to romanticize her.

Another change was that Henderson began to think more

about the war: a subject he had skillfully kept out of his mind for nearly thirty years. Now he could sit and remember every experience, remember the sort of person he had been. Specifically, he thought about Cassino.

He had been with the McCreery X Corps, 56th Division, which had begun its attack on January 17th, in an attempt to roll up the German flank and draw away German reserves that might hamper the Anzio landing five days later. They rolled the Germans up to Ausonia and were rolled right back down again. There followed weeks of mountain fighting. It either rained or sleeted every day. They were constantly fighting in cloud, constantly wet, constantly freezing. They were always up to their knees in mud. There were no roads, only mule tracks, and mules brought in the supplies in an endless stream. Their position was a straggling line of stone "sangers," where one or two soldiers would lie hidden. There was no one to talk to.

After a while, England seemed not only far away. It had never existed. Nothing could be counted on except the rain. Everything else was temporary, tedious and boring. At first, Henderson had been very self-protective, always keeping his head down, taking no unnecessary chances. Then he began to take risks.

Because of the higher German positions, daylight attacks were too costly. Instead, they specialized in night raids. The Germans were spread out like the British. At night, Henderson and others would crawl out of their hiding places and stab or strangle the Germans in their sleep. They were also armed with revolvers. Some soldiers ended in taking a comic delight in these raids. Henderson's mate—he couldn't remember his name—contended it was better to kill only one German per hole because the discovery would be such a nasty surprise for the man's friend in the morning.

Henderson finally alleviated his boredom by turning the

raids into a kind of game. Since the Germans were expecting them, he began to take pleasure in how careless he could be and still not be caught.

Then one night he and three others stumbled into a squad of Germans who had been waiting for them. But the Germans hadn't heard them coming and they were all mixed together before they realized what had happened. Panicking, Henderson had been unable to move. Two of his mates had run and were instantly shot down. Henderson began to fire wildly. He could see nothing, but because of the nearness of the Germans he scored several hits. Then he was shot twice himself: once in the right lung, once in the left arm. He began slashing violently with his bayonet, so violently that the Germans thought there were more soldiers than they had assumed, and retreated, shooting. Realizing he was alone, Henderson made his way back to his line. On the way, he found one of his mates who was still alive. Henderson dragged the man back with him.

The fact that he received a D.S.C. for this embarrassed him terribly. He wanted to tell them that he had meant to run. Instead, he lay quietly in his hospital bed while nurses fluttered about and his commanding officer told him that he was the sort England was depending on.

Sitting in his office Tuesday morning, Henderson again recollected the incident and again experienced the embarrassment. He wondered if Trevor had been in the war. Too young, probably. Perhaps Korea.

Henderson tried to interrupt his thoughts by going over the final details of the carpet sale he had been negotiating with the hotel chain. He was due to meet with the chain's representatives in a week. The chain wanted to buy about fifty carpets to show off in their lounges and smoking rooms. Henderson planned to ask for ten thousand pounds, which he considered a low price. Because of the size of the sale, he was handling it, instead of Mrs. Clavering.

He continued to go over his material—samples of fabric, photographs, the histories of individual carpets—until twelve thirty. Then he went out to find Sandra. He had asked her out to lunch the afternoon before, partly in reaction to his hesitation and indecision about her. She had accepted. They would go to the Baker & Oven on Paddington Street. Henderson found her filing invoices for Mrs. Clavering.

"Are you ready?" he asked.

She nodded and got up. Then she took a small mirror from her purse and looked at herself briefly.

"You look perfect. What more can you do?"

"One always hopes," she said, smiling.

Getting their coats, they walked to the door and down the stairs. The weather was still good, for some inexplicable reason, although it was chilly. Small, terrible white clouds scudded across the face of the sun.

Henderson began looking for a cab. Beside him, Sandra made a slight gasping noise. He turned, startled. "What is it?"

She pointed across the street. "There's that American again."

Trevor was standing on the sidewalk across from Henderson's office. It was a little after twelve thirty. He was waiting calmly. From a deep place inside himself, he was laughing. An expensive Nikon camera hung from a strap around his neck.

When Henderson came out with Sandra, Trevor stepped back behind a parked car in order to hide himself a little. Then he saw the girl say something. Henderson jerked around and looked at Trevor. It was only for a few seconds, then he turned away. Trevor could see the muscles standing out along Henderson's jaw and neck. Henderson took Sandra's arm and they began to walk down the street.

Trevor walked quickly around the parked car and hurried across the street. He was smiling. Running ahead of Henderson and Sandra, he turned, focused the camera and began taking pictures, changing the angle as he moved, shooting them from as close as five to fifteen feet.

"What's he doing?" Sandra asked Henderson. "Who is he? Why is he doing this to you?"

Henderson tightened his grip on her arm and began to walk faster. There had been a moment when Trevor thought Henderson would jump him. He had hung on the edge and then slipped back into his shell.

Trevor kept shooting them as they hurried down the street. He was now audibly chuckling.

Sandra tried to break away from Henderson. She wanted to speak to Trevor. Henderson kept a tight hold on her arm. "What do you want?" she called to Trevor. "Can't you leave him alone? Can't you stop bothering him?"

Henderson turned to her angrily. "Don't speak to him. Ignore him!"

Trevor kept laughing. Then he shot the last of his roll and stopped. Henderson and Sandra passed him, moving toward a waiting cab which Henderson had flagged. Trevor watched them climb into the cab. He still wondered if they slept together.

Trevor continued down the street, turned down Half Moon and walked to Piccadilly. Then he crossed over into Green Park. He intended to see Mitchell but he was in no hurry. It was peaceful in the park. People were feeding the pigeons and saying goodbye to the sun. He dodged across the Mall by the Victoria Memorial, which looked like a massively ornamented wedding cake plopped down in front of Buckingham Palace. Then he passed into St. James's Park, walking along the south side of the lake, looking at the odd ducks. The park was full of civil servants eating sandwiches on the grass. Trevor had a momentary desire to see the pelicans perched out on their rocks at the far end of the lake. He had always been particularly fond of them. Whatever changes went on in London, the pelicans would remain the same, just as their predecessors had done ever since the Russian ambassador had given the first brace to Charles II.

Trevor shrugged and turned off toward Great George Street. They didn't matter. Off to his left he could just make out the pelicans sleeping on their rocks. A tourist was standing illegally on the grass bordering the lake, trying to throw them bits of bread. The pelicans didn't notice.

Mitchell was in a poor mood due to the fact that Sergeant Fawcett was being more incompetent than usual that morning. The sergeant had begun the day by announcing his intention to investigate a well-known M.P. in connection with the death of his wife. The woman had died of cancer following an illness of fifteen months. Fawcett believed the husband had poisoned her because he could no longer endure the expense. He had then gone on to suggest that they arrest Trevor in order to "get something out of him." After several hours, Mitchell had brought the enthusiasm to a halt with broad hints about police work in Manchester.

But it had been difficult and he was in no mood to be chatty with Trevor, who appeared at his office at one o'clock. Barely listening to Trevor's account of the picture-taking, he reached out his hand for the film. "We'll have this developed. Possibly there's something we can use."

"How?" Trevor's mild exuberance was rapidly changing to an empty feeling, which he had been experiencing for the past few days despite his short rest in Surrey. He was beginning to fear that only the presence of Henderson would allow him to feel any strong emotion.

Mitchell unscrewed the stem of his pipe and held it up to the light, trying to look through it. Then he sighed. "They could be sent anonymously to his wife. Their very innocence would suggest guilt."

The idea struck Trevor as unfair, although obviously no worse than anything he had been doing.

"At any rate," Mitchell continued, "we won't do that for a while. I think you can step up your activities tomorrow morning with no fear that Henderson will try to stop you."

Trevor nodded. "Have the Moroccan police come up with anything yet?"

"Can chickens fly? They say they're watching Ahmed. Oh, yes, there is one new development. An old woman across the street from Jacobs' flat apparently saw the murderer."

Trevor felt his insides give a leap. "Was it Henderson?"

"Of course not, but then we knew that, didn't we? She saw a man wearing coveralls leave the building at seven thirty. She knows it was seven thirty because she then turned away to watch her favorite program on the telly, "Gunsmoke" I believe. At first, she thought the man was a repairman. We've talked to the people in Jacobs' building again, however, and nobody had anything delivered, fixed or taken away by a man in coveralls. It still might be a valid deliveryman, but I doubt it."

"Hadn't you talked to this woman before?"

"Yes, but the man in coveralls had gone quite out of her mind. Then she happened to think of it and found it strange that the man should be working on Sunday. She herself, she said, had never been able to get a repairman on a Sunday. It's astonishing. If you put on a pair of coveralls, you simply disappear. People look right through you."

"What did the man look like?" Trevor still hoped it would be someone recognizable.

"Young man, blond hair, average height, weight, everything. She thought, however, that the man might be wearing quite a few rings."

"She could see that?"

"Apparently. Her flat is on the second floor front. She said they were very flashy rings. At first she thought he was wearing 'those brass knuckles that Americans wear,' as she said."

"Good eyes."

"She apparently watches a lot. In any case, I've turned the matter over to Sergeant Fawcett. Hopefully, it will keep him out of the building."

"I still wish it had been Henderson." Trevor had no doubt about Henderson's guilt, but he wanted it to be provable guilt.

"Cheer up," said Mitchell, a trifle maliciously, "you'll make him jump soon enough. Perhaps tomorrow morning."

It rained for most of the night, but by morning it had stopped. Trevor was standing under a dripping tree across the street from Henderson's house. The Nikon was around his neck.

Up and down the street, men in expensive raincoats and carrying expensive umbrellas were kissing their expensive wives goodbye. Cars purred. A few people glanced curiously at Trevor, who only smiled.

At precisely seven thirty, Henderson opened his front door and came out with his daughter. Harriet stood behind him in the doorway. Trevor walked quickly across the street, raised the camera, focused it and began taking pictures, moving in a tight semicircle around Henderson and his family.

There was a moment of stunned silence as Henderson's wife and daughter looked at Trevor with amazement. Trevor was aware of other people on the street pausing to look, trying to understand what was happening.

Henderson's daughter recovered first. "What's he doing, Daddy? Why is he taking our pictures?"

Henderson stood there without speaking. His face was white stone. Harriet looked at him with a worried expression. "What is it, dear? Why is he taking pictures?"

"Why, Daddy?" Elizabeth sounded a little frightened.

Trevor moved back and forth around them, focusing and taking more pictures. The shutter kept clicking.

"Daddy, say something."

Henderson took hold of himself. "Go back inside, Harriet. This is for a magazine piece. Come along, Elizabeth, I'll drive you to school this morning."

Harriet began to protest, but Henderson told her again to go back inside. Then he firmly took his daughter's hand and walked her quickly to his car. Trevor followed, still taking pictures.

"But why does he want all those pictures, Daddy? Why don't you say something to him?"

Henderson shook his head and pushed his daughter into the car. Trevor ran around to the front, taking pictures. The car started with a muffled roar. Henderson accelerated quickly. The car lunged forward, forcing Trevor to jump out of the way. He watched the car turn onto Fitzjohn's Avenue. He was smiling.

12

ADDED TO THE complete lack of privacy was now the unpredictability of Trevor's attack. It was Tuesday, October 17th. Henderson hadn't seen Trevor since Thursday, when he had appeared with his camera as Henderson was leaving work. The street had been busy and a number of people had stopped to watch, assuming that Henderson was somebody important, perhaps an actor. Mrs. Clavering had watched from the office window, then Sandra, then Cecilia. He had felt so powerless, although he had managed to appear unruffled. At least he hoped so. But he was afraid that someday he wouldn't, that he would break to pieces. He was even afraid he might cry. Henderson had long since given up the hope that Trevor would lose interest. But he tried not to think of the other alternatives.

At the moment, Henderson was preparing to leave his club on Jermyn Street, where he had been lunching with the two representatives of the hotel chain. They had just completed two hours of near-Moroccan haggling over fifty or fifty-five carpets, depending on the side of the haggle. The representatives (they called themselves assistant vice-presidents) were willing to pay ten thousand for fifty-five carpets. Henderson would only offer fifty for that price. Actually, he found that he didn't care, but felt some protest was necessary. He didn't even care about the sale.

What he minded was his apparent indifference to the part of his business which had always been the most interesting to him. He felt tired and terribly bored by his fears. He was tired of the way Trevor filled his mind. Although he had taken great precautions about the meeting, he was almost certain Trevor would be waiting outside with his camera.

The two representatives were being irritatingly jolly. Their voices had a northern twang which grated on Henderson's nerves. He had at last given into their demand for fifty-five carpets and they felt they had scored a smashing victory.

They were the sort of businessmen Henderson particularly disliked. Taking themselves and all their actions terribly seriously, they completely lacked a sense of humor except for an inclination toward risqué puns. As they went down the wide stairs of the club, one of the representatives —a fat red-faced man wrapped in the history of massive dinners—put his hand on Henderson's shoulder. "Hard luck, old fellow. Don't let it get you down. We're all honest men here."

Henderson managed a smile, although irritated by the man's assumption that he was worrying about the carpets. Smiling again, he opened the door onto the street.

He didn't see Trevor until they were all out on the sidewalk. Then Trevor leapt forward in that maniacal way he had developed, darting in a tight semicircle around them. He was wearing his tattered raincoat and his longish red hair was windblown and fell over his forehead. Henderson watched the hotel representatives shrink back into their own personal crowd.

"Who the devil is this man?" cried the red-faced representative, raising his arm.

"Here, you, what's the meaning of this?" said the other, who was bald and had a set of false teeth like a marble frieze.

"I say, get away from here," said the red-faced man.

Henderson didn't move or speak. To his surprise, he found himself thinking how bright the day was, air so clear that each edge seemed to be scraped with a knife. A cab driver slowed down to look at them and then waved, for some obscure reason of his own. Shoppers moved to the curb to avoid them. Henderson was aware that in a far corner of his mind something was trying to get out.

"I demand to know the meaning of this," said the bald man.

Trevor laughed unexpectedly. "Ask Henderson. He knows."

The red-faced businessman turned to Henderson while the other belatedly covered his face with his hat. "I say, Henderson, this is really too much. You agreed to let us handle the publicity."

Henderson managed to summon up some control. "This has nothing to do with you, gentlemen. I suggest you ignore him."

The red-faced businessman snorted and took up a protected position behind his colleague. "How can we believe that?" He looked nervously at Trevor who was still taking pictures.

"As I said, gentlemen," pursued Henderson, "this has nothing to do with you. It's a private matter between me and this man here." He pointed at Trevor. Then he looked at him. Trevor slowly lowered his camera and stared back. For a few seconds, the two men gazed at each other. All that had happened between them was communicated in that look. Henderson felt he was staring at stone. He turned away and walked off down the street, leaving the hotel representatives open-mouthed behind him. Trevor watched for a moment, then followed.

Henderson walked directly back to his office. Several times, people had to dodge out of his way to avoid being run down. He was thinking of Trevor's face and the hatred he had seen there. Reaching his office, he went to his window and waited until Trevor took up his position across the street. Then he stared at him. Stone can be broken, he thought. It was three o'clock when he returned. At four, he was still looking out the window. Trevor was leaning against a wall, swinging his camera.

Sandra knew something was decidedly wrong and knew it concerned the American. Having seen Henderson standing like something nailed to the floor for over an hour, she at last went in to speak to him.

"Is anything the matter? . . ." She stopped, as if struck by the absurdity of the remark.

Henderson kept his back to her. After a while, he said, "No, nothing."

"Is it that man across the street? Why don't you call the police? Why do you let him torment you?"

"Because it has nothing to do with the police." Henderson spoke very quietly. He continued to stare out the window.

"Then let me call the police." Sandra seemed about to cry.

Henderson turned and looked at Sandra standing in the doorway. She was wearing a dark-green dress with a yellow collar. "No, don't do that. I'm all right now. In fact, I think everything will be all right." He walked over to her and took her hand. "There's no need to worry." He paused, and glanced toward the window. Then he said, "I'm going out for the rest of the afternoon. Tell Mrs. Clavering to lock up, won't you?"

Sandra nodded, surprised by the touch of his hand. Henderson turned and left the office. Out on the street, he ignored Trevor and continued down Chesterfield Street to Queen Street, then crossed Curzon to Half Moon. When he reached Piccadilly, he turned left, walking so quickly that Trevor almost had to run to keep up. Henderson crossed Piccadilly at the Ritz, standing like a French urban chateau at the edge of Green Park. He continued toward Piccadilly Circus, past expensive shops, Fortnum & Mason with its reed baskets of jam and caviar in the window, Hatchard's with its books in hand-tooled leather; past the high bow-fronted windows of the Piccadilly Arcade. Henderson was almost running now, forcing his way through the crowds of shoppers: past shops selling ornate military toys, umbrellas, watercolors; past the massive plate-glass window of Pan American Airways; past a Midland Bank; then St. James's Church, a crouch of brick tucked back toward Jermyn Street, then into the Circus itself with its garish advertisements and crowds of people.

Henderson dashed down the steps of the underground station. Crossing the large and busy circular foyer, he continued down an escalator. At the bottom, he turned left down a tunnel marked "Exit Only" and took another escalator going up at a different angle.

When he reached the top, Henderson went through the station to the Haymarket exit and out onto the street. He walked quickly south, crossed Haymarket to Panton Street, turned, passing the Comedy Theatre and several movie houses, and hurried toward Leicester Square. He had stopped worrying about Trevor.

Henderson badly wanted a telephone. He went into Lyons' Corner House just off the Square, which was half full of late afternoon snackers. There was a telephone booth in the lobby. For a moment, he was afraid he might have lost the number, but, searching his wallet, he discovered it on a dog-eared calling card of Ahmed's. He looked at it, still unable to make up his mind, then he shook his head and dialed.

It rang fifteen times before a man answered. "Hallo?" The voice sounded drunken.

"I wish to speak to Frank," Henderson said.

There was a pause, followed by a fit of coughing. The man cleared his throat. "You do, do you, and who might Frank be? . . . My name's Harold. . . ."

"A young man with blond hair. I don't know his last name."

"Ah, mate, you ought to be careful about last names. I've had lots." The man was obviously drunk,

"Is there anyone else I can talk to?" asked Henderson desperately, and immediately regretted it.

There was a long pause followed by another fit of coughing. "Well," said Harold thoughtfully, "there's a lady wheeling a pram; there's a gent with an Alsatian, a mean looking brute; there's a boy with a vanilla ice; and a Pakistani reading an English grammar. Who suits your fancy? Shall we have a try at the lady?"

Henderson was astounded. At last he said in almost a whisper, "Where are you?"

"Pardon me?"

"I said, where are you?"

"Well, I've been having a drink and . . ."

"But where are you?"

"Don't shout, mate. I'm in a bright red call box. Shall I fetch the lady?"

"What call box?" Henderson felt frightened.

"A call box in Hyde Park, right on the banks of the Serpentine, you could say. Shall I fetch . . ."

Henderson hung up the phone. It hadn't occurred to him that Frank's number might be false. Henderson left the booth and walked back toward Leicester Square. Then he stopped.

What if he called Ahmed? He was unsure of this because Ahmed had been very cool lately. Henderson considered flying to Tangier. He thought of sitting in white tiled rooms drinking mint tea. But he couldn't go there yet. He'd call Ahmed. Henderson walked across the square to the Post Office on Charing Cross Road at St. Martin's Place.

It took some time to get through to Tangier. The suspicious operator called his office to double-check his credentials with Sandra. At last she made the connection, although Henderson had to wait five more minutes for Ahmed to come to the phone. Henderson wasn't aware that he was behaving stupidly or even dangerously. He just wanted Frank.

"Hello, Ahmed, this is Henderson. You know that chap you put me in touch with about a month ago? Frank, his name was." There was a pause of about fifteen seconds. "Hello, Ahmed, can you hear me?"

"Yes, I can hear you." Ahmed spoke very softly. While his English was exact, there was still a kind of lilting accent.

"Do you remember that chap Frank you put me in touch with? I need to see him again, I . . ."

"I am very sorry, Henderson," Ahmed interrupted, "I know no one by the name of Frank."

There was static on the wires. Henderson had to strain in order to hear. "Of course you do, don't be absurd. You gave me his number, but it turns out to be a call box in Hyde Park. I must get in touch with . . ."

"You are mistaken, Henderson. I know no one by the name of Frank. Think, Henderson. You must be mistaken."

Henderson felt very cold. He braced himself against the sides of the booth. "Please, Ahmed, something serious has come up. I have to . . ."

"There is no way I can help you, Henderson. It is impossible. I am very sorry." He paused. Henderson could barely hear him. "It is impossible." There was a click.

"Hello, Ahmed? Ahmed?" Henderson flicked the button up and down. "Hello?"

The operator came back on the line. "I'm afraid your party has rung off, Sir. Shall I try again?"

"Yes, . . . No, never mind, operator. Thank you anyway." After hanging up the phone, Henderson walked back out to the street. He stood thinking. His mind felt like wet cotton. Then he slowly walked back to Leicester Square. He needed to sit and sort things out. The image of Trevor overshadowed everything else in his mind.

Entering the Square, Henderson sat down on a bench facing the huge statue of Shakespeare. The Square and the streets around it were crowded with people deciding where to go. Bright new American movies were playing at the theaters. Nearby, a tattered man stood on a bench quietly talking about God. An equally tattered but much older woman stood looking up at him with her mouth open. Henderson looked at the great plane trees and then at the dolphins balancing inexplicably on their chins at the base of the statue. Some young people with packs sporting Swiss flags were collapsed on the next bench. They looked as if they had walked all the way from Geneva in their bulky vibram-soled boots. They were quarreling quietly.

Trevor. He had to think of Trevor. Henderson sat for three hours as the crowds moved around him, wrapped in their noise and busy destinations. Dogs sniffed at him. Pigeons came to see if he had any crumbs. Henderson continued to sit, a small island of silence. There was a wet feeling on his right arm, something hot. It grew dark. At last he shook himself, like a creature waking from a long sleep. He got up and walked out of the Square.

13

AFTER HAVING LOST Henderson in Piccadilly Circus Station, Trevor spent the rest of the afternoon trying unsuccessfully to reach Mitchell by phone. According to Sergeant Fawcett, Mitchell was out. He wouldn't say where, except, of course, it was somewhere important. Trevor left messages which the Sergeant said he would try to leave for Mitchell, but he couldn't promise anything. Trevor went so far as to say that Henderson had run and this was very important, but since Fawcett believed Henderson was innocent he accepted the news as only another example of Trevor's stupidity. Trevor considered going over to Mitchell's office to wait, but he knew if he were alone with Fawcett, even for a short time, he would probably try to throw the Sergeant out the window.

Several times during the day and early evening, Trevor went back to Henderson's office. There was no one there, although Henderson's Bentley was still in the garage on Curzon Street. Shortly after six thirty, he called Henderson's home. His wife hadn't heard from him. "I don't know where he is. He's always home by at least six and he said he'd be home early tonight. Who is this? Do you think he's all right? Do you think . . ." Trevor hung up.

Then he checked Henderson's club and some pubs he had visited in the past. There was no sign of him. After that there was nothing more Trevor could do. He considered calling Eva, whom he hadn't seen since leaving her bed-sitter eleven days before. Although he had been fairly successful in keeping her out of his mind, he knew he had behaved more than badly. It was another thing to feel guilty about. But he felt he had had little choice. In a way it had been an action between him and Jacobs, and Eva became the medium. But it didn't seem that he could just forget about her. Sentimentally, he felt he owed her something. He decided to call her after he had eaten.

Trevor treated himself to a venison dinner at Maggie Jones on Kensington Church Street as a means of consolation. Then, instead of calling Eva, he went back to St. James's for a drink at the Red Lion, a small pub on Duke of York Street, crammed full of Victorian mirrors and cut-glass screens. Wherever he turned he saw his own worried face looking like a message of what he ought to do. Making Henderson jump had not given Trevor the feeling of justification he had expected. Despite his weeks of doubt, the jump found Trevor apparently indifferent. The only moment of exhilaration had been when the two men stared briefly at each other; when for an instant there had been no pretense. Trevor told himself angrily that that was nothing to what he would do next.

His thoughts reverted to Eva. He definitely owed her something. She would have been wondering why he hadn't called. Although he didn't want to see her, he couldn't be so unkind as to ignore her completely. He walked over to a phone on the wall by the door, remembering that she would be at work now. He looked up the number of the Coach and Horses and dialed.

Because of the noise, Trevor had difficulty making himself understood to whoever answered the phone, but at last Eva came on the line. She asked him what he wanted.

"I just wanted to talk, see how you were." Trevor had cupped his hand over the mouthpiece and was almost shouting into it. He felt faintly embarrassed.

"Why?"

"I just did. Can I see you?" He could barely hear her. Eva said something he couldn't make out. "What was that?"

"I said there's no reason to."

"Sure there is."

"I don't think so."

Trevor felt that people in the pub were staring at him. Looking up, he saw a red-haired man standing by a telephone. He found himself thinking the man looked old, before realizing it was only one of his reflections. "Are you all right?" he said.

"Is there any reason I shouldn't be?"

"What are you going to do?"

"What do you mean?" Her voice sounded quiet and detached.

"I mean, what are you going to do now?"

"Continue."

"Pardon me?"

"I said, continue. What else is there to do?"

Trevor didn't know what to say. He wished he could drop the phone and leave this place of mirrors. "Well," he said at last, "I just wondered. Let me know if there's anything I can do for you." He hung up before she could reply. Then without looking back, he left the pub, feeling that he had been tricked in some way.

Out on the street, he told himself to forget about it. The girl was being foolish. He had more important things to do than bother about her. But he still couldn't get over the feeling that he had been outmaneuvered. It was foolish.

After all, he didn't need her. He congratulated himself on the fact that Clare had more sense.

It began to bother him again that he hadn't talked to Mitchell. Trevor felt slightly cut off, as if he were all alone amid the life of the city that was going on around him. He decided to get his car and see if he could find anyone he knew in one of the Fleet Street taverns, before calling Mitchell.

He drove first to the El Vino, had a double Scotch, but found no friends. Occasionally he saw Eva's face in his mind. This worried him, so he left to try another tavern. He went to the Cock Tavern farther down the street, then the Punch Tavern with its flowered mirrors, also on Fleet Street; then the White Horse on Fetter Lane, an old coaching inn. He called Mitchell at home. His wife said he wasn't there but was expected shortly. Trevor went on to the Printer's Devil, farther up the Lane.

By the time he reached the Pigeon on Shoe Lane, near the offices of *The Evening Standard,* he was feeling rather comfortable. There he found Don Somerset, a New York correspondent whom he had known in Washington. The tavern was crowded and the great darkened beams seemed to press the smoke down upon the drinkers.

Having at last found company and support, Trevor told Somerset to wait while he made a phone call. This time he found Mitchell at home. Although Fawcett had told him Trevor had called, the Sergeant hadn't mentioned Henderson.

"When I transfer him," Mitchell said, "he'll be fortunate if it's to such a nice place as Manchester. Don't you think you may have pushed Henderson a little hard?"

Trevor was surprised. "I thought we wanted to make him jump."

"Certainly, but we'd like to have a little control over the

direction. It would be a shame if he became dangerous."

"Shit."

"I'm quite serious. Remember his army record?"

"That was nearly thirty years ago. It's a long way from there to a ritzy house in Hampstead."

Mitchell didn't seem to be convinced. "Well, we don't wish to carry him back. By the way, we may have a line on the actual killer. A porter on the Edinburgh train remembers finding a pair of coveralls under a seat. He also remembered the man who wore them. He remembered because the coveralls were brand new and because he thought it strange to see a workman going to Edinburgh on a Sunday. He described the man as about twenty-four, blond hair, hawkish face, average height and weight and wearing four or five gaudy rings. It was Fawcett who traced him. I was forced to congratulate him."

"Fine, maybe you'll catch the guy someday." Trevor had no interest in the young man with four or five gaudy rings.

"I'm sure we shall. He probably flew out of Edinburgh. I'm having that checked. In the meantime, I'll put out an alert on Henderson. We ought to have him followed officially from now on."

After agreeing to call Mitchell the next day, Trevor went back to Somerset, whom he found sitting at the bar, surrounded by five empty glasses.

"Hear you got a special story," said Somerset. He was a bearlike dark-haired man with the capacity to consume great quantities of lager. He was also constantly apprehensive that major events were taking place without his knowledge.

"Maybe ten 'graphs when the time comes. I'm just cementing my relations with Scotland Yard." Although he didn't want to talk about Henderson or Mitchell, he didn't care to arouse Somerset's interest. He also wanted to get away from that part of his life for a while.

"About time I did that," said Somerset dreamily. "They really hate me." He had done a series of stories on police corruption in the detective division of New Scotland Yard.

Surrounded by a crowd of people and the smoky yellow-and-brown atmosphere of the tavern, they retreated into a comfortable conversation of their world, gossiping about other reporters, criticizing their stories, praising, mocking and rewriting their leads. They discussed dirt that had come to light in Whitehall and various embassies. They discussed who was sleeping with who and what the Queen must be like in bed. They discussed scandals in Parliament, homosexuality in the House of Lords, sodomy among the bishops. They had that enjoyable conversation which journalists engage in, casually reviewing the horrors and stupidities of the world, activities barely fit for their attention, that wouldn't be fit at all if they weren't basically absurd and even, occasionally, funny.

By the time the tavern closed at eleven, they had been joined by Dermot, the reporter Trevor had lied to on the night of Jacobs' murder, plus an AP correspondent and a writer for the *Washington Post*. Although they had all been drinking heavily, they were not ready to quit. Trevor contended he was sober enough to drive them to the New Chelsea Club, even though he had been drinking tequila with beer chasers. No one protested.

They packed themselves into Trevor's Austin Mini and started off. Wails of pain erupted from the tiny backseat as Trevor kept hitting the curb. Buses honked at him on the Strand. Taxi drivers in Trafalgar Square told him to go back to the zoo. He nearly smashed into the Admiralty Arch and a bobby blew his whistle at him. He drove around the Victoria Memorial three times before getting on to Buckingham Gardens heading toward King's Road. At last

133

Trevor brought them to the doors of the New Chelsea Club without injury, although the AP writer swore that he would never ride with him again. Trevor shrugged and walked inside.

They avoided the dancing room with its exotic drinks and the lounge with its classical music jukebox in favor of the hard-drinking room on the third floor. There were long tables with benches, a small bar and gray walls covered with the photographs of race horses.

Sitting down, Trevor began a long, rambling story of the "execution-type slaying" of a Chicago lawyer, which had been one of the first stories he had ever covered. The lawyer had been found in his study at home with tape over his eyes and a small bullet hole behind his left ear. The murder was vaguely similar to Jacobs' death. Trevor kept losing his place and starting over.

He was just approaching the part of the story where he had stolen family photographs of the man in order to keep them out of the hands of other reporters, when he was interrupted by the arrival of Eddie Wolfe, a thin foxlike reporter who worked with Trevor. He had been working late on an IRA-in-London story. Feeling kindly toward everyone at that particular moment, Trevor bought him a double Scotch. Wolfe was suitably grateful.

After they praised each other for a while, Wolfe said: "By the way, Trevor, someone called the bureau this evening asking about you."

"What'd he want?" Trevor tried to focus his mind on what Wolfe said.

"Wanted to know who you were, what you did, where you lived. You been balling somebody's wife?"

Trevor thought for a moment. "Did you tell him all that stuff?"

"Not me, I didn't talk to him. Lawrence was there. He

talked to him for about ten minutes." Jack Lawrence was the youngest of the four correspondents at the bureau. His work often suffered from enthusiasm.

"Did Clare tell you about the shit I've been having with Belton?" Wolfe continued. "He tried to kill a story about a family from Nebraska that got cheated and robbed in London. Jesus, it was good stuff with art showing this farmer's black eye and torn shirt. Belton calls it an 'isolated incident.'" . . .

But Trevor was trying to focus his mind on who might be calling about him. He kept trying to think about it while Wolfe went on to tell his story of suffering to Somerset.

Trevor knew he ought to talk to Jack Lawrence, but he was so drunk that he hardly knew why. At last he gave up and ordered a fresh double tequila before joining a pointless discussion comparing baseball to cricket.

When they left the club at two thirty, Trevor was almost too drunk to walk, much less drive a car. Somerset convinced Trevor to come home with him. He lived with his wife and small son only a few blocks away, on Cheyne Row. The walk seemed to take hours. Trevor kept looking up at the sky, trying to find the Big Dipper, while trees ran into him and shrubbery enfolded him in prickly embraces. Somerset cursed, threatening to leave him behind. Trevor groaned.

Somerset's Irish wife wasn't pleased to see him. She warned him that if he threw up on the couch or woke her four-year-old son, she would be forced to disembowel him with the electric eggbeater. Trevor was in the act of groaning again when he passed out on the couch.

During the night he had long dreams about Eva, but when he rolled off the couch at 9:00 A.M. he couldn't remember what they had been. He seemed to remember her in a dark place. It had been raining. It hurt Trevor's head to think and he gave up. His head felt like a whirling ride in a second-rate August Bank Holiday concession on Hampstead Heath. Something had died in his mouth.

Opening his eyes, Trevor saw Somerset's son, Ralph, staring into his face from a distance of three inches away. Trevor shut his eyes with a snap.

"Your eyes look funny," said Ralph, a plump red-haired child whose behavior was described as precocious. "Do my eyes look funny? Daddy's eyes look really funny."

"Get away," said Trevor.

"The rest of you looks funny too. Your hair looks funny. Your nose looks funny. Your mouth looks funny."

"Get away before I hit you."

Ralph backed to a safe distance of six feet and continued the conversation. He was used to his father's friends. "Your ears look funny. Your clothes look funny. You have red marks on your face. They look funny. The holes in your socks are funny. . . ."

As Ralph continued to describe Trevor—a description he could feel down to the roots of his being—Trevor was slowly putting on his shoes and pushing his own red hair back away from his eyes. Then he got up, grabbed his coat and headed for the door.

Somerset's wife stuck her head out from the kitchen. She looked fresh and attractive. The sight of her made Trevor feel tired. "Coffee or tea?" she asked.

"Neither," said Trevor as he left.

A little later he was sitting in a Golden Egg on King's Road, counting the varied architectural styles used by the mad team of interior decorators hired by the restaurant. What he particularly appreciated was the combination of Aztec and Cape Cod. It reflected how he personally felt. As he waited for his breakfast of eggs, sausage, toast and coffee, he remembered there was something he had to think about. It lay at the bottom of his mind like a murder victim at the bottom of a disused well. It had something to do with the bureau, something he had heard last night. Just as his food arrived, he remembered. He practically ran to the phone.

Fortunately Jack Lawrence believed in being at work by nine thirty. Lawrence didn't, however, know who had called about Trevor.

"He just wanted to know if you really worked here and for how long. He also wanted to know where you lived, but I didn't tell him that. Then he wanted to know where you hung out. He said he wanted to talk to you about some story you're doing."

"Did you tell him?"

"Not really, but you're never here and if it's really important I thought you'd want him to find you. So I gave him the names of the El Vino and the Cock Tavern, the usual touristy places, and the press club of course."

"That was kind of you." Trevor felt cold inside.

"How was I to know; besides, it's stuff he could learn from anyone. He sounded perfectly legitimate, you know, an educated voice. He could have been a cabinet minister."

"Sure," said Trevor, and hung up. He didn't care to think about what the information implied. There was a heavy sensation at the bottom of his stomach which he hoped was just old tequila. He decided to call Mitchell. For once he got through to him without difficulty.

Mitchell was in one of his jolly moods. His cheerful voice went through Trevor's head like a colony of earwigs. "Certainly we found him. No trouble at all. Guess what he was doing?"

"Getting information about me," Trevor growled. He wondered what the penalty was for hitting a detective inspector.

Mitchell was mildly surprised. "How did you know?"

Trevor told him, then added, "What do you plan to do?"

"Nothing. What can we? Does it bother you? Poor Trevor." Mitchell laughed. "Actually, I put a man on him just in case he turns vicious."

Trevor stood in the booth wishing he could go someplace and sleep, someplace where his good friends would leave him alone. "What do you want me to do?"

"Stay away for a while, stay away from your flat."

Trevor was amazed. "You think he's after me?"

"I'm not certain, but you'll only be an interference if you stay here. He's moving now and we must not interrupt him. We found him at the Cock Tavern about nine thirty last night. He was asking about you."

"What did he learn?"

"I have no idea."

Trevor wondered what would have happened if Henderson had wandered into the Pigeon. He put the thought out of his head. "Well, I was thinking of going down to Surrey this weekend. I'll just leave today instead. Okay?"

"Much the best thing. You'll keep in touch?"

"Sure, there's no phone but you can leave messages at the Green Dragon in Haslemere." They hung up.

Trevor left his breakfast, which looked like a mass of cold margarine that someone had stepped in, and drove to his flat to pick up some clothes and take a shower. He thought a little about Mitchell. How much was the man using him? Well, as long as Henderson had jumped, it didn't matter.

He decided to call Clare to see if she wanted to come down on Friday by train. They could have a good weekend together.

14

TREVOR'S MOST relaxing occupation in the country had always been chopping wood. He was doing that now. It would have been easy to buy the wood he needed for his fireplaces in Haslemere, but the actual process of swinging the ax and splitting the logs was so basic that he did it contentedly for at least three hours each time he came down.

It was while chopping wood that Trevor always thought seriously of leaving London, and cities in general, in order to buy a farm. Not that he would farm it, of course, although he would have a large garden. He thought he could buy a place cheaply in northern Michigan or southwestern New York. There he could teach and do some freelancing, perhaps string for some area paper. He would buy two large dogs and learn the names of birds.

As a child Trevor had owned a small, spotty mongrel. Because of its thin fur, Trevor's father had named it Henry, after the bald youth in the comic strips. During a bitter period in his life when his younger brothers were both babies demanding attention, Trevor had made Henry his sole receiver of secrets. Then one day his mother let the dog out of the apartment and it was never seen again.

Since then Trevor often had been tempted to buy a dog

but he was never living in the right place. Big dogs weren't suited for cities. And if he couldn't have a big dog, then he wanted no dog. But at those times when he was chopping wood, Trevor could have accepted any dog as long as it was companionable. He even felt he could live happily in the country with Clare. Perhaps he could. But like many sentimental people, he never carried such subjects to their logical conclusions.

It was about six o'clock. Trevor had been chopping wood for over an hour. The wood pile was on the far side of one of the two large oaks that framed the front door of the cottage. He had more than he needed for the kitchen and drawing-room fireplaces even if it got quite cold. It was now almost too dark to see. The sun had gone down shortly before and although the day had been clear, storm clouds were moving in from the west. Sparrows were chattering in the oaks.

Trevor split one more log and stacked the pieces on the pile. He picked up the ax again, meaning to stick it in the block. He had bought it when he had been down before and there was still a shine to its double blades. Swinging it over his shoulder, he brought it down toward the block. The ax glanced off and struck a rock, nicking the blade. Swearing, he swung it again toward the block, sticking it firmly in the center. Then he picked up an armful of wood and walked to the cottage. Acorns crunched under his feet.

He noticed it was later than he had thought. He'd have to hurry if he were to be on time for Clare's 7:15 train. Going into the bathroom, he turned on the water for the tub, hoping there would be enough hot water to rise above his ankles. He hated washing in a puddle. For the tenth time, he promised himself to write to Bethune about a new water heater. He shrugged. Trevor was feeling too content to be bothered about anything for long.

For two days, Trevor had been fussing about the cottage, repairing cracks and loose tiles that didn't need repairing, fixing a broken window, pulling up summer weeds in the weedy garden, raking leaves and collecting dead branches from the oaks, and in general behaving like a typical homeowner. Henderson was a creature from another world. London was some place in a vivid and desperate dream. The cottage seemed to be in the middle of a wilderness, although the nearest neighbors were only a hundred yards away.

Trevor again considered buying a farm, as he lowered himself into the shallow and tepid water, a farm with dogs and a large water heater. Perhaps he could even raise dogs. It wasn't natural living in cities; it made him unpleasant. He was continually aware of a level of anger barely beneath the surface. But then, Trevor thought, that makes people keep their distance.

Despite the tepid tub, Trevor dawdled. It was exactly seven when he backed out of the gravel driveway, telling himself he couldn't be late, no matter what. The clouds had moved up and it was about to rain. The headlights of the car swept across the cottage and large oaks, the woodpile with its chopping block. Seeing the ax, he cursed himself for not putting it inside. It would get rusty. Well, there wasn't time now. He drove toward Haslemere like a Le Mans dropout.

Trevor pulled into the parking lot as the train drew into the station. Clare ran up to him, kissing him on the cheek. She was cheerful and glad to be out of the city. "I want a drink," she said. Trevor took her bag. Her raincoat was open and Trevor was pleased to see that she was wearing a short blue dress he had given her for Christmas.

"Drinks it is. We'll eat afterward." She took his arm and after putting her bag in the car, they walked to a pub not far from the station. Large drops were just beginning to fall.

The Dog and Fox was not the pub he had mentioned to Mitchell, but Trevor wasn't thinking about that side of his life. Even if he had been, it's unlikely he would have gone to the Green Dragon. Trevor and Clare settled themselves with double Scotches and complimented each other on how well they looked.

"I wish I could have three months off," said Trevor, "so I could come down here and be idle. Even better, I might go up to the Highlands."

"Wouldn't you be bored?"

"Probably, but that would be part of the fun. I'd write a book or something. All reporters want to write books—stuff like Hemingway. Sometimes they even get published. At least I'd keep busy."

"You'd be a wreck after the first week. Wouldn't you be lonely?"

"Umm, maybe."

"And women?"

"I'd take you of course, supply you with entertainment and keep you in bed."

Clare laughed. "What makes you think I'd go?"

Trevor looked at her for a while. "I have great kidnapping abilities."

Pushing her hair back from her eyes, Clare laughed again. "Perhaps you wouldn't need to use them."

Finishing their drinks, they had another round and continued talking. About eight thirty, they went down the street to a restaurant that served traditional roast beef and Yorkshire pudding, despite its plastic and modern atmosphere. It was now raining steadily and they ran to avoid getting too wet.

After ordering, Trevor told Clare about life in Washington and Chicago. It seemed almost interesting to him after an absence of two years.

The only rough spot was when Clare asked him about his work with Mitchell. "But when do you think you'll finish?"

Trevor shook his head. He didn't care to think of it. "I have no idea."

"But it's been over a month. Is it investigative work?"

"You could call it that."

"If you don't want to talk about it then you should say so, instead of being rude." Clare was beginning to get angry.

"I don't want to talk about it."

But Clare wasn't quite finished. "Does that man who has been asking about you have anything to do with it?"

Although Trevor was interested in what Henderson was doing, he was more interested in keeping him out of his mind. "I don't want to talk about it." Then he added, "Look, I realize it's been interfering but it won't go on much longer. I came down here to get away from it. I don't want to think of it. Besides, it's not very interesting."

"Anything secret is always interesting, but, well, I promise not to ask anymore. At least that strange woman has stopped calling." Clare tossed her head slightly. She was a little irritated but not particularly cross.

By the time they reached dessert, everything was smoothed over; and by coffee Clare was laughing as Trevor described a sergeant he had known in Germany. The sergeant had been badly shell shocked in Korea and couldn't be approached from behind. "When I knew him, he was so tight that any sudden noise would send him spinning around, swinging his fists."

Speaking to Sergeant Kowalski entailed running around to the front and approaching from a recognizable distance. Everyone knew this. "But then this major came onto the post. One of those guys who always knows best no matter what, like he's the only guy who can make a bed, peel a

143

potato or clean a latrine. He goes running after Kowalski one day for having a dirty shirt, that's the kind of guy he was. A corporal's running after him saying, 'Ah, Major, ah, Sir, perhaps it would be better . . .' This major had everybody nervous and the corporal wasn't trying too hard. He knew what was going to happen. . . ."

Trevor told the story with grimaces and swings in the air, but at the end he felt depressed. He had been fond of Kowalski as one is fond of one's own mean dog. Kowalski had been court-martialed and discharged. Majors always win in the end, even when they have their jaws broken.

"Shall we go?" he asked Clare. The restaurant was beginning to close and waiters were hovering nervously.

She nodded. Trevor paid the check, leaving a bigger tip than he meant to. Driving back to the cottage, Trevor and Clare talked idly about the bothers of London life and the mythical beauties of living in the country. It was still raining. The windshield wipers clicked back and forth as the headlights swept the wet road.

Trevor was thinking about Germany in 1954. He had joined the army right after high school, hoping to be sent to Korea where he could do something brave. Instead, he had been sent to Germany.

"What are you thinking about?" asked Clare.

"The army. It used to be such an obvious thing to do, I mean join the army. Gave a kid backbone, my father used to say; although he never said it after my youngest brother went to Vietnam in '63. But I remember . . ." He paused. There was a gray Morris parked along the hedgerow only fifty yards from his driveway. Someone out of gas, he thought.

"I remember that I really expected it to change me, turn me into some big man of action. Instead, I was bored the whole time. Bob didn't want to go at all, but once they got him he chose OTS. So they make him an advisor in 'Nam. . . ."

Trevor turned into the driveway. The lights swung across the wet grass, the woodpile and chopping block, the trees, stopping on the house itself, lighting up the kitchen windows. He flicked them off. The house was dark. The only other light came dimly from the neighbor's house down the road.

Clare got out of the car and Trevor followed with her bag. "Even then, Bob thought Vietnam a bad idea. In his letters he said how they didn't even want us there. . . ." Trevor stopped. Something was bothering him, something very serious which he was forgetting. It had nothing to do with his brother or Korea or even Clare. Something about how he had spent the day. He wished he had left the porch light on. It was too dark to see.

He looked again toward the dark house. Suddenly he leapt forward and grabbed Clare's arm, nearly slipping in the wet grass. "Get back in the car! Don't say anything."

He grabbed her so sharply that she jumped, but there was such urgency in his voice that she did what he said without question. Trevor got back behind the wheel. He was sweating. "Lock your door!" He turned the key in the ignition. The starter whined for a long ten seconds before it caught. Trevor kept looking anxiously toward the house, expecting to see something running toward them through the rain. He flicked on the lights. There were only shadows. Jamming the car in reverse and grinding the gears, he accelerated quickly out of the driveway. Gravel rattled under the belly of the car.

As the headlights swept back across the lawn, Trevor looked again at the woodpile. The ax was gone. He couldn't see it on the grass or near the house. There was no sign of it. For a moment he imagined it in someone's hand, some-

145

one waiting behind one of the large oaks. The car skidded back onto the road. Trevor jammed it into first gear. The wheels spun on the wet cement as he popped the clutch. He slowed only long enough to get the London license plate of the Morris parked by the side of the road.

"What on earth is wrong?" asked Clare at last. She was breathless and nearly as upset as Trevor.

"We're going back to London."

"What?" She was amazed. "You can't be serious."

"I'm very serious."

"But whatever for?"

"I don't want to talk about it, but I may have saved your life."

"Is this your idea of a joke?" She obviously didn't think it was, because there was a note of fear in her voice. It was clear something was wrong, but she couldn't think what it might be.

"No, I'm quite serious, but I don't want to talk about it. Maybe when we get back. I've got to think now." He wasn't sure why he didn't want to tell her. Partly it was because of the privacy of his relationship with Henderson. Clare didn't say anything else but sat hunched over in her seat. Trevor couldn't tell if she was angry or frightened. Then he stopped thinking about her. After he had driven for about twenty minutes, he started to laugh. He kept chuckling all the way back to London.

15

"STOLEN? I thought he rented it or something. Shit." Trevor pushed his hand through his hair. It was midnight of the same day and he was sitting in Mitchell's office. Mitchell was tilted back in his chair, puffing on his pipe. He seemed pleased. There was a small tape recorder on the desk in front of him.

"He took it from a parking lot near Elephant & Castle. At least we assume he took it. The keys were in it. He only had to drive it away. Odd that he should bring it back to nearly the same spot."

Trevor swore again. "Sure, he's basically honest. What do you mean you 'assume' it was him?"

"We found no fingerprints and no one saw him. Not even you."

"You think I'm crazy? I'm not going to play games with a guy with an ax. Who else would drive down to Haslemere to kill me? Jesus, and you said you were following him." But along with Trevor's anger and sarcasm was the small fear that it might not have been Henderson.

Mitchell tapped his pipe on a glass ashtray displaying a picture of Buckingham Palace. It was a present from his wife. "We were following him, but it was a rather loose tail. I'm still positive he knew nothing about it. He had gone to the cinema about six o'clock: that place on Marylebone near Baker Street Station. Our man was sitting a few rows behind him. Around seven, Henderson casually got up and walked out. Our man," Mitchell gave the word a nasty emphasis, "our man mistakenly assumed he was going to the lavatory. He decided to check, found he wasn't there and ran out to the street in time to see Henderson disappearing down the steps of the Baker Street Station. I heard about it twenty minutes later and put out an alert. I even called you at the Green Dragon."

"Thanks, I didn't happen to be there." Trevor's original pleasure at having forced Henderson's hand had changed to an examination of his own motives for leaving. He didn't question that he had been scared, but fear alone was no reason not to have investigated. He told himself that he had been afraid of endangering Clare. But he didn't quite believe it.

And what if it hadn't been Henderson? What if the ax had been stolen by someone in the neighborhood? How stupid he would have looked if he had called the police to organize a manhunt for some pimply and innocent teenager. He wanted reassurance from Mitchell that Henderson had indeed been there. But he was afraid to mention it for fear Mitchell would mock him.

It seemed nothing could be gained from the incident. Nothing had happened which would justify Henderson's arrest. "So you still can't prove anything."

"No, but we're more certain. There's one other thing which will interest you. . . ." The phone rang and Mitchell answered it. After saying "Yes" three times and "Do that" twice, he hung up.

"Henderson just picked up his car. He appears to be driving home. My men are following him, so you needn't worry."

Trevor smiled ruefully. "It's not in the city that I bother about him. After all, he's a London animal."

"Perhaps." Mitchell began cleaning his pipe with an elaborate ten-bladed device. "As I was saying, there's a new development which will interest you. On Wednesday, I received a call from the Moroccan police. They said they were sending me some extremely important evidence. You can guess how little I made of that. It arrived here today. I'm afraid I was mistaken as to its value. Now I'll have to send them two boxes of cigars at Christmas, or whatever one sends to Moslems."

"What is it?"

"Listen for yourself." Mitchell reached over and flicked on the tape recorder. The reel turned with a slight hiss and then Henderson began talking.

"Hello, Ahmed, this is Henderson. You know that chap you put me in touch with about a month ago? Frank, his name was." There was a pause. "Hello, Ahmed, can you hear me?"

After listening to the tape, Mitchell rewound it and played it again. Trevor felt terribly relieved, as if something he had feared to be a hallucination had turned out to be real, proving him sane.

"So you're just going to arrest him," he said.

"On what?"

"The tape, I mean, it's all there."

Mitchell gave Trevor a pitying look. "While we both know that to be true, even a third-rate lawyer could make this tape appear as innocuous as a trip to the zoological gardens."

"Then what are you going to do?" It seemed to Trevor that Mitchell was being overly academic. "If you got him in here and played the tape, you could force a confession out of him."

"And his solicitor? He'd sit and wait patiently perhaps. Don't be obtuse, Trevor. The great pity is that Ahmed apparently suspected that the police were eavesdropping, otherwise we could have set up a lovely trap with which to catch the lot."

"With me as bait?"

"Quite."

"No thanks." Trevor didn't care to be the target for a hired killer. His memory of the murdered Jacobs was too vivid; and he was not pleased with Mitchell who seemed to feel they were carrying out an experiment with exhausted white rats. "But what are you going to do?" he asked again.

"I think we'll wait a little. I want to see which way Henderson will go."

Trevor shook his head. The incident at his cottage had frightened him a great deal. He was in no mood to let Henderson rest. "I want to keep after him. He must be right on the edge."

Mitchell looked at him for a few seconds. There was a slight smile on his mouth. "No, we need to let him become comfortable with himself. You should do the same. We are not, after all, helping you with your personal vendetta and nothing else. I wish to see the man tried and convicted. You're the only one interested in punishment."

Trevor angrily got to his feet. He stood for a moment glaring at Mitchell, then turned away. There was a picture of the Queen on the wall. He turned again and looked out the window. The rain had stopped, although the streets were still wet. He had a great desire to leave and pursue Henderson on his own. But he knew he needed Mitchell. Trying to keep his voice calm, he said, "Henderson's gone and made this a very personal affair. I want to get him now."

"Only because your pride was hurt." Mitchell was staring

intently at Trevor. It didn't occur to Trevor that the policeman was baiting him for a reason.

"What the hell do you mean by that?"

"You ran. He scared you and you ran. Worse than that, Clare saw you run. That's the reason you didn't tell her."

Trevor stepped forward and slapped his hand down on Mitchell's desk. It was a few seconds before he could bring himself to speak. "You son of a bitch, he could have killed Clare, too. You were supposed to be watching him, remember? What was I going to do, catch him with my bare hands?"

"It's pointless to discuss it now."

Trevor sat back down in his chair. "Jesus Christ."

"I think you should drop the whole matter and let us handle it from now on."

"Forget it. I'm going to keep pushing either with your help or without it. And you can do me a favor by not telling me again about his army background."

Mitchell was smiling at him. "As you wish. But leave him alone for the weekend. The tension should make him uncomfortable."

Trevor was growing suspicious of Mitchell's mood. He couldn't tell what the man's intentions were. Slowly he began to suspect that he was one of Mitchell's white rats.

While the two men were making their plans, Henderson was sitting in his study at home, drinking a small glass of brandy. He was thinking of how calm he felt.

Not killing Trevor had been his own choice. From his position behind one of the oaks, he could have easily run out and split Trevor's skull.

But the girl had been a surprise. It never occurred to him that Trevor had actual human contact with other people. He had never imagined him in a normal situation.

Trevor was too much his own personal devil. Seeing him with the girl had made Trevor seem like someone else. For a moment Henderson hadn't known who he was.

And then there was the girl. Henderson hadn't, as yet, reached that mental state where he could have considered killing her. Therefore she would be a witness. It made him question what he would do after killing Trevor. That would have to be thought out. But at this juncture he was primarily interested in his own change of feelings.

Henderson sat on the couch rubbing his arm. The sensation of wetness still bothered him. He was thinking about Trevor with some surprise. He was struck by the fact that he was no longer afraid of him. Too much had happened.

Henderson was tired. He was tired of waiting to see what Trevor would do next. He was tired of feeling like a creature on a leash. He was tired of feeling so exposed, of having no privacy.

Earlier in the day, he had talked to John Carlton in Tangier. Carlton had been worrying about Ahmed. "If I didn't know him better, I'd say he was getting ready to pull out," Carlton had told him. "He said he'd contact you, but he acted so strangely that I thought you had better know about it."

Henderson had accepted this without surprise. He knew Ahmed had been upset by his call concerning Frank, but there must be more to it than that. Perhaps Ahmed had returned to smuggling and was in difficulties with the police. Although Henderson was vaguely curious, he didn't care enough to find out.

Nor did he really care that the hotel chain had decided not to buy the fifty-five carpets after all, presumably because of Trevor's picture-taking. His indifference bothered him, but it didn't bother him a great deal.

What bothered him more was how his life could move

along so smoothly for twenty-five years and then take such a sudden turn. It was as if a wall had been placed across its path. He wondered if it had always been there; if his whole life had been directed toward this point; if he had been born with a wall across his forty-seventh year, as if the wall were the punch line and he were some sort of joke.

Although he saw Trevor as responsible for the collapse of his business and life, Henderson was beginning to separate him from it, making him a kind of isolated force. This didn't diminish Henderson's hatred for him. Trevor was between him and his thoughts, between him and the life he had expected to have. It was as if Henderson were locked in a small windowless room. Trevor was the room.

From the beginning, Henderson had accepted Trevor's presence with his normal fatalism. Beyond that he knew Trevor had his own motivations. He dismissed the idea that he had been a friend of Jacobs; Jacobs wasn't that sort of person. But Trevor was a reporter; and because of Henderson's position any news story connecting him to murder and dope smuggling would be quite a coup. Apart from that, Henderson believed that Trevor was caught by the very intimacy of the relationship. It would be impossible for either one of them to give up before the end. Henderson would continue, driven and pursued as if by one of the Furies of Greek tragedy.

He wondered how long he could accept this. It made him mad to be a creature who was acted upon, who took no responsibility for his own future. But what recourse did he have? It was obviously too late to contact the police. Could he hire a killer? It was absurd how ignorant he was of such things, despite his passive life of crime. Was he to wander through the slums of the East End asking questions and making offers? He realized it was this very passivity that hurt him most. He was too willing to be acted upon. He had spent too much of his life just putting up with things. If there were a wall across his forty-seventh year, he bore responsibility for its being there. And if the wall were to be removed, Henderson wanted to do it himself. He realized he didn't want a hired killer. His relationship with Trevor was too personal. If Trevor had to be killed, Henderson wanted to do it himself.

The attempt on Trevor with the ax had been extremely foolish, but in finding out about Trevor, he had learned of the cottage near Haslemere and learned that Trevor had gone there. Henderson had followed, completely governed by his own hatred, with no thought beyond killing Trevor. Fortunately the presence of the girl had made him question what he was doing. Whatever happened, he couldn't allow himself to act emotionally. It would be pointless to sacrifice himself to his own hatred.

Henderson got up to fix himself another brandy. He was aware of another emotion which both bothered and embarrassed him. Thinking back on how he had waited behind the tree with the ax, he remembered experiencing a feeling of exhilaration. Henderson wasn't sure what to make of this. It made him uncomfortable, as if he were extracting pleasure from something of which he disapproved. In his relatively passive life, exhilaration was a rare emotion. The exception to this was his years in the army, where exhilaration in the face of danger was the only alternative to boredom. Now, however, the emotion made him feel a little guilty. It seemed unclean.

He pushed it out of his mind and began wondering about his own safety if he decided to kill Trevor. Why should the police suspect him? In learning about Trevor, he had talked to people on the phone or in pubs. He doubted that the people who had seen him would be able to give the police an adequate description. After killing him, he could leave the country for a while, go to Tangier. Even so, it would be dangerous. There was too much he didn't know. Perhaps it would be possible just to scare Trevor off. If only he could contain his hatred; but, more and more, his response to Trevor's pressure was a blind desire to obliterate him.

Henderson walked over to the desk in the corner and pulled open the top drawers. He told himself he had to be ready for any possibility; that if he were forced to kill Trevor, he would have to do it without hesitation. After looking under the papers in the drawers, he shut them and pulled open the drawers underneath. He knew that somewhere in the house was his service revolver, a .38 Smith & Wesson, and he thought he remembered putting it in his desk so that the children wouldn't find it. Several times since the war he had considered turning it in, but the revolver was linked to so many memories that he had been unable to let it go. Henderson was beginning to think it must be in some trunk in the attic when he found it buried beneath papers in the bottom drawer.

He took it out, handling it as if it were terribly fragile, and inspected it carefully. It needed oiling, and there were no bullets, but those were not serious problems. He knew that in another part of the house there was also his bayonet. Five years before, he had used it as a hunting knife when he had taken his family on a disastrous camping trip into northern Norway. He suspected it was now in his son's room along with his medals and campaign badges. Well, that could wait.

Henderson began to feel that he was behaving ridiculously. Here he was, arraying himself like some American desperado for a situation which would most likely never arise. But even as he told himself this, he felt another surge of hatred at Trevor's interference in his life.

He felt tired and knew he ought to go to sleep. Looking

again at the revolver in his hand, Henderson raised it and sighted down the barrel. He pulled the trigger. There was a click as the hammer hit against the empty chamber. He put the revolver back in the drawer and got up to fetch some blankets from the linen closet. As he did so, he thought that his hatred was the most dangerous thing with which he had to contend. It blocked all his reasoning power and could force him to act with no thought of his own safety. He would have to be careful. Henderson spread the blankets out on the couch and began getting undressed. His shoes were already out in the pantry, waiting to be scraped by the maid.

Harriet had been irritating about that, making a fuss over the muddy shoes and wet clothing, calling him worse than one of the children. He told her he had been out on the Heath.

"In this weather?" she had said. "You'll catch your death."

Henderson had nearly laughed. Now, settling himself on the couch and smoothing out the pillows, he smiled at the absurdity. He was still smiling as he drifted off to sleep and long dreams of pursuit.

16

AGAINST HIS OWN best advice, Henderson took Sandra to dinner on Monday evening. Trevor had appeared only twice during the day, remaining for about fifteen minutes each time and then leaving. Henderson had the uncomfortable feeling that something was going on that he should know about, but there didn't seem to be anything he could do. This minor harassment wasn't worthy of response. But if Trevor increased the pressure, Henderson would have to act. He knew Trevor's habits and most of his hiding places; he knew where he spent his time. Henderson felt as if he were listening for something which would take place miles away: the sound of something falling or breaking. But until it happened, he could only wait.

Henderson took Sandra to Wilton's on Bury Street in St. James, a small Edwardian restaurant decorated in an art nouveau manner. They ate lobster, talked about the theater and the best ways to collect china. Henderson kept the conversation impersonal. Afterward they went to Ronnie Scott's in Soho to hear Buddy Rich and his band. It was too noisy to talk comfortably.

He found it strange to experience the same anxieties he had felt on dates more than twenty-five years before. The fact that he hadn't outgrown them both elated and depressed him. He was afraid of showing Sandra his feelings, afraid of a rebuff. Intellectually, he could see that she enjoyed being with him. Intellectually, he believed that she would go to bed with him. The thought made him uncomfortable.

They talked generally, avoiding all mention of "the American," as Sandra called Trevor. Henderson talked about Tangier, remembering a tiny bar there called the Segovia, which was practically filled by the massive head of a bull, and dozens of caricatures of the proprietor, who looked like Mr. Pickwick.

He remembered one evening at the Segovia when a small Spaniard, practically a midget, sang "Granada" in a high tenor while tears ran down his rouged cheeks. Two Berbers laughed and called the Spaniard homosexual. A thin, aging American, whose wife had left that day for Reno and a divorce, kept saying, "Isn't this the life" and "Women, who needs them?"

The bar was at the end of a small arcade, and it bothered Henderson that he couldn't think of the name of the street which then ran down to the bus station and the market. The English library was right on the corner.

"What's the matter?" Sandra asked.

"I've forgotten something, nothing important." But it ruffled him enough so that he wanted to go back to his office to look at the map of Tangier on his wall.

"My father flies to Tangier occasionally."

Henderson had almost forgotten that her father had his own plane. For an instant he was filled with a desire to hunt out the man and have him fly him and Sandra to Morocco. This was followed by the feeling that he would first have to settle with Trevor. The strength of this feeling surprised him.

"Perhaps he can take us there sometime," Henderson said at last.

Sandra smiled at him. "That would be nice."

Henderson felt embarrassed and was about to change the subject when an idea occurred to him. "As a matter of fact, I've occasionally thought of hiring a plane to take me there. Sometimes I leave on short notice, and often I have to make trips from Tangier to Fez and Marrakech. Trains are such a nuisance in Morocco."

Sandra had been making a design in some salt that she had sprinkled into a small pile. Now she looked up at him. She was wearing a red dress with large white flowers.

"I wonder if he could do it?" continued Henderson. He felt like a terrible hypocrite. "It would depend on whether or not he could leave without much advance warning."

The band had finished its set some minutes before and Henderson's voice seemed absurdly loud in the comparative quiet of the room. Waiters circled with drinks. "I'm sure he could," said Sandra. She spoke rapidly and stared at Henderson with an expression of great kindness. "It would mean a lot to him. Business seems to get worse and worse. Do you really think you'll do it?"

Although wincing internally, Henderson nodded his head. "Perhaps you'd better give me his name and address. Does he have a phone? Write that down, too." He gave her his pen and notepad. As Sandra wrote down the information, Henderson cursed himself for dragging her even further into his affair with Trevor. On the other hand, if he had to leave the country quickly . . .

Henderson continued to feel uncomfortable until they left Ronnie Scott's. Then he saw Trevor standing across the street, half-hidden by the crowd of people searching out Soho entertainment. Trevor was staring at him with a kind of leer. Although Henderson had no plans with Sandra after leaving the jazz club, his immediate desire upon seeing Trevor was to put her in a taxi and send her home alone. Being watched like this made all his thoughts seem suddenly public. There was no privacy. It was almost as if he were watching himself from across the street. The leer was disgusting.

Henderson flagged down a taxi. Sandra hadn't seen Trevor because of the crowd. She was obviously surprised when Henderson, with no warning, bundled her into the back of the cab.

"I've forgotten something," he said lamely. "I'll see you in the morning." He shut the door and walked off toward his car which was parked down the street. Trevor followed him.

Later, at home, he was furious. He seemed without power, unable to do anything. Several times he looked out the window to see Trevor under a street lamp across the road. The beams of light were like mooring ropes binding him to a tiny and cluttered world.

Henderson believed he had humiliated himself in front of Sandra, that he had cheapened himself by his plan to use her father. She must have seen some of this. What could she think? He began brooding again about Trevor, and the wall across his forty-seventh year. He wished he could force his mind to work clearly, make it the tool with which to defeat Trevor. He could barely force it to move in one direction.

In order to function in the past month, Henderson had had to screen out many thoughts and anxieties. But by reducing the conscious portion of his mind, he had opened himself up to thoughts and pictures which he otherwise would not have allowed. It bothered him that mixed up with his brooding about Trevor would be erotic fantasies about Sandra and Tangier; that he would suddenly see her lying naked upon some Moroccan bed. White walls rose around her. There was a palm-leaf window surrounded by red tiles. He could hear vendors shouting in the street outside. He was aware of the heavy smells of incense and mint.

Henderson couldn't understand why these fantasies existed alongside his hatred of Trevor. They even grew with it. Although it seemed to Henderson that he had intercourse with his wife fairly regularly, he had never considered sex as being necessary to his life. Thinking about it now, he had no idea when he had last made love to his wife or what it had been like. He drifted off into a fantasy about taking Sandra to Tangier, of sleeping together in cool, tiled rooms. Then he shook himself out of it. Damn Trevor for being there.

Henderson went to the window again and, drawing the curtain aside a little, looked at Trevor. After a moment, he walked back to the center of his study and stood thinking. He started to move toward his desk, then stopped. That alternative was too dangerous. He walked over to the door, turned off the light and left the room. Then he turned off the hall light, and the night light in his bedroom. His wife was sleeping peacefully. After making sure the house was dark, he came back downstairs and watched Trevor through the curtain.

About ten minutes later, Trevor turned and began walking down the street toward the church. Quietly, Henderson opened the door and slipped out. It was shortly past midnight. The sky was clear and the air quite cool. Henderson followed Trevor down the street.

Shortly before the church, there is a lane for pedestrians that runs downhill between the graveyard and the gardens of the houses of Church Row. There are no streetlights. The lane is cluttered with loose stones and the roots of the oaks that grow in the graveyard. Henderson stood at the top, watching Trevor carefully make his way down to the bottom. Trevor walked with his shoulders bent forward, rounding his back and making him look as if he were crouching. To Henderson it seemed that Trevor was being transformed into some other sort of creature, something homeless. There was a moment when he almost felt sorry for him. Then he smiled at his foolishness and went after him, hurrying along by the wall of the graveyard.

At the bottom, he turned onto Frognal Way. Trevor was about seventy-five yards ahead of him, walking swiftly past the dark angular houses built by the rich fifty years before. Both men crossed Frognal to Frognal Lane. The streets were completely quiet. Henderson walked on the grass to keep his feet from clattering on the pavement. Reaching Greenaway Gardens, Trevor turned right. Henderson hurried to the corner in time to see him ascending the steps of the third house on the left. In the darkness, it seemed to be one of those large, ugly brick villas which has been converted into a warren of bed-sitting rooms.

After a minute, a light came on in a second-story room. Henderson caught a glimpse of Trevor before he walked to the window and pulled down the blind. Henderson stood looking up at the window, thinking. Then he went up the steps to the front door. It wasn't locked. Turning, he went back down the steps and stood for a moment on the sidewalk. The air felt colder and there was a red tinge in the sky from the lights of the city. At last he moved off down the street, walking home.

Sitting at his desk the next morning, Henderson still had the sensation of waiting. His mind switched from subject to subject and he kept thinking of the previous evening. He kept seeing Trevor walking down the dark hill. He kept remembering the comfort he had felt with Sandra. He told himself there would be no more dates, that it wasn't fair. He believed this, but he also knew it wouldn't effect his actions. Henderson was still trying to convince himself to leave Sandra alone when a package arrived around ten thirty.

Sandra brought it into his office. "A deliveryman just brought this. It looks like a box of roses, but it's quite heavy." She put the box on his desk.

Henderson looked at it distrustfully. It was indeed a box for long-stemmed roses, but he didn't believe it held any. There was no return address on the wrapping. He ripped the paper off the box and broke it open.

Inside was Trevor's ax.

"What an odd gift," said Sandra. "Look, there's a card."

Henderson picked it up. "Better luck next time," it read. Walking slowly over to the window, Henderson looked out and saw Trevor leaning against a wall across the street. Henderson's first reaction was as if someone had hit him soundly in the stomach. This was followed by a moment of intense fear, then anger, then emptiness and finally, relief.

He went back to the ax and stared at it.

"Is anything wrong?" asked Sandra.

"No, not for me at least." He kept rubbing his arm. He was aware that Sandra was still talking, but he didn't pay any attention. Everything was settled. Trevor had chosen and now bore complete responsibility for whatever happened. Henderson considered himself no more than an instrument, a very exact instrument.

Trevor remained outside Henderson's office, trying not to think about what effect his gift might have. It bothered him to discover that the possibilities worried him. He felt restless. Although he knew everything was coming to a head, all he could do was wait; and waiting was what he was poorest at. Trevor wanted it to be over. He wanted to get back to his own life. Tired of the slow-mounting pressure and the ambiguous response, he wanted everything clear and precise. He wanted Henderson to come out and say, "Yes, I killed Jacobs. This is how I did it. . . ." The confession would be broadcast over the BBC. Afterward the listeners would write Trevor, saying he had done the right thing.

He had made Jacobs into a symbol of betrayed trust. He had exaggerated the circumstances surrounding Jacobs' death to the point where he saw himself as having delivered the Judas kiss. Although he partly knew this was absurd, the idea remained with him in the way people can believe something is true and know it is false.

Beyond Henderson's public confession, Trevor wanted assurance that he himself would return unchanged to his former life. He was afraid that the alterations he had undergone would stay with him, that he would remain the sort of person he despised. He saw himself as becoming like Jacobs: petty in all his ways, a man of little evils. The irony of this fascinated him: that, unable to save Jacobs, he had resurrected him by taking on his personality; that he was making atonement by sacrificing himself. He wondered if that accounted for his interest in, and objectionable behavior toward Eva; why he had degraded himself with her.

He was still thinking of Eva when Henderson left his office shortly after eleven. Walking briskly, he turned left down Chesterfield Street. Trevor pushed himself away from the wall and began to follow him. Down the street in the other direction, he saw one of Mitchell's men get out of a green Vauxhall. The man gave Trevor a brief, conspiratorial nod. Idiot, thought Trevor, turning away.

Henderson continued to walk quickly. He was hatless and wore a dark-blue overcoat over a gray suit. Trevor had to run a little to keep him in sight. Owing to his general dissatisfaction, he felt lethargic and unwilling to traipse across London for no apparent purpose. He assumed Henderson was off to some luncheon meeting. Henderson turned right at Curzon Street, walking toward Hyde Park.

Despite the cold, the streets were filling with people. There was a yellow ring from the smog around the sun. Glancing behind him, Trevor saw the plainclothesman about fifteen yards away. It was almost as if he himself were the person being followed.

Henderson crossed Park Lane to the Stanhope Gate of Hyde Park, then headed left across the grass toward one of the footpaths. Trevor dropped back a little now they were in the open, while feeling it pointless to pretend that Henderson didn't know he was there. Off to his left he could hear the rumble of traffic around Hyde Park Corner and see the massive screen with its three triumphal arches and Ionic columns. Two young men in tennis shoes jogged by, followed by a small yapping terrier.

The sun seemed brighter in the park, as if drawn by the grass. Flocks of pigeons would swoop by, settle, take off, then settle again a few yards away, governed by some curious logic of their own. Trevor watched Henderson cross Serpentine Road and then Rotten Row. It was almost like seeing a movie he had seen before and had never enjoyed. There were several boats on the Serpentine. Nearby, some boys were kicking a soccer ball. Everyone was getting lots of exercise.

Henderson turned left on South Carriage Road, walking past the French Embassy and Albert Gate. Reaching the Hyde Park Hotel, he turned left toward Knightsbridge. Trevor and the plainclothesman hurried forward again while Henderson stood waiting for the light. The streets were jammed with trucks, cars, buses and taxis trying to turn off or onto Brompton Road, Sloane Street, Kensington

165

Road and Knightsbridge. It remained a source of continual surprise to Trevor that he had never seen a traffic accident in his two years in London.

He was hobbling now, having gotten a stone in his left shoe in the park. As he bent over to remove it, Trevor saw the light turn. He straightened and skipped forward after Henderson who was crossing over to Brompton Road. The stone was painful, and Trevor tried to walk on the edge of his foot to keep from coming down on it.

Henderson appeared to be heading for Harrods department store, a great red brick building, which claims to be the biggest store of its kind in the world. Trevor began a limping run, not wanting to lose Henderson in the maze of halls inside. As he pushed through the crowd of people at the door, a tall middle-aged woman grabbed his arm and deftly slipped a red flower into his lapel. "Give something to the homeless children, Sir?"

Trevor attempted to pull away but the woman kept her grip on his arm. Furious, he reached into his pocket for some loose change. The plainclothesman walked past him into the store, grinning widely. Trevor pushed some money into the woman's hand and tore himself away, the red flower contrasting sharply with the anger on his face.

There was no sign of Henderson in the store, nor could Trevor find the plainclothesman. He wandered through a large area devoted to selling food, and into a bank. An early Rolls Royce was on display in the center of the bank, gleaming black with white carnations in small silver vases attached to the sides. A hushed crowd of about thirty people stared at it reverently, perhaps seeing it as the just reward for a life of labor and saving. Henderson and the policeman were nowhere to be seen. Trevor sat down in a soft leather chair and removed the stone from his shoe. Noticing the flower in his lapel, he made a move to get rid of it, then he stopped. After all, it had cost at least fifty new pence. He left the flower where it was.

For the next thirty minutes, Trevor wandered fruitlessly through the store, idly looking at imported French clothing, bridal gowns, Rembrandt prints, costume jewelry, furniture and raincoats. Clerks in pin-stripe suits offered him their assistance. Trevor growled at them.

At last he gave up and went in search of a telephone. Since he found himself unexpectedly free, he decided to call Clare to see if she would meet him for lunch. He caught her just as she was leaving the office. She said she would meet him at the Avery Coffee House in Hind Court, off Fleet Street. Trevor was pleased that she sounded friendly. More and more he wanted to tell her about what had happened at Haslemere; even to ask her advice. But he was afraid she would disapprove of what he was doing.

Leaving the booth, he walked to the main entrance of the store and was let out by a doorman wearing a top hat and green coat. As he walked up to the Knightsbridge tube station, Trevor noticed a double-breasted trenchcoat in the window of a fashionable boutique. It had the advantage of being almost like the coat he was wearing, with the additional qualification of keeping out the rain. He made a note of the shop, meaning to come back when he had more time.

Turning away, he glanced back toward Harrods and was certain he saw Henderson in the crowd of people on the sidewalk. Looking again, there was no sign of him. Trevor walked back a short way toward the department store. Henderson wasn't there. But Trevor was sure he had seen him, at least he thought he was. This bothered Trevor; it didn't seem he could spend this much time following Henderson and then make a mistake about seeing him. He shrugged and turned away. Even if he's there, thought Trevor, I don't have time to worry about him now.

But as he walked toward the tube station, he began to wonder, if he had seen Henderson, just why the man was there. He considered going back to make certain, but he knew Clare would be furious if he didn't meet her.

The tube station was jammed with people. It seemed the entire population of London had decided to pass through Knightsbridge that lunch hour. Trevor forced his way through the crowd, waited in line for his ticket, then pushed his way through more people to reach the platform. He walked up to the end to avoid the crush, moralistically telling himself that it was during times like these that people fell onto the tracks.

Trevor stood near the edge, reading the old advertisements across the tracks, wondering if they were ever changed and trying to avoid being jostled. There was a high roar as the train swept in. People pushed forward. For a brief instant, Trevor was afraid he would stumble. He shoved himself backward as the train shot past him, braking to a stop. "Here, watch it," someone said crossly.

As he was pushed into the car, Trevor looked behind him. Henderson was staring at him from a distance of ten feet away. Trying to look again, Trevor found a fat woman with an armful of packages obscuring his vision. A West Indian brushed past him, knocking the flower from his lapel. Someone else stepped on it, leaving a red smear on the floor. The car doors slid shut. Trevor strained to look back as the doors closed. Henderson wasn't there. But Trevor was positive he had seen him. He was now equally positive he had seen him minutes before, on the street. What did he want? Trevor wondered what would have happened if Henderson had been closer to him on the platform. Had he really been there? Trevor couldn't have been mistaken twice. Again he wondered what would have happened. He looked uneasily at the people around him, as the car rocked back and forth through its long tunnel.

For the rest of the day Trevor was thoroughly uncomfortable. He felt vulnerable and kept continually looking over his shoulder. Again and again he went over those moments in Knightsbridge, trying to decide if he could have been mistaken. The possibility that Henderson had been following him was frightening, but the possibility that he was hallucinating was worse.

Trevor remained with Clare until shortly after two o'clock. Then he went back to Henderson's office. He didn't want to but he was afraid his disinclination to go there was caused by fear; so he forced himself, despite his feelings.

Clare had been very soothing during lunch, listening quietly as he told her there had been someone whom he didn't want to see waiting at his cottage. Trevor didn't mention the ax. He wasn't sure that Clare quite believed him, but she was concerned enough not to question what he said. He didn't mention Henderson, still feeling she wouldn't approve or would say he had only brought it on himself. He was even surprised to find a small amount of guilt in himself because of what he had been doing to Henderson.

At five o'clock Henderson emerged from his office and walked to his car. Trevor almost winced to see him. The plainclothesman hadn't returned, or at least not while Trevor had been there. The man's car was gone.

Trevor followed Henderson home, driving along the same route he had followed for weeks, passing Regent's Park and Lord's Cricket Ground. The trees were bare, the leaves having fallen, with Trevor hardly noticing them. He didn't see them now. For the whole distance, he stared at the back of Henderson's head, as if trying to will him to make some sign, showing him to be the person whom Trevor had seen in the tube station. There was none.

Several times Trevor had considered calling Mitchell to tell him what had happened. But he was afraid Mitchell would laugh. The thought made him angry. It was beginning to seem that he no longer had any control over his own life. He was just moving along, led by Henderson and directed by Mitchell.

Reaching Henderson's home, Trevor drove on to his bed-sitter, parked his car and walked back. Going up the lane by the graveyard, he realized how jumpy he was, as he kept looking toward the dark trees and staying away from the wall. But Henderson was still at home. Trevor could see him walking by the windows when he took up his position across the street.

Trevor remained outside of Henderson's until seven thirty, when he walked down Church Row to call Clare and get something to eat. She had asked him to come over that evening. He hadn't been able to decide at the time, saying he would telephone later. Even now, he couldn't decide. He felt he ought to watch Henderson, that something would happen, but he was so nervous that the thought of an evening watching Henderson's house was almost more than he could bear.

Reaching Clare at home, Trevor was still indecisive. "I don't think I'll be able to make it after all. There are some things I've got to do."

"Can't you put them off? Surely it can wait? I don't mean to pressure you, but I think you need a good rest."

Trevor was aware that his behavior with Eva made him uncomfortable with Clare, as if he had partly used Eva to hurt her. "Maybe, I don't know. This is almost over. Jesus, I hope it's over. I was a fool ever to get into it."

"Can't you stop it?"

"No, it's not that sort of thing. I've got to see it out."

Clare was silent for several seconds. "Are you going to come over? I wish you would."

"I can't decide." Trevor felt like an idiot. He had never

considered indecision one of his problems.

"All right, why don't you decide later. But if you can come why don't you do it before midnight. I'll expect you until then."

"Okay, I'll see what I can do." Trevor hung up the phone, and after getting a sandwich at a carry-out place up the street, he walked back to Henderson's.

He noticed the green Vauxhall near the corner. Trevor walked over to it. The plainclothesman rolled down the window, grinning at him. He had a round, blond, sallow face. "What happened to your flower?"

Trevor looked down at his lapel. He couldn't remember. "I don't know."

"You Americans are such charitable blokes."

Trevor stood with his back to the car, trying to look like he wasn't talking to anyone. He disliked such melodrama. "By the way," he said, "where did Henderson go? I lost him at Harrods."

The policeman shook his head. "So did I, mate. I went outside to see if I could spot him leave, but there wasn't a trace." The man spoke with an unexplained cheerfulness that made Trevor feel tired.

"Did you see me leave? That would have been around noon."

"No, can't say that I did. That's odd, because I was looking for you."

Trevor grunted and continued down the street. Everything seemed destined to go wrong. Reaching his spot across from Henderson's house, he leaned back against the lamppost to wait.

Looking out the window at eleven, Henderson could see him still there. Satisfied, he sought out his wife in the living room. She was watching an Oscar Wilde play on the BBC, and knitting. It struck Henderson that she had always tried too hard at domesticity. He wondered how much of that was his fault. He felt a little sorry for her.

"Harriet, I'm going out for a while. When you go to bed, I want you to turn out the lights. Don't bother leaving anything on for me."

His wife looked up a trifle anxiously. "Where are you going? Will you be late?"

"No, I'm just going out for a bit, but I want to avoid that man across the street. Will you turn out the lights at midnight?"

"Yes, but, well, who is he?" Henderson knew that his wife had avoided mentioning Trevor for fear of irritating him. There didn't seem to be anything he could tell her.

"He's a business competitor. It's very complicated, but he'll be gone tomorrow."

"Is what you're doing concerned with your business?"

"Yes, that's why I don't want him to see me." He walked to the door leading out to the hall. "You'll turn out the lights? That's important."

"Certainly, if you wish it."

Henderson left the room and walked to the back door. Although he didn't particularly think of himself as an honest man, he disliked lying. He also disliked what he was doing to Harriet. Over the years he had reached the point where he had to focus on her in order to see her. Otherwise she was just there, an innocuous presence in his house. Now he was putting all that behind him.

He took a dark-blue raincoat off a hook and opened the door. Then he reached under his coat, tucking something securely into his belt. He had been right about the bayonet. It had been in his son's room after all.

17

BUT TREVOR didn't go back to his bed-sitter that night. Instead, at the last moment, he went to Clare's. Early the next morning, he was returning to his bed-sitter to change his clothes before following Henderson into the city.

He was tired, having had about three hours' sleep, and was now remembering the night with some displeasure. Although Clare had been kind, Trevor felt he had been weak, that he had exposed too many of his emotions, laying himself open to possible pain and rejection. He realized he had acted in response to weeks of holding himself in, of trying to keep complete control, but that was no justification.

It wasn't that Clare had led him on, rather she had been too understanding. With growing dissatisfaction, Trevor saw himself as some kind of child's pet, responding to kindness way out of proportion to how he ought to have behaved. Clare had done no more than to encourage him to take a rest, perhaps leave journalism for a while.

Trevor had said he had thought of returning to the States. Perhaps he would teach for a few years or get a desk job. Although he had considered it before, he feared that to leave journalism would be a sign of defeat. He didn't mention that to Clare, knowing she would disagree, knowing he wouldn't believe her.

Then, lying next to her in bed, Trevor had asked, "I don't suppose you'd consider going back with me?"

Clare raised herself up on an elbow and looked at him, as if trying to see how serious he was. Trevor kept his face expressionless. "Do you think you would really like that?" she asked.

Trevor was surprised by the question, thinking she had taken him almost too seriously. "Sure. We could get married or something. You'd like it over there."

Clare had laughed. "You wouldn't want that. Your privacy's too important."

Although Trevor had disagreed, he didn't disagree very strongly. He was afraid it might be true, that it was too late to admit another person into his life. He had also felt a little rejected.

Driving north on Finchley Road, he told himself he had been lucky. Clare, fortunately, had more sense than to want to come with him. Even still, he was filled with an aching loneliness, and anger at all the small rooms that stretched before him, inhabited only by himself. He shook the thought from his mind and began to abuse himself for opening up to her.

Although he hadn't been thinking of Henderson, Trevor was aware of a constant brooding in the back of his mind. He still hadn't decided about the experiences of the day before, whether or not Henderson was the person he had seen. Driving back, he had the feeling of reentering a stuffy mineshaft, where the supports were rotten and the coal was gone. He considered turning around and going back to Clare's, but that too was frightening. Besides, he was bound to Henderson. There was no way out before the finish.

Trevor turned onto Frognal Lane, then left onto Greenaway Gardens. It was about quarter to seven, and he had just enough time to change and wash before going over to Henderson's. He parked his car and hurried up the steps of the building, then to his room on the second floor. He didn't see anyone, although he could hear alarms going off in small rooms as people woke to continue their endless lives.

Opening the door to his room, Trevor stopped. The blinds were drawn. He was sure he had left them open. He flicked on the light and walked slowly into the room. It was as small as it could be and still contain a narrow bed, a chair and a chest of drawers. The wallpaper showed hundreds of dying roses. There was green linoleum on the floor. Next to the door was a small closet, and next to that a tiny kitchen with a sink and hot plate.

Trevor felt uneasy. Looking into the closet, he saw that the clothes and hangers had been pushed to one side. There was also a depression on the bed as if someone had been sitting there. He looked again at the closet. Anyone entering the room would have his back to it. Trevor went out to the hall and inspected the lock on the door. It was a simple latch which could be opened with a stiff piece of plastic, a credit card, for instance.

Trevor had the uncomfortable feeling that he was being watched. But the room was empty. The feeling continued. Either someone had been in the room or he was imagining things. Possibly it had been the maid who had cleaned the room after he had left the previous day. But she had never left any sign of her presence before.

Without bothering to change, Trevor ran down the stairs to the caretaker's flat in the basement. He found her having an early morning cup of tea with the maid. She was complaining about an Indian student who refused to pay his rent. The maid said that what the Indian did to his sheets was simply awful.

The room was full of china figurines. Trevor interrupted the women brusquely. "Who was in my room after I left yesterday?"

The two women looked up with interest. "I cleaned it in the morning, Sir, just as always." Although young, the maid was an ugly woman whose face appeared to have been cut down the middle and reattached with one side an inch higher than the other.

"No one was there after that?"

"I wasn't, Sir."

Mrs. Burroughs, the caretaker, nodded her head in agreement. "You had no visitors. Is anything the matter?" She was a talkative widow who, upon learning Trevor was a reporter, had told him she intended to write a book about all her mad tenants. She had followed the remark with a long look at Trevor.

Trevor ignored her question and turned back to the maid. "Did you move the hangers in the closet?"

"No, Sir."

"Did you close the blinds or sit on the bed?"

"No, Sir." The maid began to fidget nervously.

"Whatever is the matter, Mr. Trevor?" Mrs. Burroughs got to her feet and looked at him severely. She disliked being ignored.

"Someone was in my room."

"How could that be? Are you certain?"

"Very certain. You didn't hear anything?"

"Not a sound. Is anything missing?"

"No."

"Then it stands to reason no one was there, doesn't it?"

Trevor nodded curtly and turned to leave. As he closed the door behind him, he heard Mrs. Burroughs say to the maid, "The very idea, accusing you like that." It would give them something to talk about.

It was now nearly quarter past seven. There was no time to change; he had to get over to Henderson's. Trevor drove over to Arkwright Road, then left toward Fitzjohn's Avenue. He kept thinking about his room. It must have been Henderson. There was no one else it could be. Could he be mistaken? Perhaps he really was beginning to hallucinate, that he was the one who was breaking, not Henderson. Should he see Mitchell? He couldn't decide. No, he would have to. There was no way he could accept the possibility that he was hallucinating. It must have been Henderson.

When Trevor reached Church Row, he found Henderson had gone.

Several hours later, Henderson was sitting in his office trying to analyze how he felt. There was a growing pile of papers that he had to attend to on his desk but he couldn't keep his mind on them. Instead, he was thinking of Trevor. Henderson had indeed been in Trevor's room, having spent six hours waiting for him to arrive. He had also followed him for a short time the previous day, looking for some opportunity more out of curiosity than from any clear intention to kill him.

His reward for all this had been the look of fear on Trevor's face when he had seen him in the underground station at Knightsbridge. There was perhaps one other reward, which was now causing Henderson to question his feelings. This had been the feeling of exhilaration he had felt while standing in the darkness, waiting for Trevor. Occasionally other lodgers had come up the stairs, going to their rooms. Each time Henderson had thought it might be Trevor. Each time he had stood in the closet gripping the bayonet, until at last he realized that Trevor wouldn't be returning that night after all, and he had slipped out of the building and walked home.

The feeling of exhilaration bothered him. It seemed that if he had to remove Trevor from his life, he should do it coldly. Otherwise he was allowing his judgment to be weakened by emotion. He was taking a terrible chance in any case, but by acting less than logically he was giving himself up to consequences that he didn't care to think about.

His thoughts were interrupted by a noise in the outer office, followed by a short scream. Jumping to his feet, he thought irrationally that Trevor was out there, that he was doing something to Sandra.

He opened the door to find Sandra, Mrs. Clavering and Cecilia standing in a close group, obviously upset. Cecilia was crying. Sandra looked confused. She was holding an 8 x 10 photograph in her hand. Other photographs were on the desk. Mrs. Clavering was looking at them angrily. Henderson walked over and took the photograph from Sandra.

"They came in the mail," she said. "We each got one."

Mrs. Clavering took the photographs from the desk and tore them up. "It's disgusting. If this is someone's idea of a practical joke, it's in very bad taste."

Henderson looked at the photograph. It showed a man with a gaping hole in his forehead. More accurately, there was no forehead. The lower half of the face was obscured by blood and pieces of flesh and bone. The man was wearing a set of stereo headphones.

"Who is it?" asked Sandra.

Henderson continued to look at the photograph. "I have no idea," he said.

Mrs. Clavering picked up the phone. "I'm going to notify the police."

"No, don't do that," said Henderson quickly. "After all, there's nothing they could do. What did they come in?" Sandra handed him three large envelopes. Henderson glanced at them. "There's no return address and they were postmarked in London. The police couldn't learn anything from them."

"I still think they ought to be told," said Mrs. Clavering.

Henderson nodded. "Perhaps you're right. I know an inspector at Scotland Yard. I'll contact him and see if there's anything that can be done."

"The person must be crazy," said Sandra. She had recovered to the extent that now she, too, looked angry.

Henderson picked up the torn photographs. "I'll take care of these." Turning, he walked back into his office and shut the door after him. For several minutes, he looked at the photographs before tossing them onto his desk. The man was Jacobs. Henderson knew that perfectly well. He found himself wondering how Trevor had got them. The pictures must have been police photographs. Obviously reporters have access to such things. Henderson wasn't entirely satisfied with that conclusion.

About the same time, Trevor was in Mitchell's office. He had already told Mitchell about being followed by Henderson and about the intruder in his room. Mitchell seemed indifferent. Fiddling with a paper knife, he responded by talking about the hunt for the actual killer. He must have known that he was making Trevor angry, but he talked on, as if they had at last reached a subject of some importance.

"This chap, Frank, flew from Scotland to Paris, on BUA, I believe. I can check that later. A stewardess remembered him because of his rings. But when he reached Paris, he completely disappeared. He must have more than one passport. We have the name he was traveling under but it doesn't lead us anywhere. It's a long story. The Police Judiciaire are handling it now. They have more freedom than we have in these matters. In the meantime, Sergeant Fawcett and some men are searching the records for someone who matches Frank's description. No luck so far, but it's amazing how something will suddenly turn up. I remember one time . . ."

"What about Henderson?" Trevor wanted to reach over and knock the paper knife out of Mitchell's hand.

"What about him?" Mitchell looked surprised. He was attempting to balance the paper knife point first on his right index finger.

"Are you going to let him kill me? What do you mean to do? I told you he was waiting in my room."

Carefully holding the knife, Mitchell flipped it two feet and tried to catch it by the hilt. The knife clattered to the floor. Mitchell sighed. He appeared tired and bored. "You don't really know he was in your room."

Trevor snatched the knife up off the floor and held it in his lap. "But someone was, and what about seeing him yesterday?"

"You said yourself you might have been mistaken."

"Your man lost him."

"That doesn't prove anything."

"I suppose I was imagining things in Haslemere, too. I suppose no one was there. Jesus, Mitchell." There was a cold knot in Trevor's stomach. He was afraid he would lose control. He pictured himself crying or completely losing his temper. Glancing at the bronze paper knife in his hand, he saw it commemorated the hundredth anniversary of the Crimean War.

"We can't prove he was there," said Mitchell. He spoke quietly. "We can't prove anything. You were the one who said he wasn't dangerous. Perhaps it's your imagination."

Trevor nearly shouted. "What do you want? You want him to kill me? You want him to come in here and give himself up? You want him to cry on your shoulder? You don't believe any of that."

Mitchell sat perfectly still. He glanced up at Trevor. "I

don't know. Perhaps I don't." He paused. "Give me the paper knife, will you?" Mitchell took the knife and put it in the top drawer of his desk. Trevor watched with surprise, wondering if Mitchell really thought he would stab him.

"But one thing I'll tell you for certain," continued Mitchell, "if we had the slightest idea where to find Frank, I'd put you out of this office immediately."

"Oh, shit." Trevor leaned over and rested his head on his hands. "Mitchell, you're not serious. You know I'm right about Henderson. From now on I want him carefully tailed. Get rid of that idiot who's doing it now. I also want a gun."

Mitchell's reaction startled Trevor. The policeman began to laugh, a deep full-throated laughter, tilting back in his chair, laughing at the ceiling. After a moment he straightened up again. He was still chuckling and there were tears in his eyes. "Are you going to play cops and robbers, Trevor? Are you afraid of this little businessman of yours?" All the humor went out of his face and he looked at Trevor angrily, glancing from one eye to the other. "A gun is out of the question. I am indifferent to what happens to either you or Henderson, but I am not indifferent to unpleasant publicity. I suggest you get up and leave this office. Forget about everything. We'll handle it from now on. I'm sorry I ever allowed you into it in the first place."

Trevor slouched down in his chair. From where he sat he could just see the towers of the Houses of Parliament through the window. Although he would have liked to forget about Henderson, he knew it was impossible. There was no way he could let it be handled by outsiders.

Looking back at Mitchell, Trevor said, "No, I plan to see this through."

Mitchell shrugged. "All right, but it's going to take a much greater commitment on your part. In the past week, Henderson has frightened you. You're going to have to put up with much worse. We're no longer trying to pressure him. We're putting you out as bait, hoping he'll try to snap it up. You must be willing to do that. I'll add another man, perhaps more, but we don't want him to know we're involved. I know perfectly well that I ought to tell you to get out and not come back. I'll very likely regret it. But the situation is, if I may say so, interesting."

Trevor felt uncomfortable, as if he had exposed himself in some way. "What do you want me to do?"

"Nothing at the moment. Go home and think about it. Then call me."

Trevor nodded and began pulling on his coat. He was walking toward the door when Mitchell said, "Oh, and Trevor, don't go back to your bed-sitter. I think you were probably right about that."

Driving home that evening, Henderson was thinking about percentages and probability theory. He was thinking of Trevor. How much worse would it get? How quickly would he have to act? He told himself that he must stay calm. There was Sandra's father's plane. He would have to call the man. There was also the question of money. Although he had nearly a thousand pounds in a strongbox at home, he might need more than that. There was money in a bank in Geneva. He might have to fly there.

The situation seemed unbelievable. Henderson barely knew the person he had become, could barely remember the person he had been six weeks before. Had he been that weak? How much he must have disliked the shallowness of his past life in order to change so quickly, for it to become so unimportant.

He was planning to kill Trevor and escape. But no matter how coldly he tried to evaluate it, he was aware of how personal it was. Even if Trevor stopped his persecution, Henderson would want to kill him. Again he told himself he would have to act quickly. The pressure was becoming too great. Everything was becoming dirty, tainted. There were no clean places anymore.

Henderson turned off Fitzjohn's Avenue onto Church Row and parked his car. Despite the pride he had once had in his house, the sight of it now meant nothing to him. It was the place where he slept.

Harriet met him in the hall. She was holding an 8 x 10 photograph in her hand. She looked perplexed. Henderson thought it was another picture of Jacobs. It wasn't.

Harriet held the picture out to him. "This came by post for me. I don't understand. Who is she?" There was no note of accusation in her voice.

Looking at it, Henderson saw it was a picture of him and Sandra. They were walking down the street. She had her hand on his arm and was laughing. He was smiling at her. Henderson couldn't remember what they had been talking about, but he was surprised by the tenderness on his face. It was as if Trevor had snatched the feeling from him, as if Trevor were taking his life and breaking it piece by piece. In some way the picture bothered him more than the picture of Jacobs. It was such an intrusion.

He continued to look at it. "She's my secretary," he said at last.

Harriet stared at him questioningly, her blue eyes sweeping his face. "But what does it mean?" She was wearing a shapeless gray checked suit which made her look older than she actually was.

"Nothing. I don't know why you received it."
"Why should anyone send it to me?"
"I don't know, perhaps as a practical joke."
"But why?"
Henderson restrained himself from snapping at his wife.

Not for fear of making her suspicious; he was indifferent to that. But his very indifference made him wish to be kind to her. He remembered the first time he had met her. It was at a social club for veterans in the early fifties. One of her brothers had brought her. Henderson couldn't remember which one. She had seemed so frail. She still seemed frail. Frail and frightened by her life to the extent that she had turned herself into an object, doing and thinking only those things that she thought safe. Henderson wondered how much he was responsible for that, while realizing he had passed beyond the point where it really mattered. But at least he could be kind to her.

Henderson took off his overcoat. Then he shook his head. "It must be a joke."

"It doesn't seem very funny." Harriet looked at the picture again. "She's very pretty."

"Yes," said Henderson, "she is."

18

IT WASN'T COMMITMENT to Henderson that bothered Trevor; it was commitment to Mitchell. Worse than commitment, it was submission. From the beginning, Trevor had seen himself as the prime doer, manipulating Henderson and using Mitchell. Now he was choosing impotence, abnegating himself, turning all responsibility for himself over to Mitchell. It was nearly a religious act, almost sexual; Mitchell as pimp or priest, using him to seduce Henderson.

From the beginning, Trevor had been attempting to reaffirm his own life in seeking to punish Henderson. Instead, he had been chipping away at it. Now, in order to finish with Henderson, Mitchell was asking him to sacrifice it, to give up all control. What would be left afterward? He would be a stranger in his own life. There would be no going back. At times he felt that if he stopped now, he could still return. But he knew the knowledge of his failure and cowardice would make it impossible to live.

And afterward, when Henderson and Mitchell were gone, then what? Trevor told himself that what happened wouldn't matter, that nothing mattered that much. But although he felt this was true, it was also irrelevant. He would have to take responsibility for himself, retrieve his essential self from Mitchell; find some believable lie in which to encase himself.

He saw his former life as self-indulgent, moving not in a continuous stream but zig-zagging to whatever pulled him at the moment; and although this, too, didn't really matter, its unimportance was also irrelevant. In order to take control he would have to make it matter, find the believable lie.

While still possessed by Jacobs, Trevor was no longer controlled by him. He saw he had been using the man as another excuse to avoid his own life, until Jacobs had become the tool with which he had destroyed his life. Jacobs would have liked that. Trevor felt he had also destroyed Henderson. Sometime, he knew, he would have to take responsibility for that.

Trevor pictured himself as speeding in a car without brakes, with no steering mechanism. The doors were locked. Around him were other cars with other people speeding by him, collisions avoided only by chance. What power did he have? Maybe he could use the radio or the cigarette lighter. Maybe he could shout. That was control.

Again he asked himself what he would do afterward. Go back to the States? Trevor wasn't sure what he would do there; perhaps teach, even go to law school. Unaware of his tendency toward sentimentality, Trevor never analyzed it. He didn't realize he was formulating some punishment for himself. He would have scoffed at the word expiation. But he felt he had to retrieve himself. He didn't particularly wish to be a lawyer, and saw the three years of law school as particularly unpleasant, but it seemed necessary. At least something was necessary. Trevor didn't try to determine the motivation for these plans. If someone had accused him of wanting to purify himself, he would have been furious.

After several hours of brooding, Trevor at last called Mitchell at his home in Tooting Bec. At first Mitchell's protective wife refused to let Trevor talk to him, saying he needed his rest and couldn't be bothered by police affairs so late at night. Trevor tried to assure her that he wasn't a police affair.

When Mitchell finally came to the phone, Trevor only said, "What do you want me to do?"

"Follow him, stay right behind him, no more than fifteen feet. If he wants to kill you, he'll lead you someplace where he can do it. It shouldn't take long."

There was a silence, then Trevor asked, "Have you heard anything new from the French police?"

"Nothing at all. Don't worry about protection. I'll have other men there, although you may not recognize them. Perhaps I'll even arm them. Are you positive you wish to do this?"

Trevor searched his mind for alternatives. There weren't any. "I'll do it."

"Excellent. Get out to Henderson's house first thing in the morning. I'll take care of the rest of the photographs."

As he hung up, Trevor thought of a small feature story he had run across in Chicago. An old man who sold peanuts and balloons for years at the zoo was forced into bankruptcy by a chain of hot-dog stands. Since he had become a kind of institution at the zoo, he was offered a job as a sub-sub-keeper. One of his duties was to keep the grizzly bear from staying in its cave all day. He was told to take a long stick and hit the sides of the cave with it. The old man was then warned, "But be very careful. When the bear leaves its cave, it will go up on that ledge above it. It may try to jump down on you. Two men have been hurt that way." The old man was a dismal failure as a sub-sub-keeper. All day he stood clenching his stick, staring in terror at the ledge, while the bear slept peacefully in its cave.

* * *

Thursday morning a large envelope was delivered to Sandra at Henderson's office. It was another photograph. Opening it, Sandra thought it was another picture of the dead man. She was mistaken. It was a picture of Henderson on his doorstep with his wife and daughter. Henderson's wife looked frightened. The daughter only looked interested. Henderson was staring at the ground.

The question of why it had been sent to her led Sandra to an inference which it was impossible to avoid. She had been out to dinner with Henderson and had had lunch with him half a dozen times. She was fond of him and had been sorry when he put her in a cab after leaving Ronnie Scott's Monday evening. Someone had sent her the picture to remind her that Henderson was a married man with responsibilities. She was angry and a little embarrassed but felt that what she and Henderson did together was nobody else's business.

As for who had sent the picture, she guessed it came from the American. She couldn't understand why Henderson didn't do anything about him. Why didn't he call the police? It bothered her that he hadn't done so the day before, when they had received the pictures of the dead man. She wished Henderson wouldn't shut her out from whatever was happening. It was partly for this reason that she decided to show him the picture.

Entering his office, she found him sitting at his desk, looking out the window. She handed him the picture. "This just came for me. I don't know what to make of it."

Henderson glanced at the picture, then tossed it in the wastebasket. He looked tired. "It's a joke, a bad joke."

"That American sent it, didn't he?"

Henderson shrugged. "It's unimportant."

"Why don't you do something?" The idea of Henderson being abused hurt Sandra. She wished she could help him.

"You could, you know. There's no reason to put up with it."

Henderson turned to the window again. Everything about him seemed sad; even his skin seemed sad, as if it were the bandage of his solitude. "It's like a war," he said, "an extremely private war. You must try to understand that."

Sandra felt he was talking more to himself than to her. "I remember at Cassino," he continued, "it sometimes seemed that the whole German army was only one man, the person hiding somewhere in front of you. Often you'd get a glimpse of him, crouching behind his rock pile. You'd shoot and he'd shoot back. Sometimes you'd trade food. You'd throw him a can of something and he'd throw something back. It made a pleasant change. Everything was that one man. You were so close. At night you'd crawl out and try to kill him with your bayonet. If you managed to kill him, he'd be replaced the next day. It was as if he had come back, as if it were always the same man. It was an odd kind of immortality. There was no getting rid of him."

Although Henderson continued talking, Sandra had turned and quietly left the office.

All day Thursday and most of Friday, Trevor followed Henderson wherever he went, never more than fifteen feet behind. Although Henderson appeared oblivious to it, Trevor had twice caught him looking at him. The look frightened Trevor, not because of its hatred, but because it seemed so calculating.

Constantly Trevor tried to spot Mitchell's plainclothesmen but without much success. Several times he saw the man who had been in the green Vauxhall. Once Sergeant Fawcett walked by, glancing at him with more coldness than Henderson had ever been able to achieve. Mitchell had told him that although Fawcett had come to accept Henderson's guilt, he still hated Trevor for being involved. Trevor hoped that Fawcett would never be responsible for his safety.

Although chilly, the weather was perfect: two sunny, cloudless days in which to follow Henderson to work, to lunch, to meetings, in a walk through Green Park, home again, out Thursday evening to the King of Bohemia, a Georgian pub on Hampstead High Street. Trevor had stood at the bar, drinking a pint of lager while Henderson talked to some acquaintances nearby about the war, specifically the Italian campaign and Cassino. Trevor didn't believe his stories.

But despite the clear sky, Trevor felt he was in a very gray place. He seemed to exude his own London fog, and his private weather pressed around him like a shroud. He felt he had no power, that Henderson might try to kill him at any time. It was like not having hands. He was afraid he might panic when Henderson finally acted. Each night he returned to the small hotel room he had found in Hampstead, and couldn't sleep. The room was expensive, and Mitchell's willingness to pay for it showed Trevor more than anything else that the policeman thought Henderson would act in a very short time.

On Friday afternoon, Trevor followed Henderson up Regent Street to Austin Reed's, a large and expensive men's store. Trevor lost him immediately in the crowd and maze of aisles. He looked around for any recognizable plainclothesmen, but didn't see anyone he knew. He was certain that Henderson had lost him on purpose. He found himself constantly looking over his shoulder, expecting something to come at him through the mass of people. After several minutes, he couldn't stand it any longer. He left the store and took a cab directly back to Henderson's office. An hour later Henderson returned, apparently oblivious to Trevor's presence. Trevor felt a little foolish.

Mitchell had chided him about it when Trevor called him

later in the evening. "You can't just bolt the moment he does something unexpected. You must learn to relax. Shall I have Sergeant Fawcett bring you some tranquilizers?"

"Well, I couldn't find him." Trevor thought again of the old man watching the ledge where the bear was supposed to appear.

"You'll have to do better than that. My men stayed with him easily. There was nothing to worry about."

Trevor felt even more foolish, although he didn't admit it to Mitchell. "Where did he go?"

"He made several phone calls. Perfectly innocuous." It didn't occur to Trevor that Mitchell might be lying. "Over the weekend, I want you to stay with him, no matter what. I think he'll try to do something."

Trevor said that would be nice. He also considered asking Mitchell for those tranquilizers in order to help him sleep, but he was afraid Mitchell would take it as a sign of weakness.

When Henderson got home Friday evening, he found his wife hysterical. She had received the photograph of the murdered Jacobs. Taking it from her, Henderson looked at it coldly while Harriet asked, then pleaded, to know what was happening. Henderson went to the medicine closet to get his wife several tranquilizers. Afterward he went to his study where he remained for the rest of the evening. Again he asked himself how much worse it was going to get. Again he wondered where Trevor had gotten the photograph.

Shortly before midnight, the telephone rang. At first Henderson thought it was some new tactic of Trevor's. He was wrong. The call came from Ahmed. Henderson had almost forgotten about him.

"Is it safe to talk, Henderson?"

Henderson was startled. "Certainly, why shouldn't it be?"

There was static on the line. Ahmed's voice was an electronic whisper.

"The police here are being difficult. They have been listening to my telephone conversations."

"Whatever for?"

"That is what I thought you might be able to tell me. In Tangier, I lead an honest life. I take pride in the community. I involve myself in no questionable affairs." There was a brief chuckle which sounded like paper being crumpled together. "What I wondered was about your life. Are the police still interested in you?"

Henderson was genuinely surprised. "Why should they be?"

"Surely, Henderson, you haven't forgotten. You yourself called recently to ask for Frank."

"That was for something else," said Henderson with some confusion. "The police here think that other business was mixed up with blackmail. I haven't heard from them for over a month."

"They have no interest in you?"

"None at all."

"You are certain?"

"Very."

"But you are still in difficulties?" Disturbance on the wires made Ahmed's voice rise and fall. The last question came through as a yell, making it a statement about which there was no doubt.

"It's nothing I can't deal with." Henderson decided not to mention Trevor.

"Then I can't understand it. Perhaps it is the government. The King is in difficulties and people leave quickly. No matter. I'm sorry, Henderson, that I was unable to assist you last week."

"That's all right." Henderson paused, then asked, "Frank is safe?"

"Yes, I believe he suns himself in the south of France. He is a clever boy. Then there is nothing I can do to help you?"

Henderson considered for a moment. "There is one thing. If something goes wrong here, I may have to leave quickly. Could you get me Moroccan papers? I could be old French. There must be thousands of them. Also a passport. Could you do that? I'll send photographs right away."

"Yes, I think so. It may be expensive."

"That doesn't matter."

After hanging up, Henderson thought over what Ahmed had said. Then he dismissed it. The police had lost interest in him weeks ago. Even so, he wondered if he were forgetting anything, if he were attempting to balance too many things in his mind. He sat in his chair, rubbing his arm. Well, Trevor wouldn't bother him after the weekend.

Saturday passed without incident. Henderson went shopping with his wife, came home and went out again, leading Trevor on a long, rambling walk through the twisted maze of small streets between the Heath and Hampstead High Street. Some were so narrow that Trevor could stretch out his arms and touch each gray wall. He would have been uncomfortable if there hadn't been so many workmen and deliverymen on bikes. Trevor suspected some of these were plainclothesmen. He also suspected that Henderson was trying to see how easily he would follow. Trevor followed like a child's toy all over Hampstead.

Twice he saw Fawcett, who glared at him. Once, Mitchell drove by in a taxi and gave him the victory sign. Trevor felt he was being played with. Fawcett's presence worried him a little. He couldn't remember if Henderson had ever seen him as a policeman. Apparently he hadn't, but Sergeant Fawcett looked so much like a policeman that Trevor wished he would remain hidden.

When the lights went out in Henderson's house that night, Trevor was still outside. He felt more comfortable in the darkness, as long as he knew he was alone; the world as blank and empty as he was trying to keep his mind; giving up personality, becoming the victim. After a while he walked back to his nondescript hotel. From an upstairs window, Henderson watched him leave.

19

IT WAS LATE Sunday morning, October 29th. Henderson and his wife were walking leisurely up Hampstead High Street, looking into shop windows: old maps, Mexican jewelry, contemporary paintings and furniture, expensive clothes. Henderson's wife was wearing a long fur coat. Trevor, across the street, thought it might be mink, but he could never be certain about that sort of thing. Henderson was wearing a dark-blue overcoat. They looked exactly like other couples window-shopping on High Street.

It was quite cold. Although it had rained earlier, a stiff wind had pushed the rain clouds east. Now smaller clouds moved quickly across the face of the sun, changing it from white to dull yellow to golden, changing the shadows on the street from light to dull gray. In the varying light, the mood of the people seemed to alter from cheerful to depressed, innocent to sinister. It made Trevor feel as if he were seeing more people than were actually there. Trevor's own mood was solid gray. He believed he had given up any free will he might have had. There was even, to his disgust, a faint pleasure at this submission.

Henderson and his wife continued to walk up the hill until they reached the top, where the road forked: North End Way to the left toward Golders Green, Spaniards Road to the right along the northern boundary of the Heath to Highgate. The area before the fork was taken up by Whitestone Pond, completely encircled by traffic. Despite the weather, small boys were sailing boats: expensive toy yachts large enough to sleep dozens of lascivious and pleasure-seeking mice. Interfering fathers showed sons how to do it.

Henderson and his wife watched them briefly before continuing up Spaniards Road. Trevor crossed over to the pond. A yellow retriever was swimming frantically after one of the yachts. Bystanders were yelling encouragement. The small owner of the boat was getting ready to cry at the first bite.

Trevor watched as the dog neatly retrieved the boat without breaking a single mast. Its tail wagging like a semaphore above the water, the dog paddled back toward its owner, who was standing with his eyes closed. Trevor felt a tinge of sympathy. The boy's father, a large man, was also heading toward the owner of the dog. Trevor calculated they would both reach him at the same moment.

Glancing back at Henderson, Trevor was startled to see that he and his wife had parted. Harriet appeared to be returning to town, while Henderson continued to walk along Spaniards Road. Looking again at the dog owner, Trevor saw he was being shouted at by the boy's father. The dog was sitting quietly, waiting to be patted. Everything seemed very distant. Trevor turned and hurried after Henderson.

It was only after he had crossed the road that Trevor began to feel suspicious about this sudden parting between Henderson and his wife. With the suspicion came a return of his fear. Instead of getting closer to Henderson, Trevor remained back about twenty yards. He looked around for Mitchell's plainclothesmen. He thought he recognized one sitting in a car by Jack Straw's Castle. Then he saw Sergeant Fawcett, standing beside an ice-cream truck which Henderson had just passed. The Sergeant was eating a chocolate ice and had a green plaid golfing cap pulled down over his forehead. He looked like a spy in a Marx Brothers' movie. The ice-cream truck was between him and Henderson.

Abruptly, Henderson turned left, down a steep path onto the Heath. Trevor stopped. He had no wish to follow Henderson into a place with so many trees and dark areas. On a day like this there would be few people: dog owners, some children, perhaps a fisherman near the Vale of Health. Henderson could easily lead him to a place where they wouldn't be interrupted. Trevor saw Sergeant Fawcett waving at him impatiently. Hesitating for another second, Trevor began to move forward. His legs felt heavy. When he reached Sergeant Fawcett, he asked, "Where's Mitchell?"

"He'll be along shortly. You're not frightened, are you, Sir?" There was an unpleasant edge to the Sergeant's voice.

"Fuck off," said Trevor, as he turned and plunged down the hill onto the Heath.

In the distance, he could see London wrapped in its nest of smog. Besides the high-rise office buildings, he could pick out the Post Office Tower and the dome of St. Paul's. He felt separated from it by time rather than space. The path was still muddy from the rain. Trevor walked carefully, trying not to fall.

A hundred yards ahead of him, he saw Henderson turn left into a grove of trees, away from the Vale of Health and Hampstead. Again Trevor hesitated, but he was aware that Sergeant Fawcett was watching him. He began walking again, very slowly. Other than Henderson, there was no one else to be seen on the Heath. Trevor saw himself as drawing a knife across his own throat, of having passed into a place without hope. Following Henderson into the trees could only end in his own death. It gave him no pleasure that the police would catch the guilty man.

The trees were black and leafless. Heaps of leaves lay on

the ground like beds. Although Trevor had been on the Heath before, he had no idea where he was going. Somewhere in front of him was Kenwood House, but that must be almost a mile away. There were more trees now: large oaks and maples were the kinds he could recognize. Others had twisted trunks bending almost parallel to the ground, as if put there as couches for the public. Sparrows and starlings quarreled in the branches. The ground was rolling. Way ahead he could just see Henderson through the trees. Trevor found himself wishing it were a sunny day. The sun had disappeared completely. This was not the sort of day he would have chosen to die on. Some of the trees were so large that five men could have hidden behind them easily.

Walking through the wet leaves, Trevor asked himself in a shocked interior voice what he was doing. He wasn't cowardly, just sensible. He could think of thousands of places where he would rather be, even unpleasant places. He was amazed at the chain of circumstances that had led him here; amazed that he had allowed it. The trees pressed around him like the grayness of his mind. He would have to pass through them if he were to reach a brighter place. Where were Mitchell's plainclothesmen? He thought he heard someone walking quietly through the leaves off to his right. Looking ahead toward Henderson, Trevor couldn't see him. He had disappeared through the trees. He could have stopped. Trevor came to a halt. His legs stopped working. It seemed he was breathing through a thick cloth over his mouth. What alternatives did he have? Again he began to move forward.

Stuck through his belt, the bayonet pressed against Henderson's leg, but it wasn't that which made him feel uncomfortable. He was standing quietly behind a large plane tree. His whole body felt silent as if it had been molded out of darkness. He could hear Trevor walking toward him through the leaves. There was also a slight rustling off to his left, but he couldn't see anyone.

He was thinking of the man eating the chocolate ice and wearing the absurd cloth cap; the man who had turned away as he approached. Henderson's mind circled him as a hawk circles a field. He took a pair of gray gloves from the pocket of his overcoat and drew them on. When the man turned away, Henderson had had the impression he had seen him before.

Trevor was getting closer. The rustling to his left had stopped but now Henderson thought he heard something in the other direction. Squirrels most likely. The wood was very still. Water dripped from the branches. Everything seemed centered on Trevor moving through the leaves. Fires made similar sounds. Even the sparrows had stopped their bickering. It seemed quite dark between the trees.

The man was in some way linked with Mrs. Clavering. Her boyfriend? Surely not. Then had he seen him in the office? Henderson slipped the bayonet out of his belt and held it against his leg. For a brief instant he imagined a curved Berber knife with a gold inlaid handle. There was a prayer engraved on the blade, spots of rust. Trevor was less than ten yards away.

There was an official feeling to the memory of the man. Postman? Repairman? Inland revenue officer? Henderson ran his gloved hand over the blade of the knife. It made a slight cut in the gray leather. Was he from some assurance company? Was he a policeman? That was absurd. When had a policeman been to his office? There was that inspector, of course, asking about Jacobs. Had he come alone?

Trevor continued to come closer, walking very slowly. Henderson could hear the murmur of cars from Spaniards Road, the muffled roar of a motorcycle, a bus. All other sound had stopped.

No, the inspector had had a man with him who talked to

Mrs. Clavering. Henderson had only seen him for a second before taking the inspector into his office, but he was positive it was the man in the cloth cap. What did that mean? Henderson thought again of what Ahmed had said: Were the police still interested in him? Of course not. Where had Trevor gotten the photographs of Jacobs? Reporters have access to such things. Why was the policeman up on the road? Hundreds of people come to the Heath. In this weather? Why had he turned away?

Trevor had apparently stopped. There was no sound from that direction, but something was rustling off to his right again. Henderson suddenly imagined that he was surrounded by policemen. Trevor had been working with them all along. They had led him into a trap. But he could still kill Trevor. The impulse to do so was stronger than ever. He looked at the bayonet in his hand. Again he told himself that he couldn't let his emotions control him. Why should the police know anything? He was being paranoid. But there did seem to be enough of a possibility to make it foolish to do anything now.

Henderson couldn't decide. His desire to get rid of Trevor once and for all was equally balanced against the knowledge that he should wait. Everything was quiet except for the drip of water from the trees. Trevor seemed to be standing still. Why should he hesitate? If he didn't suspect anything, why had he stopped? He must suspect something. Then why had he followed him into the woods? Henderson thought again of those other noises. But balanced against it in his mind was the image of himself grabbing Trevor, slashing the bayonet across his throat, feeling the blood run down his right arm.

Trevor was unable to move. He knew he must get closer, that Mitchell's men would be unable to act unless Henderson acted. It seemed that he was taking himself, his whole personality, and denying it. But in order to retain anything, he must do that; he had to move forward into the darkness between the trees.

Henderson was there somewhere. There were a dozen trees which he could be hiding behind. And where were Mitchell's policemen? He had heard them in the undergrowth, but could they act in time? No doubt they would shoot. Presumably they were armed with rifles. Trevor didn't find that particularly reassuring.

But to move forward, to commit himself completely to Mitchell's care in the face of Henderson's hatred, could he do that? All of Trevor's muscles felt stretched and weak. Where was Henderson hiding? Which tree? Trevor couldn't allow himself to move. But if he didn't, he would have nothing. He had to take the chance.

He pushed himself forward, nearly stumbling, forcing his legs to take a step, then another. As he did so there was a noise from behind the closest of the tall trees bordering the path. Suddenly Henderson stood before him, less than ten feet away. He stared at Trevor with intense anger. His eyes were like hands on Trevor's face. Henderson's whole body seemed rigid, as if he were being pulled in several directions. The two men stood frozen for nearly a minute. Then Trevor turned slightly, looking for some sign of Mitchell's plainclothesmen. As he moved, Henderson whirled around and walked off in the other direction.

Trevor watched him, barely able to make his mind follow what was happening. He felt he had been jerked from one place and deposited in another. Despite his shock, he found himself thinking that at least he had moved forward. Jacobs wouldn't have done that. Ahead of him, Henderson was disappearing through the trees. Trevor followed.

* * *

Several hours later, Mitchell and Trevor were quarreling in Mitchell's office.

Trevor felt better than he had for days. "He must have recognized him. What alternative is there? Henderson was all set to kill me, and suddenly he changes his mind. Maybe his conscience bothered him, right?"

"Sergeant Fawcett assured me that Henderson couldn't have recognized him."

"But he was in his office. Henderson must have seen him. You blew it, Mitchell. Everything was set and you let it fall apart." There was a self-complacent tone to Trevor's voice. He enjoyed seeing Mitchell on the defensive. The pleasure had been growing ever since Trevor, Mitchell, Sergeant Fawcett and about eight plainclothesmen had been standing around Spaniards, brooding about Henderson, who was casually drinking a pint of lager inside. Two marksmen had returned their rifles to a police car. One policeman had a yellow retriever on a leash, while another held a tennis racket. The picture of their defeat substantially cheered Trevor.

Mitchell reached across his desk, jabbed a button on an intercom and barked Fawcett's name into it. The Sergeant appeared in the office moments later. He looked wary.

"Could Henderson have recognized you?"

"No, Sir." Sergeant Fawcett had the sort of vain ignorance that didn't believe someone would notice something that he wouldn't notice himself. He glanced suspiciously at Trevor.

"Weren't you in his office?" asked Mitchell, looking down at his desk as if Fawcett were one of his loose pencils.

"Yes, Sir, but Mr. Henderson didn't see me."

"What makes you think that?"

"He was talking to you, Sir. The two of you went into his office."

"You mean he didn't even look at you?"

"Perhaps just a glimpse, Sir, but he went into his office with you right away."

"Just a glimpse? Did he pass you today?"

"Yes, Sir, but I turned away and a van was between us."

"Were you wearing that cloth cap?"

"Yes, Sir."

"How were you wearing it? Put it on."

Sergeant Fawcett drew the cap out of his pocket and put it on. Then he pulled it down over his forehead, again making him look like a spy in a Marx Brothers' movie.

Mitchell looked up, staring at him for several moments. "Get out of here," he said softly. Sergeant Fawcett turned and left.

Leaning back in his chair, Mitchell glanced at Trevor. "But there must have been something else." He straightened up again and reached for a brown paper bag on his desk. "At least we have this, although there were no prints on it." He opened the bag and took out Henderson's bayonet. There was mud on the blade. Mitchell held it up to the light coming in through the window. The bayonet was about a foot and a half long. "This would have made quite a hole in you. My men found it behind a tree. Henderson had driven it into the ground to hide it."

Trevor looked at it coldly. When he spoke, he tried to keep all emotion out of his voice. "So what do we do now?"

"We continue. It should be easier."

"Why? We still aren't sure if he meant anything."

"Don't be foolish, Trevor. You can't allow yourself to question that."

Trevor heard the phone ringing in the outer office. Sergeant Fawcett answered it. Seconds later there was a knocking on the door, followed by the Sergeant's entrance. He scowled at Trevor. "Someone wants to speak to you. He says it's terribly urgent."

Mitchell got to his feet immediately. "Did you tell him he was here?"

Sergeant Fawcett looked surprised. Before he could speak, Mitchell asked Trevor, "Does anyone know you're here?" As Trevor shook his head, Mitchell ran to the outer office. Trevor heard him shout, "Hello!" several times. Then there was a crash, as the telephone fell to the floor. Mitchell stalked back into the room. "Sergeant Fawcett, if Siberia were a British possession, you would be there tomorrow. Get out of here! I'm sick to death of seeing your face!"

Mitchell flung himself back into his chair. Getting up again, he walked to the window where he stood with his hands behind his back, apparently watching the tourists. Then he turned to Trevor. "It may not be so bad. Henderson's in an odd position."

Trevor looked at the policeman curiously. He had never seen him like this before. "What do you mean?"

"He can't do anything. He's changed a great deal in the past six weeks. He just can't return to what he's been doing."

"Sure he can." Trevor hoped that at least Henderson could go back.

Mitchell shook his head. "It's too late. What's he going to do about you? He hates you too much to forget about you. He still has no choice. He's moved away from his fatalism and he must take control if he is to survive."

"What's that supposed to mean."

"He's going to kill you."

"You're not serious." He thought he was finished with Henderson.

"Well, he's going to try."

20

THERE WAS a small package on Henderson's desk. He knew what it was and why it had been sent. It was a challenge. But he wasn't sure what to do about it. From the outer office he could hear the sound of typewriters and the occasional murmur of voices. The sound of traffic came up from the street: cars honking, the squeal of brakes. The room itself was like a well of silence. Henderson was trying to climb up out of it.

For six weeks, Henderson had been moving in a new direction. Now he either had to stop, denying what he had learned, or take advantage of his new knowledge and mold another life. What would it mean to stop? Go back? Where had that been? He could hardly remember.

In the past six weeks, he had gained control over his life. Was he to give that up to return to a life controlled by accident? Much of the control came in reaction to Trevor's manipulation, but it certainly wasn't limited by that. Henderson didn't worry that it would be difficult to move beyond Trevor.

It was as if the six weeks had been spent perfecting a new tool. The time had come to use it or put it aside. But putting it aside meant returning to a life he had destroyed.

Using it meant trying to control his future. Could he do that? Did he have any choice? There was always suicide. The thought disgusted him.

If Henderson were to continue, he would have to kill Trevor. He had become such a symbol. Trevor had acted as a crutch, enabling Henderson's new life to come into being. In order to walk, he now had to kick away the crutch, even though the crutch included Inspector Mitchell and Scotland Yard. Henderson didn't feel that his logic was controlled by hatred. The hatred was part of what he had become.

Could he control his future to the extent of killing Trevor and getting away? That, too, seemed like suicide. But did he have any choice? To admit defeat meant greater destruction. If he confessed to the murder of Jacobs, the resulting scandal would be impossible to endure. To be dragged into the courts, to have his name in all the tabloids—suicide was certainly preferable to that.

But if on one side stood death, what did he have to lose? At least he would have made his play; and if he lost, he would have lost nothing. Besides, the possibility of killing Trevor and outwitting Scotland Yard was worth the chance. It might even be possible, if he acted quickly enough. He had money, a way out of the country and a place to go. And though the odds were against his success, they were better than suicide.

What if he left without killing Trevor? Henderson pictured himself in Tangier, walking through the market. There was Trevor. He saw himself sitting at a table at the Café Paris. There was Trevor. The only way to separate himself from Trevor was to kill him. Otherwise, Henderson would be always waiting for him to appear.

Then kill Trevor. Take the bait from Mitchell's trap and escape. He felt he had the advantage that the police didn't know the sort of person he had become. They would learn quickly. He had already talked to Sandra's father. Today he would talk to him again. Tomorrow he would be in Morocco.

Looking again at the package on his desk, he reached out and drew it toward him. Then he ripped off the paper and broke open the box. It contained his bayonet. He withdrew it and balanced it on his palm. There was still mud on the blade. Grasping the hilt, he lifted the bayonet over his shoulder, and brought it down with all his strength on the desk, driving the point two inches into the wood. He left it there as he got up and walked over to the window to look at Trevor.

Trevor remained outside of Henderson's office until eleven that morning. Then he left. Mitchell had told him to only put in an appearance, so he would be there when the package arrived. Afterward he could do whatever he wanted. Tomorrow there would be another push, then another and another until Henderson broke.

Trevor thought Mitchell was being too relaxed. It even occurred to him that Mitchell was trying to appear relaxed, as if he were protecting Trevor from his own fears. Trevor didn't care about that anymore. He was restless and wished the whole business over.

What he had wanted to learn about himself he had learned the day before, when he had moved after Henderson, despite his knowledge that Henderson was waiting for him between the trees. The strength he had drawn from this would keep his life together, but he didn't feel he could use it until he was free from Henderson and Mitchell. He didn't think he might be overestimating this strength. He was only glad he had found it.

He spent an uncomfortable day. He felt like a person

about to leave on a journey who keeps being detained. First he can't find his suitcase, then he has to change a tire, then he can't find his wallet, then he loses his keys and it begins to rain.

After lunch, Trevor went home, thinking he could catch up on some reading, but his books bored him. The new books on chess seemed like intricate forms of torture. He tried to write some letters, but they all fell into the pattern of "I am fine. I hope you are fine. It is raining here. I hope it is not raining where you are." He was reminded of a phoney Chinese proverb he had once composed: "He who rides the tortoise wonders why he got on." At last he spent several hours cleaning his flat.

It began to rain in a slow, endless downpour. Trevor decided to use his time by buying the raincoat he had seen in the boutique in Knightsbridge. The purchase would be a constructive act.

Reaching the boutique, he learned that while that particular raincoat was now on sale, his size was no longer in stock. The salesman assured him that his was the only size unavailable. If he didn't mind a coat a little too small or a little too large, they could easily accommodate him. Trevor suggested they order the raincoat in his size. He didn't care if it was on sale. He was told that particular model had been discontinued. There was no way to order it. Again the salesman assured him he could have any other size he wanted. He even implied there was something not quite fashionable about Trevor's particular size. It was so usual. Trevor left the shop in a contained rage. It was now raining harder than ever.

He considered calling Clare, but rejected the idea, deciding to wait until he had finished with Henderson. Instead, he went to the New Chelsea Club where he had an early and uninteresting dinner. Then he began going to pubs, having a drink at one and moving on to another. Shortly after 10:00 P.M., he was sitting at the bar of the White Star Tavern on Fleet Street, drinking his sixth Scotch of the day. He was feeling a little better.

Nearby a UPI correspondent he knew was telling a lithe blond girl about the uses and abuses of the American electoral college. The girl was falling asleep. The correspondent spoke in an endless monotone and prefaced each sentence by saying, "In point of fact . . ." Trevor considered battering him about the ears and dashing out of the pub with the girl over his shoulder. It's not the girl, it's the exercise, he told himself.

The pub was crowded with damp drinkers and the smell of smoke and wet clothing. It was a long narrow room with signed pictures of past celebrities on the wall. Trevor recognized some as film stars of the thirties. All wore toothy smiles reminiscent of the façade of the National Gallery. Trevor had thought of this before, had pictured the celebrities now growing old in small rooms. Coming into familiar bars meant thinking the same things again and again.

He was still looking at the photographs when the bartender called to him. "Your name's Trevor, isn't it?"

Repressing a desire to deny it, Trevor nodded his head. The bartender pointed to the phone. "You've got a call, mate. Don't talk all night."

Trevor finished his drink and walked to the phone near the back door. "Hello?"

"Trevor? Mitchell here. You're a difficult fellow to reach."

"So what?"

"I want you to stay there until two of my men arrive. Then I'd like you to come down to the Yard."

Trevor was startled and thought absurdly that he was being arrested. "Why?"

"We've lost Henderson."

"And you want me to bury my head?"

"He's looking for you and he may well be armed."

There was a long silence as Trevor considered this. "How do you know?"

"I'm afraid I wasn't quite truthful when I described Henderson's activities after he lost you on Friday. Besides the phone calls, he bought shells for a .38 revolver at Cogswell & Harrison on Fleet Street. At the time, I thought it would be better if you didn't know."

"And he's looking for me now?" Trevor spoke softly. He could hardly believe what Mitchell was telling him. It was as if he were being tricked back into an old story he had thought finished.

"At eight o'clock he was seen at the Press Club. Shortly after nine, he visited the New Chelsea Club. A little later he went to the Punch Tavern. We're putting police into the area but he's very elusive. There's no doubt that we'll catch him, but I thought you'd like to know. Actually, you're as difficult to trace as he is. So be a good fellow and wait there, will you? My men should be arriving at any moment."

Trevor looked quickly toward the front door where someone was just entering. It wasn't a policeman. From a distance of about thirty feet, Trevor and Henderson stared at each other through the crowd of drinkers. Trevor could hear the UPI correspondent still discussing American politics. Keeping a hand in the pocket of his blue overcoat, Henderson began pushing through the crowd. There was a slight smile on his face. Trevor felt the muscles tighten in his stomach. He dropped the phone and made a dash for the back door.

The door opened onto Wine Office Court, leading back into a maze of streets and alleyways filled with businesses related to the printing industry. It was empty at night.

Trevor paused in front of the rough-beamed exterior of the Cheshire Cheese and looked back down the short dark tunnel which led to Fleet Street. Somewhere in his mind, he heard himself say, "This is where Dr. Johnson drank and where Yeats met with the Rhymers Club. It's safe here." Then he saw Henderson step out of the darkness of the tunnel. Trevor turned and ran.

The streets were so narrow that the dark walls of the four-story brick buildings seemed to meet at the top. It was still raining slightly. The small street lamps gave off a dim light surrounded by a yellow nimbus. The reflection of the light on the wet paving-stones made them look like the tops of hundreds of skulls. Trevor stumbled over them, slipping and almost falling, regaining his balance against the side of a building, running faster, stumbling again, his leather-soled shoes sliding over the stones. He could hear Henderson's feet skittering on the pavement behind him.

Trevor kept thinking of characters in books who wouldn't have run, who would turn and fight, be missed by the bullets, unhurt by the blows; who would stand in a dark doorway waiting for their chance. There was no way he could bring himself to turn and face Henderson. The strength he thought he had achieved earlier in the day was meaningless in this situation. All he could do was run.

Trevor rounded the corner into Gough Square, scraping his hand on the brick, steadying himself on a street lamp. Through the rain he could see Dr. Johnson's red brick house leaning into the far side of the L-shaped square. It was absurd. Running was absurd. Trevor wanted to turn and tell Henderson it had all been a joke. All's well that ends well. Forgive and forget. He had never meant this to get out of hand. Let's just stop and have a drink. He kept on running.

He turned the corner into Great New Street, running toward Crane Court, hoping to reach the open area of Fetter Lane. He felt certain that Henderson was gaining. The footsteps sounded louder. Water was trickling down Trevor's face and neck, soaking his shirt and jacket. Henderson was closer. Trevor had to know where he was. Trying to look over his shoulder, he slipped. Henderson stopped. Trevor saw him raise his arm. Although he was expecting it, the shot took him by surprise. The shot echoed and reechoed in the small court. The bullet smashed into the wall above Trevor's head and whined off. Bits of stone cut into his face. Trevor regained his feet and dodged away. He wanted to scream, shout at Henderson to stop. There was a second shot. The sound filled the air like a fist. Trevor could feel it all around him. The bullet hit the wall and ricocheted down the street with a high whine.

Trevor lost control. He began running wildly, bursting across and up Fetter Lane to Greystoke Place and Cursitor Street. He ran with no thought of direction, expecting any moment to get a bullet in the back. If he could only outrun it. He kept slipping on the wet stones, beating his arms like wings, flailing them to keep his balance. He splashed through pools of water. He stumbled against the curb. Turning the corner into Chancery Lane, he headed back toward Fleet Street. Every thought was directed toward running. He sucked air into his lungs with tight painful gulps. He was aware of nothing but the pavement before him. He didn't see the policeman standing in front of the old Public Record Office. Barreling into him, Trevor thought it was Henderson and began swinging his arms. Suddenly he received a sharp blow to the head and fell back to the pavement, splashing into a puddle. The bobby stood over him with his nightstick, ready to hit him again if necessary.

"Here, what's this?" he said indignantly.

"There's a man chasing me." Trevor tried to scramble to his feet but the policeman pushed him back.

"What, did you hit him, too?" He did, however, take a few steps toward Cursitor Street. There was no one in sight.

"But someone was chasing me." Trevor felt as if he had been gutted and left empty. He didn't try to get up.

The policeman looked at him thoughtfully, pushed his face toward Trevor's and sniffed. "Been doing a bit of drinking, haven't you? Perhaps you'd better come with me."

21

HENDERSON HAD NO WISH to merely frighten Trevor. He would not have been satisfied by a number of close attempts on his life. He meant to kill him.

After shooting twice, Henderson had stopped, deciding to wait until there could be no doubt about hitting his target. He knew the police were looking for him. He knew he would only attract attention by pursuing Trevor wildly. Therefore he had cut back, crossing Fleet Street, and walked briskly through Old Mitre Court and The Temple until he reached Victoria Embankment.

As he crossed Fleet Street, he noticed quite a few policemen. They didn't frighten him. Instead, he saw them as an obstacle which he meant to avoid. Other than that his mind was filled with Trevor. It was a physical presence, and there was no room for Sandra or even Tangier.

Walking through the rain, along the Embankment toward Temple Station, Henderson listed in long repetitions all that Trevor had done to him. It was like listing the price of carpets. Without thinking of Jacobs, he saw Trevor as the kind of pointless disaster which sometimes comes into people's lives. He would now work as tirelessly to remove it as a relief worker at a flood. Or as he had worked during those weeks at Cassino, killing the enemy.

Reaching the tube station, Henderson took a Circle Line train to Notting Hill Gate. Then he walked up Holland Park to Trevor's flat on Portland Road. The .38 Smith & Wesson in his overcoat pocket bumped against his right hip. Although he had been outside the building before, he had never gone in. This time he did.

Trevor's flat was on the third floor front. The door was thin and Henderson sprung the lock without difficulty. He would have kicked it down if necessary. The flat was empty. Henderson meant to wait for Trevor's return, but now he felt restless. He prowled around the flat, talking to himself and flicking on lights. He took off his wet overcoat and threw it on the couch in the living room.

It was a small four-room flat: living room, bedroom, kitchen and study. Trevor had taken it furnished with square and shabby 1930's chairs, end tables, a square uncomfortable bed, a couch with two broken springs. The predominant color was faded green: solid green wallpaper, a green rug with pale flowers, heavy green drapery which looked like a hiding place for bats.

Henderson could feel Trevor's presence but could see no sign of him in the objects of the flat. He kept talking to himself: "Where are you, Trevor?"

Henderson poked through Trevor's records which were mostly classical, with some jazz. He poked through Trevor's books, scattered on tables and in the large wooden bookcase in the living room, glancing at the new books on chess, the science fiction, the histories of Scotland and the First World War. He tossed them aside.

Henderson glanced at the magazines: *Punch, Newsweek, Time*, a quarterly on foreign affairs. He took a piece of hard candy from a jar on the low coffee table, tasted it and threw it away.

"Where are you, Trevor?"

He looked at the pictures on the walls: a copy of a print

showing a knight on horseback talking to Death, another of an old woman crawling across a yellow field.

He went into the kitchen, rifled through cans of beef and kidney pies, canned spaghetti, cans of pressed meat. There was a single blue coffee cup with a chipped handle in the aluminum sink. There was faded green tile on the floor, and a mop missing half its strings.

Henderson went through Trevor's study. He nosed out clippings in file cabinets, copies of speeches by members of Parliament, a worn copy of the bureau's style book. He found bits of a novel which Trevor worked on occasionally with a kind of despair. It was about growing up in Chicago. Henderson tossed the pages onto the desk. There were a few letters on a small table and Henderson read them. One was from Trevor's younger brother, James, a schoolteacher in Chicago. "I don't mean to keep nagging you about this but if you really mean to invite Mother to England, I wish you would do it now. Martha's pregnant again. . . ."

There was also a letter from the mother, criticizing James for the way he brought up his children. The letter concluded with a few lines about a third brother, Robert, killed in Vietnam nine years before. "I keep thinking he is not dead but in some foreign city, like you are, and I worry because he is so young." Henderson dropped the letters on the floor and went back to the living room.

"Where are you, Trevor?"

There was no trace of him. These signs of human habitation were not quite believable to Henderson. He couldn't reconcile the Trevor he knew with these evidences of another existence. It was as if Henderson were in the wrong apartment. The smells of old food and dirty laundry, the closeness of the air, the damp—they belonged to someone else.

Henderson felt impatient. He didn't want to give his

anger a chance to relax. He continued prowling around the flat, going through the closets, looking in cupboards. He glanced through Trevor's pills: tranquilizers, aspirin, pills for upset stomachs. He poked at toothpaste and mouthwash, deodorant and shaving lotion. He found contraceptives. He found a photograph of Trevor, sitting on a wooden fence in front of a weathered farm house, smiling intently at the camera. Great trees surrounded the house. There was a child playing with a large dog. There was a flat field stretching out until it disappeared into the horizon. Trevor looked young and full of energy. Henderson took the picture and slowly tore it in half. The tear separated Trevor's face, destroying the smile. Henderson tore the picture the other way until there was nothing left of Trevor's face but four unidentifiable pieces. He wadded the pieces into a small ball and dropped it on the floor.

Henderson waited until one thirty. Then he left, feeling terribly bored. He found a cab on Holland Park Avenue and directed it to the New Chelsea Club. There he had a small brandy and asked if Trevor had been in. He hadn't. The bartender pointed to another man at the bar. "He might know."

The man was Somerset. He had been there for three hours and was quite drunk. "Trevor? Sure, he's probably at Clare's. Clare Strickland. You don't know where she lives? Here, I'll draw you a map."

Charlie Meadows, the owner of the New Chelsea Club, had been warned by Mitchell to keep an eye out for Henderson. Always cautious about his own relations with the police, he was careful to do so. When Henderson left the club for Clare's flat, Meadows noticed him and made sure he got the number of the cab. He then telephoned Mitchell's office, which relayed the message on to the radio car which was taking Mitchell and Trevor out to Hampstead.

"He's looking for you again," said Mitchell as the car made a U turn on Park Road. It was raining harder now. There was very little traffic.

"You mean 'still,' " said Trevor. He was tense and had not yet recovered from being shot at. His clothes were sodden but he barely noticed it. He was trying to keep his mind away from what had happened, but it kept going back, going over every moment. He tried to regain some of the feeling of strength he had experienced earlier in the day. There was no trace of it. The thought of Henderson searching for him made him feel lonely and frightened. He wished he were someplace warm and well lit.

"We'll have no difficulty catching him now that we have the number of his cab." Mitchell busied himself with the radio, alerting other police cars.

Trevor nodded. He had no faith in Mitchell's optimism. He was essentially shocked and could force himself to do very little. All sorts of pictures moved through his mind. He saw himself sweating over a journalism exam at Northwestern, certain he would fail. He saw himself taking his wife, Louise, to a Chicago steakhouse before their marriage, where he hoped to get her drunk and permissive. He saw Clare walking away from him down a broad street. He saw himself running down Wine Office Court with Henderson behind him with a massive revolver. Henderson raised the revolver and pulled the trigger. There was no sound. Trevor bucked forward, stumbling, grabbing at his back with his hands, falling, rolling over on the wet cobblestones.

"We've located the cab," said Mitchell after a few minutes. "Now we'll see where it went."

Trevor nodded again. It seemed as if he were watching everything through dark glass: the wet streets, the gleam of the passing cars, the rhythmic glare as they passed streetlight after streetlight. The windshield wipers clicked back and forth as if measuring out Trevor's fears. He saw himself and Henderson dispassionately, as if he were watching the odd activities of strangers. There was a solid core of self-dislike and surprise, but other than that he was beginning to feel empty. Only with the greatest concentration could he keep his mind on what was happening around him.

Mitchell was talking into the radio again. "What? . . . Say that again?" The radio crackled. Trevor shut his eyes. He tried to concentrate on the hiss of the tires, the click of the windshield wipers.

"I don't understand this," said Mitchell over his shoulder. "Do you know anyone who lives on Victoria Road in Kensington?"

Trevor opened his eyes. He knew someone who lived there, but it seemed like a long time ago. Then he remembered. "That's Clare's address." He felt frightened.

Mitchell began talking into the radio again. The driver turned up Knightsbridge and accelerated. Then he flicked on the siren.

22

"WHAT DO YOU mean pushing your way in here like this?" It was 2:00 A.M. and Clare was furious.

Henderson didn't look at her. "Where's Trevor?"

"I don't have the least idea. If you don't leave immediately, I'll call the police."

Ignoring her, Henderson walked into the small living room. There were art nouveau posters of Gibson girls on the walls. A pink begonia in a green pot took up most of a clear plastic end table. A few of its flowers lay on the floor like broken promises. Henderson sat down in a chrome and leather chair next to the plant.

"Where's Trevor?" he asked again.

Having followed him into the living room, Clare now stared at him, unable to believe his rudeness. She assumed he was one of Trevor's drinking companions.

"I'm afraid I haven't made myself clear," she said, standing with her arms crossed over her green bathrobe. "I'm asking you to leave. I have no idea where Trevor is. Try the New Chelsea Club. I'm quite serious about calling the police."

"He's not at the New Chelsea Club." Henderson looked at the woman for the first time. He found her completely uninteresting. He looked away.

"Couldn't you have a drink there by yourself?" asked Clare sarcastically.

"I don't want a drink." His voice was flat. "Do you expect Trevor this evening?"

Clare felt confused and began to worry. She didn't understand what was happening. "Does he owe you money?"

Looking at her again, Henderson shook his head. "No, I intend to kill him."

Although she assumed Henderson was joking, she grew more frightened. There was a coldness about him that made her decide to be careful. His obliviousness to his wet clothes and shoes, his matted hair, made him seem like someone who had moved beyond polite society to a place where the rules were his own.

"He won't come here tonight. He really won't."

Henderson got to his feet. There was a dark stain on the chair from his wet raincoat. He took Clare's arm, not roughly but very firmly. "You're telling the truth?"

"Yes. He won't be here tonight."

Henderson looked at her carefully, staring into her face. She could almost feel the pressure of his eyes. She had a sudden desire to pull herself away and run. At last Henderson let go of her arm. Then he nodded and walked out, leaving the door open behind him. Clare followed, shutting and bolting the door. Pushing her hair away from her face, she stared at the mud on the floor, trying to decide what to do.

Outside, Henderson walked up to Kensington Road where he caught a cab back to Trevor's flat. Trevor wasn't there. He considered waiting but felt too restless. Trevor filled his mind like a wind. Going back out onto the street, he caught another cab and directed it to Fleet Street with the vague plan that he could find Trevor somewhere in the area. But he knew this was a poor idea. He felt rushed and began to fear that he wouldn't find Trevor. He told himself that he had to relax. Basically he had no doubt that he would both find Trevor and shoot him. He would erase him from his life.

It was still raining. The empty streets were like a movie set for a film about the end of the world. Henderson began to think of Tangier. The cab was driving along Bayswater Road, bordering Hyde Park.

Henderson could let his mind move over Tangier as if over a map. There was the main post office with its massive yellow stone and rude French clerks. There was the boulevard with its palm trees, embassies and houses of the rich. Small mad cars leapt from lane to lane. There was the city at night, stretching down from the patio of a café in the Medina which specialized in mint tea and hashish. He could see freighters in the harbor. Nothing was moving. Somebody was playing a flute; quarter tones piled on quarter tones. The air was heavy and oppressive. From the hill, the city seemed foreboding, as if it were about to collapse, slide down into the harbor.

With no warning, he began to think of Sandra. The thought of her took his breath. She entered his mind like a bright color and remained there without fading. Not thinking of the time or his own situation, he decided he wanted to see her, to be with her.

The cab was going down Oxford Street. Henderson remembered that Sandra lived somewhere near London University, in Bloomsbury. There must be a telephone box someplace which would give him the address. The more he thought about it, the more he decided it was what he wanted to do. Getting his bearings, he told the driver to stop at Tottenham Court Road. The driver pulled to the curb. Henderson paid him and got out.

The driver assumed Henderson was going off into Soho. "Good hunting, Sir," he laughed.

Henderson walked up Tottenham Court Road with its used furniture shops and gray stone. He found a telephone box outside Goodge Street Station and looked up Sandra's address. She lived on Ridgmount Street, a few blocks away. Henderson left the box. The streets were completely empty.

At the same time, Mitchell and Trevor were leaving Clare's flat. Sergeant Fawcett was off looking for the cab that had taken Henderson away from Clare's. Although it would take some time before it was found, Mitchell guessed correctly that Henderson had gone to Trevor's flat. Trevor was staying very close to Mitchell.

They had arrived at Clare's just as she had been telephoning the police. She had been glad to see them, relieved to find that Trevor was all right, while irritated that they wouldn't say what was happening. She told them about Henderson's visit.

"Was he serious? He said he meant to kill you. He was joking, wasn't he?"

Trevor had shrugged. Mitchell had asked, "Did he give you any idea where he was going?"

"No. He said he'd been to the New Chelsea Club. Is he really trying to kill you, Trevor? Why don't you say something?"

Although he had a strong desire to stay with her, Trevor couldn't bring himself to speak. His life seemed to be fragmenting around him.

"Are you all right? Do you want to stay here? Of all the . . ."

"That might not be a bad idea, Trevor," interrupted Mitchell. "I'll post some men outside."

"No."

"You'd be safest here. I'll come back after this is straightened out."

"No."

Clare took his arm. "Tell me what happened. Someone, please." Her voice sounded desperate, although she was trying to smile.

"No. I'm going with Mitchell." Trevor kissed her lightly on the cheek. "Everything's fine. I'll call you in the morning." He tried to pull away.

Clare began crying. "For God's sake, can't you see that you matter to me. Don't just ignore me."

Mitchell had retreated to the door and was watching the pair of them closely.

"It's my life," said Trevor. "I've got to go."

Turning away, Clare wiped her eyes on a corner of her robe. "And what about me? Don't you think I care?" She turned back to him angrily. "It's not just your life."

Trevor shrugged and walked to the door where Mitchell was waiting. "I'll call you in the morning."

Clare followed him. "Do you think you can live like a solitary animal? What about other people? You can't do that to yourself." She was speaking calmly, while keeping her arms folded tightly across her breasts.

"I said I'd call you in the morning. Let's go, Mitchell." Trevor turned and left.

Mitchell stood for a second and then hesitantly patted Clare's shoulder. "Don't worry. I'll leave a man outside." Frowning slightly, he followed Trevor out of the flat.

"Bastards," said Clare, closing and locking the door.

As they drove toward Trevor's flat, Trevor tried to draw the strings of himself together. Nothing would settle in his mind. He tried to think about Clare, but instead he kept seeing himself running and hearing Henderson running behind him. He kept hearing those two shots. It was as if his life had stopped at that point and that from now on he would go around and round those few desperate minutes like a trapped beast on a merry-go-round.

What helped clear his mind more than anything Clare could have said was the sight of his flat. It frightened him almost more than being shot at. It wasn't so much messed up as violated: Books were out of place, letters and pictures were on the floor, old manuscripts were scattered about. Trevor had a keen sense of having been pawed at. There was an obvious lack of direction to Henderson's prowling that was casual and indifferent. This shocked Trevor.

"He's out of his mind. Look at this? What did he do it for?"

Mitchell looked depressed. He was beginning to feel that no matter what happened, he would be blamed for involving Trevor. He was sorry he hadn't forced him to stay at Clare's, under armed guard if need be. Seeing the flat, Mitchell realized for the first time how far Henderson had been pushed. Mitchell felt relieved that he wasn't the one being searched for.

"I wish you'd consider going back to Clare's," he said at last.

Trevor wandered through his apartment, picking up papers, looking into corners as if tracking an animal. "Oh, no. I'm in this all the way. Jesus, just look what he did. Why did he do it?"

Mitchell shook his head. He was holding the picture that Henderson had destroyed. "Remember that I warned you."

When she answered her door at 3:00 A.M., Sandra thought she would find her father, drunk and needing a place to stay. The last person she expected to see was Henderson. He stood leaning against the doorjamb. His clothes were wet and muddy.

"May I come in?" He spoke very softly.

She stepped back to let him pass. Her flat was on the top floor of an old house, and small: two rooms and a tiny kitchen under a sloping ceiling. Henderson seemed to fill it. She could see there was something dreadfully wrong with him. His clothes, his expressionless face, his depression, made her realize he needed taking care of. She was fond of him and still regretted how their evening had ended the week before. She assumed he was shy, nervous about his wife. Nothing had prepared her for a 3:00 A.M. visit.

She didn't ask any questions, saying only, "This is a surprise," and leading him into the kitchen for a hot cup of tea. Although she was curious, she didn't believe she could be curious and helpful at the same time.

Henderson stood in the kitchen, looking at the blue Spanish tiles that Sandra had hung on the wall. Then he sat down on the one straight chair. It creaked under him. "It's comfortable here," he said.

The tone struck Sandra as the tone of a person who never expected to be comfortable again. "Are you hungry?" she asked, stepping around him to the small gas stove.

"No." Restlessly, Henderson got up and walked into the living room. There were more blue tiles on the wall and a Klee print of Sinbad the Sailor. There were blue burlap curtains over the windows. A large, dark-red armchair stood next to a brass floor lamp. Some straight chairs were gathered around a table. Wandering around the room, Henderson looked at books and magazines, occasionally having to lower his head to avoid hitting it on the ceiling. He explored the flat as he had explored Trevor's. Here, however, he recognized the person.

Sandra brought him a cup of tea. Henderson took off his raincoat and hung it carefully in the closet. Then he drank the tea from the green ceramic mug. He didn't speak or sit down but continued to walk around the small room like a cat in a new house. Sandra couldn't think what was wrong. Henderson put the empty mug down on the table. "Would you like some more?" Sandra asked a little helplessly.

"No, thank you."

She was standing a few feet from him. Very slowly, he reached out and took her arm high up by the shoulder, then, still slowly, he drew her toward him. She could feel the tension in his hand, squeezing her arm almost painfully. She moved forward to kiss him.

They stood kissing in the center of the room, gently at first, then almost desperately as Henderson relaxed. He took off her robe and tossed it on the chair. Underneath she was wearing an old-fashioned white nightgown which trailed on the floor. It was warm, comfortable and the last thing she would have worn if she had known Henderson was coming.

He touched her breasts and began roughly to undo the buttons of the nightgown.

She brushed his cheek with her lips. "You'll tear it."

Henderson stepped back. "Then take it off."

He stood watching as she got undressed, as if staring at a bright light. Then he took off his damp clothes and muddy shoes. They looked at each other, not touching. At last Sandra took his hand and led him into the bedroom.

Later as they lay in bed, Henderson talked constantly of Tangier. Sandra was frightened for him. He was running like a machine which is out of control. It was only with difficulty that she could understand him. She lay next to him, trying to comfort him, soothing him with her hands. Slowly he began to relax. He seemed so fragile to her. She wanted to pick him up and put him in a hot tub, to wrap him in something warm. At last he fell asleep, almost in midsentence. She remained next to him until he was breathing deeply, then she got up to make sure the door was locked and to put Henderson's clothes in front of the electric fire to dry.

Henderson's revolver fell out of his jacket as she picked it up. She stood looking at it, not wanting to touch it. In the end she forced herself to pick it up, put it back in the pocket. After folding the clothes, she walked over to the window and stared out at the black buildings. She was still standing there when the sun began to rise.

23

"SINCE HE can't kill me, he screws her. Jesus, that's really logic."

"We have no evidence that they slept together."

Trevor and Mitchell were in the back seat of a police car which was on its way to Henderson's office. It was shortly after 9:00 A.M. The rain had stopped a few hours before and a brisk wind was clearing the London sky. The city was full of people going to work, living their usual lives on a usual Tuesday morning.

"Sure they slept together. Why shouldn't they?" asked Trevor irritably. He was slouched over and staring out at Coventry Street. There had been no chance to change his clothes or wash. He needed a shave. His long red hair looked like a mass of twine. As the car stopped for a light at Piccadilly Circus, a few people looked at him curiously, apparently thinking he was a dangerous criminal who had been caught at last.

Mitchell also needed a shave, but unlike Trevor, he didn't look like a threat to society. He was annoyed with himself and annoyed with Trevor. He hadn't found the cabdriver who had driven Henderson to Tottenham Court Road until about six o'clock. Like the driver, Mitchell had assumed that Henderson had gone into Soho. Consequently, he had directed his efforts to combing the area for him.

After about two hours, Sergeant Fawcett had mentioned that Sandra lived not far from there. Trevor had joined in by saying he suspected Henderson and Sandra were having an affair. This was the first Mitchell had heard of it.

As if offering final proof, Sergeant Fawcett had said, "But he took her to Wilton's last Monday night."

Mitchell had felt too tired to be angry. "You might have told me."

"You only asked to be told anything out of the ordinary, Sir. What could be more natural than taking a young woman to dinner?"

This was an old dispute between Fawcett and Mitchell. Fawcett's inclination was to heap every bit of information onto Mitchell. Mitchell responded from the bottom of the pile by begging only for what seemed important, with summaries of the rest. At that time last week, he had been primarily concerned with checking the records for a man with many rings. He had neglected to read the summaries.

"If I thought it was important," Fawcett had continued, "I would have told you."

"And if you had told me," snapped Mitchell, "Henderson would be in jail at this moment. I want men over there immediately. Check her flat, talk to neighbors. Be careful he doesn't see you and shoot you, Sergeant Fawcett. It would ruin my day."

Sandra's flat had been empty, but a brief search had shown that somebody else had been there. A helpful insomniac across the hall told Fawcett the visitor had been a man and that he had arrived "very, very late." The insomniac, an elderly woman with an eye for her neighbors' affairs, had added that the activities of the young were quite shocking. Sergeant Fawcett agreed.

Armed with this information, Mitchell had decided to talk to Sandra. The police car passed out of the Circus onto Piccadilly.

Trevor was still worrying about the apparent relationship between Sandra and Henderson. Such behavior made Henderson seem more human, more open to conventional interpretation than the creature who had been pursuing him. He didn't want Henderson to appear human. Trevor had justified his own behavior by telling himself that Henderson was out of control. But with evidence to the contrary, he again began to suspect his own motives. He suddenly wished he could talk to Henderson, discover the sort of person he had become. But the thought frightened him and he returned to thinking about his relationship with Sandra.

"But why should he go over there?" he asked.

"He needed a place to rest," Mitchell answered. The subject didn't interest him.

"But he could have rested anywhere. Why see her?"

Mitchell looked at him crossly. "How psychological do you wish to be? Perhaps she counteracts whatever horrors he has in his mind. Perhaps they just like each other. I myself prefer the latter opinion."

Sergeant Fawcett turned around in the front seat. "He must have taken advantage of her."

"I'm not interested in your beliefs, Sergeant Fawcett."

Fawcett withdrew from the conversation.

"Do you think she knew?" asked Trevor.

"Knew what?"

"Knew that Henderson's a killer, that he's dangerous."

Mitchell laughed. The conversation irritated him terribly. "When you were chasing Henderson all over London, did that girlfriend of yours know about it?"

"Come on, Mitchell, there's a difference."

Mitchell turned away and glanced out the window. The

231

police car turned off Piccadilly onto Half Moon Street. "We are observing a man in the process of being caught," he said at last. "The girl may know that or she may not. We shall probably learn which quite shortly."

Seeing Sandra, it was clear to Trevor that she had something to conceal. She looked embarrassed and nervous when Mitchell introduced himself. Trevor felt uncomfortable watching her. She was wearing a yellow cotton dress with a green border. Trevor could not stop thinking about her and Henderson. Mrs. Clavering was also there, superintending the interview.

"Where is Mr. Henderson?" asked Mitchell quietly. He liked the appearance of the girl and didn't wish to be hard on her.

Sandra stared at Trevor, recognizing and disliking him, but curious as to why he was there. "I have no idea," she said.

"I don't believe you're telling the truth. He's in a great deal of trouble. It would be better if we knew where he is."

"I have no idea where he is," repeated Sandra, still staring at Trevor.

Mitchell paused before he spoke again. "He shot at this man last night."

Looking up, Sandra seemed surprised, even though she had seen Henderson's revolver. "Why, why should he do it?"

"Because I know he murdered a friend of mine," said Trevor.

Both Sandra and Mitchell looked startled. Mrs. Clavering made a noise that sounded like the air brakes of a truck.

"A friend of yours, but who . . . ?" began Sandra.

"Come along, Miss," interrupted Mitchell. "We know Henderson spent the night at your flat. It will go poorly with you if you don't tell us where he is."

Although she was upset, she still said, "I have no idea where he might be."

Mrs. Clavering clucked at her. "But he telephoned you this morning, my dear." She looked helpfully at Mitchell.

"Did he?" Mitchell barked.

Sandra nodded. She's going to cry, thought Trevor.

"Where did he go after he left your flat?" Mitchell demanded.

"I really don't know," said Sandra softly; then she added, "He borrowed my car."

"What kind of car?"

"A Morris."

"Describe it."

She gave him the number. It was a blue Morris convertible, belonging to her father. Then she began to cry, quietly and completely to herself. Mrs. Clavering patted her shoulder. Trevor felt depressed. It seemed that even if Henderson were caught nothing would be solved. The survivors would all continue. It didn't basically matter.

"Did he have a revolver when you saw him?" asked Mitchell.

Sandra nodded.

At that moment, the blue Morris was parked half a block away. Henderson sat behind the wheel, watching the police car parked in front of his office. He was still looking for Trevor. He was devoid of any feeling. This surprised him, because it seemed he ought to be thinking of Sandra.

Henderson had already looked for Trevor at his flat and office. There had been policemen at both places. Then it occurred to him to look outside his own office, where Trevor had been standing for weeks. He had arrived to find the police car. Henderson parked the blue Morris and waited. The revolver was beside him on the seat.

After about ten minutes, Trevor came out with Mitchell. Henderson had expected the two would be together. It didn't alter his intention to kill Trevor. There was no place to go back to. He thought of the plane that was waiting to take him to Morocco. It could wait a little longer.

The police car pulled away from the curb and drove up to Hill Street, where it turned left. Henderson followed it. He could see Trevor talking excitedly in the back seat. The two cars circled Berkeley Square to Bruton Street. Reaching New Bond Street, they turned right toward Piccadilly.

Henderson meant to wait until the police car stopped and Trevor got out. Then he would carefully shoot him. He had decided to take as few chances as possible. Because of the police, he knew he would have only one opportunity. The cars merged with the heavy morning traffic on Piccadilly, driving toward the Circus.

At the Circus, Henderson noticed a policeman at a call box. The policeman waved at Mitchell's car. Then he glanced idly at Henderson in the blue Morris convertible. Suddenly he looked as if he had been kicked. He grabbed the phone and began shouting into it. Both cars turned down Haymarket.

"Behind us?" Trevor tried to turn but Mitchell grabbed his arm.

"Be careful, we don't wish to show our hand." Mitchell was rather embarrassed. He had no idea how long Henderson had been following them. It wouldn't have occurred to him that since Henderson was searching for Trevor, all they had to do was wait. Mitchell had never been hunted before. It was an unpleasant feeling. Sergeant Fawcett was making indignant and protesting noises in the front seat.

"If you let me have your pistol, Sir, I'll jump out and get him at the corner."

Mitchell shook his head sadly. He could think of nothing worse than a shoot-out in front of American Express for the entertainment of all the tourists. Think of the questions raised in Parliament. "You will do nothing of the kind," said Mitchell. "You will sit there quietly until I tell you otherwise. Give me the radio!"

Mitchell gave directions to other police cars in the vicinity, bringing another car up behind them and setting up a roadblock at the foot of Northumberland Avenue. He hoped the avenue would be fairly free from traffic.

Putting back the microphone, he grew aware of Trevor beside him. The man was shaking. Mitchell grabbed his arm. "What's wrong with you?" he demanded angrily.

"He did it, didn't he? You know he did it." Trevor was about to panic.

"Stop it. What I said for Fawcett goes for you, too. Amateurs. You're disgusting!"

Henderson was aware that they knew he was behind him. He was laughing at it. Even at this point he believed he could get away. He was still laughing when he noticed a second police car, in his rear-view mirror. All three cars drove sedately around Trafalgar Square and onto Northumberland Avenue, heading toward the Thames. A short way down the avenue, Henderson noticed a roadblock being set up at the other end. This didn't lessen his confidence about killing Trevor. He would only change his plans.

There is a wide lane, where buses and cars are sometimes parked, down the center of Northumberland Avenue. Henderson swerved into it, slamming on the brakes. The Morris skidded in a wide circle. The tires squealed. The car was still moving when Henderson jumped from it.

By the time the two police cars had stopped, Henderson was disappearing down tiny Northumberland Street, which cuts off from the avenue at a forty-five degree angle directly across from Great Scotland Yard. Henderson ran around the pub the Sherlock Holmes, which stands on a triangle bounded by the two Northumberlands and Craven Street. He was still laughing to himself as he ducked into a narrow doorway and stopped.

Behind him he could hear police whistles and the sound of people running. Henderson cocked the revolver and pressed himself flat against the doorway. The police were only accustomed to people running away. They had no suspicion that Henderson might wait for them. Three policemen ran by, followed by Sergeant Fawcett. Henderson could hear somebody shouting. It was Mitchell shouting at Trevor.

"Dammit all, get back to the car! Don't go through there!"

Trevor was waving back at Mitchell, as he came even with the doorway. Henderson calmly stepped toward him.

"Trevor!" he said. Henderson watched as Trevor turned to face him. He was surprised to see how pinched and drawn he was. He looks ill, Henderson thought.

Trevor stared at him, startled, as if trying to recognize who he was. Then he ran forward a few paces, shouting, "Did you kill him?"

Henderson had no idea what Trevor was shouting about, nor did he care. Raising the revolver, Henderson pulled the trigger, shooting from a distance of five feet. The bullet entered Trevor's stomach, ripped through his left kidney and exited from his lower back. Henderson fired a second time as Trevor stumbled toward him. Striking his chest at an angle, the bullet glanced off his breastbone and ruptured his right lung before lodging in the muscle of his right arm. The force of the bullet knocked him backward. The sound reverberated through the narrow street.

Henderson was about to fire a third time, into Trevor's face, when Mitchell tackled him, cursing terribly. As he fell, he saw Trevor still standing as if he were about to speak, holding himself together with red hands. Henderson began fighting desperately with Mitchell. He had no intention of being taken by the police.

The strength of Henderson's fury took Mitchell by surprise. The two men rolled silently on the pavement, each trying to cripple the other. Grabbing Henderson's throat, Mitchell attempted to reach the hand with the gun. It was too late. Henderson brought the butt of the revolver down solidly on Mitchell's skull. The policeman let go and Henderson twisted away, getting to his feet. Groaning, Mitchell pushed himself onto his knees, then fell back again.

Henderson gave a brief glance to Trevor, who was lying on the pavement as if tossed into a pool of his own blood. He assumed he was dead. In any case, it didn't matter any more. His anger had gone. It was enough to have shot him.

Several policemen were running toward him, shouting. Henderson turned and ran back around the Sherlock Holmes to Northumberland Avenue. If he could only reach Charing Cross tube station . . . As he ran down the street, his mind began filling with pictures of Tangier, as a sink fills with water. First he could see the lush green of the trees and plants, then he could smell it, smell the mint, the spicy food, the stale urine, all the smells of people packed together; smells of leather and wet wool; the smell of the small dirty cars. They were so strong as nearly to block out what was happening at the moment.

He stopped and looked up at the massive plane trees and sooty red brick of the buildings. There were banks and some African embassy. There was the headquarters of the Anti-Vivisection Society and the War Office with its four cupolas and Corinthian columns. The few people he could see were tending their own business as if nothing had happened. Henderson wiped his face with his hand and began running again.

As he passed the Whitehall Theatre, he saw three policemen running toward him from the roadblock. He swerved in toward the station only to see two more policemen standing under the bridge. Turning on his heels, he ran back toward the Victoria Embankment, then left under the railway bridge. He hoped to get into the station by the other entrance. He still thought he could escape, that he could meet Sandra and be safe, never be bothered again.

Two policemen were coming out of the station. Sliding into them, Henderson raised his arms, knocking them aside. Before they could recover, he was running up the steps of the Hungerford Footbridge. There were people in his way. He pushed through them. He still had the revolver in his hand. Again and again, he kept telling himself that he had to get across. With Charing Cross closed to him, the only possibility left was Waterloo Station. It was bigger and he would stand a better chance of losing himself in the crowd.

Reaching the top of the bridge, he was almost blinded by the view: the huge white and gray stone of Royal Festival Hall with its green roof, then the City stretching off to his left: Waterloo Bridge, high-rise office buildings, the wedding-cake steeple of St. Bride's, the dome of St. Paul's glittering in the October sun. The sky looked like an inverted sea. After the relative dark of Northumberland Avenue, the scene took Henderson's breath away. He paused, but, hearing footsteps running behind him, didn't stop.

He kept thinking of Sandra's father, who was waiting for him at Gatwick Airport in Horley. If he could only reach the other side. People were shouting and pointing at his revolver. They fell down or flattened themselves against the steel grating of the bridge. They raised their hands as if he possibly wanted something from them. There were a pair of German tourists with a movie camera. A heavy man in a Bavarian cap pointed the camera at him. Henderson could hear it faintly whirring as he pushed people away.

Like music in the back of his mind, he kept seeing Tangier: beggars crouching in doorways, veiled women breast-feeding their babies on curbs, men selling water from polished bronze cups, old women leading donkeys loaded down with sticks, the marketplace with its shouting and the smells of hundreds of fruits.

A train crossing the bridge cleared Henderson's mind again. The bridge shook and the air filled with its roar. About fifteen feet in front of him, an old man with a harmonica was dancing up and down, playing a tune drowned out by the train. It was as if he were dancing silently. Turning a little, he saw Henderson running toward him, his eyes focusing on Henderson's gun. The man's clothes were torn and dirty. He dropped the harmonica and flattened himself against the railing, staring in horror as Henderson ran by.

The end of the bridge was less than thirty yards away. Henderson was beginning to think he would reach it, when he saw a blue uniform appear at the top of the stairs. He raised the revolver and kept running. The policeman didn't know anything was the matter. He just happened to be crossing the bridge. He was young, with blond hair. He was talking cheerfully to someone behind him.

Henderson stopped and aimed the revolver, holding it with both hands. The bridge was still shaking from the train. Someone was screaming. The policeman turned and stared at Henderson, not understanding what was about to happen. The two men looked at each other. As Henderson began to squeeze the trigger, he could see fear sweep over the policeman's face like a wind. Henderson paused. Then he dropped the gun. Everything was wrong.

There are cypress trees in the garden of the King, royal palms and a riot of purple and yellow flowers; the tower of the mosque is covered with small purple and yellow tiles. Henderson could hear the chanter at the top calling the people to prayers. Running again, he put his hand on the railing and vaulted over the side, twisting in a wide arc, making no sound, falling end over end into the Thames, fifty feet below.

STEPHEN DOBYNS

Stephen Dobyns was born in East Orange, New Jersey, in 1941; he was raised in New Jersey, Michigan, Virginia, Pennsylvania and Michigan again, moving every year or two. He was educated at Shimer College, Wayne State University and the University of Iowa. He spent two years in college news service work, two years as a college instructor and nineteen months as a reporter for the Detroit News. *His book of poems,* Concurring Beasts *(Atheneum), was the Lamont Poetry Selection for 1971. He is presently teaching at the University of New Hampshire.*